WOLF VALLEY: A VERY GRUMPY HOLIDAY COLLECTION

THE COMPLETE SERIES

WOLF VALLEY: A VERY GRUMPY HOLIDAY
BOOK 6

SHAW HART

WANT A FREE BOOK?

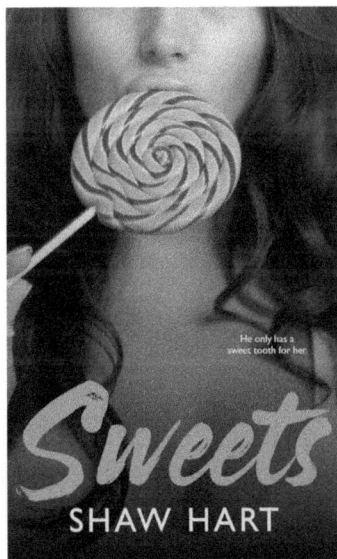

You can grab Sweets **Here.**
**Check out my website, www.shawhart.com for
more free books!**

*

Looking for some grumpy sunshine holiday romance books? If you love steamy romance books with alpha heroes who are head over heels in love with their plus-size women, then you'll love the Wolf Valley: A Very Grumpy Holiday Collection!

Books in this collection include:
    A Very Grumpy Valentine's Day
    A Very Grumpy Halloween
    A Very Grumpy Thanksgiving
    A Very Grumpy Christmas
    A Very Grumpy New Year

A VERY GRUMPY VALENTINE'S DAY

*

This Ex-Army Ranger has met his match...
Mira:

Getting out of my parents' house was meant to be a chance for me to spread my wings.

Instead, I seem to have picked up a new babysitter.

Townes Monroe is grumpy and bossy.

Every time I turn around, he's there.

The man seems to know exactly how to press my buttons.

I'm just not sure if that's a good thing or not.

Townes:

I've never wanted to be tied down.

Not until I see Mira Lane.

She obviously needs someone to look after her, and that person is going to be me.

I just need to get her on board with that plan.

With Valentine's Day coming up, I know that this is my chance to win over my girl and finally make her mine.

I just hope that my plan is good enough.

ONE

Mira

"THANKS FOR STAYING LATE," Saffron says as she sniffles.

"It's no problem," I assure her. "I hope that you feel better soon. Now go get some rest."

She smiles weakly as she gathers her things and heads for the door. I turn back to the bookstore once she's gone and look around at what I have left to do tonight.

The Shelf Indulgence Bookstore is empty at this time of night. To be fair, most of the shops in Wolf Valley are closed by now, so there's not much reason for people to be out. The only other store that's open is the other shop I work at, the Wet and Wild adult toy store.

I grab the Clorox wipes and start wiping down every surface that Saffron may have touched today. Disinfecting like this is second nature to me. I was sick a lot as a kid and teenager, and I can remember my mom wiping down every surface in our house nearly every day. It's hard to tell if my mom was doing that because she was worried about someone else getting sick or if it was her own OCD that made her do that.

Growing up in my house was kind of rough. My mom was a germaphobe with untreated OCD who was afraid of everything. She never wanted to leave the house and hated to let me leave the house either. I would come home from school and have to immediately take a shower and change my clothes. I used to have to wash my hands so often that they would be red and raw.

I was isolated in that house. The only person that I had to talk to was my mom, and as you can imagine, that wasn't a whole lot of fun.

When I was a little older and started driving, I tried to gain a bit more freedom and independence. That didn't go over well.

I was the weird girl at school, so I didn't have many friends. Even if I did, it's not like I could have gone out or done stuff with them. I couldn't have had them over to my house either.

I made a plan when I was seventeen to save up as much money as I could and get out of there. I worked at a grocery store throughout high school and saved up every penny. I didn't have anything else to spend the money on since I was barely allowed out of the house.

When I turned twenty, I tried to convince my mom to go to therapy to get some help. I had brought up the idea before, but kind of vaguely, and she had always just kind of brushed me off. That time was different though. Instead of ignoring me or brushing my suggestion off, she blew up at me, telling me that nothing was wrong with her and insisting that she didn't need therapy or any help at all.

I ended up leaving home the very next day and I haven't

been back since. I have no plans on going back either. It's been two years, and I haven't heard from her once.

I try not to think about my mom because it hurts too much. I want to focus on the positive, which is the fact that I got out, that I'm supporting myself, that I have friends and my freedom. I'm still trying to find myself and see what I like. Still, every now and then, I wonder what my mom is doing and if she misses me.

I push those thoughts aside and finish unboxing the newest shipment of books. It's almost closing time, so I set them on the counter to log into the system and put them on the shelves tomorrow. I leave a note for Saffron next to the books in case she's feeling better tomorrow and decides to come to work. Then, I gather my things and get ready to lock up.

As I close the door and pocket my keys, I'm not surprised to see Townes leaning against the side of the bookstore.

Excitement and arousal bubble up inside of me, and I try to force it down. Townes is hot, but he's also overbearing and a bit of a grump. He's always trying to do things for me, and I both love and hate it. Either way, ever since I moved to Wolf Valley five months ago, I seem to have picked up a new babysitter.

At first, I liked his attention. Being in a new town and all alone was kind of scary, but he always made me feel safe. Then he started trying to take over for me. He was always grabbing my groceries before I could, carrying boxes into the bookstore when I was doing inventory, opening water bottles for me, and just generally hovering around me.

"Mira," Townes says in his deep voice.

"Shadow," I reply, using the nickname I gave him when he first started popping up.

"How was work?" He asks, ignoring the nickname.

"Good."

"I didn't think that you closed tonight," he says, and I side-eye him.

"How did you get my schedule?"

"It's the same every week," he points out.

"Saffron wasn't feeling well," I tell him, and he frowns.

"What about you?" He asks, reaching over to feel my forehead with the back of his hand.

I get a flashback to my mom doing that to me and I flinch, stepping away from him.

"I'm fine."

"You look tired. Come on, I'll buy you some soup at the diner and then walk you home."

He starts heading towards Nosh, the diner a few blocks away, and I roll my eyes. Townes has a habit of ordering me around and expecting me to do as he bids. I never do.

"I'm going home, but you have fun," I call, turning and heading towards my apartment.

"Wait," he says as he grabs my arm.

I don't know how he can move so quickly or so quietly. The guy is huge, but I feel like he's always sneaking up on me.

"Are you really feeling alright?" He asks again, his hand going to my forehead, and I sigh as I let him take my temperature. "You look kind of pale."

"I'm fine," I tell him again, pulling out of his grip.

He frowns down at me and I turn and start to walk faster towards my apartment. I only live two blocks from the bookstore, so the walk is over quickly.

Townes falls into step beside me, easily matching my steps with his long legs.

"Did you eat enough today?" He asks, and I roll my eyes.

He asks me this question a lot. It seems like he's always trying to feed me. I'm already curvy and plus size, so I definitely don't need the extra calories, but that doesn't stop him from trying.

A few guys stumble out of the Wolf Pack Bar on the corner, and Townes moves closer to me, pressing me closer to the building next to me as we pass them. I glance over at Townes as the guys laugh and push each other as they trip and stumble in the opposite direction. Townes is glaring at them, watching until they turn the corner and disappear from view.

"Down, boy," I joke, and he frowns at me.

He's been frowning at me a lot lately. Maybe he's getting tired of me.

That thought hurts, and I clear my throat and look up at my apartment building.

"You shouldn't be walking home alone," he tells me.

We have this conversation about once a week, and I sigh.

"I never do. You're always there, shadow."

"It's not safe for you to be out here after dark by yourself," he continues, acting like I didn't say anything.

"Uh huh."

"I'm serious, Mira."

"I'm *fine*," I stress, and I don't need to look at him to know that he's frowning again.

My steps slow automatically as I dig my keys out of my purse. I turn towards Townes to say goodnight, and my breath stalls in my lungs as I see the look in his eyes.

There's heat and longing in their blue depths. He's been staring at me like that when he walks me home for the past few weeks, and I keep waiting to see if he's going to kiss me or make some kind of move.

"Good night, Mira," Townes says quietly, and I nod.

"Night."

I try not to let my disappointment show as I unlock the door and head up the stairs to my apartment.

"Lock the door," he calls through the wooden front door, and I want to scream.

He's always telling me to do the most basic of tasks. It's like he thinks I'm an idiot or incapable of taking care of myself in any way.

I ignore him as I let myself into my apartment. I live in a tiny one-bedroom apartment above Manci's Pizza Parlor. The place always smells like tomatoes, garlic, and oregano, and I've found myself craving pizza more than ever since I started living here.

I toss my things down on the kitchen counter and sigh as I look around the cramped space. I shower and get ready for bed. As I crawl onto the mattress, an image of Townes tonight flashes behind my eyes. He's staring down at me with that longing look in his dark eyes, and a shiver of lust rushes through me.

As I lay down and close my eyes, I know that I'm going to dream of Townes again tonight.

TWO

Townes

I'M DISTRACTED two mornings later, looking out the windows of the Nosh Diner for any sign of Mira walking by.

"Earth to Townes," my best friend, Xavier, says, and I blink, turning back to our table.

I'm having breakfast with my friends, and I'm meant to be catching up with everyone, but all I can think about is a certain curvy brunette.

"Sorry, what were you saying?" I ask, trying to focus on my friends.

"We were asking what your plans were for the weekend," Foster says.

I grab my coffee and peek back at the windows to see if I can spot any sign of Mira.

"Um, I'm not sure yet," I tell them.

"Maybe you'll have a date," Xavier says with a pointed look.

Xavier knows about my crush on Mira and has been pushing me to make a move or ask her out for weeks now. He just got together with his girlfriend, Olive, right before Christmas, and now that he's in love, it's like he can't wait for me to be with someone too.

To be fair, having someone like that does look nice. Xavier went from being a complete grumpy loner to a complete grumpy loner who just happens to be in love with the curvy baker in town. Now he gets out more, mainly because Olive wants to do something, and he would just do anything to make her happy.

That's how I already feel about Mira. I mean, I wait outside in the freezing cold at least three times a week just to walk her home and be around her for five minutes. She's all that I can think about, all that I dream or fantasize about.

Xavier calls it a crush, but what I feel for Mira is so much more than that. She's it for me. I've known that since the moment that I laid eyes on her. I had frozen right in my tracks and just stared as she walked down the sidewalk and disappeared into the bookstore. I ended up following her in just to get another look at her. Then I went back the next day, the next week, and the next week.

I've tried talking to her and flirting with her, and it's gotten me nowhere. She doesn't seem to pick up on the fact that I like her or that I'm trying to flirt with her. She's been keeping me at arm's length. Sometimes, I feel like maybe I even annoy her, but then there are days when it seems like she might like me too. It's those moments that keep giving me hope.

"Maybe," I lie to Xavier, and I see him and Foster share a look.

Foster is equally in love with his best friend, Lilliana. Xavier, Foster, and Ford grew up in Wolf Valley, and apparently, Foster has loved Lilliana since they were kids. She felt the same way, and it took her coming back to town for them to finally admit how they felt for each other.

I don't want that. I don't want to spend years pining for Mira. I need her, and I want to be with her.

"What about you guys?" I ask.

Ford, Foster's twin brother and the owner of the Nosh Diner, heads our way with our food, and I welcome the distraction.

"How's it going?" Ford asks, and I smile.

"Pretty good. What about you?"

"Staying busy," he says as he passes out the plates.

The door of the diner opens, and Cameron rushes in wearing a waitress uniform.

"Sorry that I'm late, boss!" She calls to Ford, and he just nods, his eyes glued to her.

"Dial it back, brother," Foster whispers to Ford, and he snaps out of his stupor and turns back to our table.

"You two should form a group," Xavier says with a laugh.

"Yeah, the lovestruck grumps," Foster adds. "Ransom could join too."

"Shut up," I grumble.

Ford just rolls his eyes and heads back behind the counter, and I dig into my breakfast. Foster and Xavier are busy eating too so I take the moment to look out the window again.

Mira still hasn't walked by, and I frown. I know that she had to work at the bookstore today and should have gone by before now.

Could she have overslept? Is she alright? I should go check on her.

The door of the diner opens, and Saffron rushes in and

up to the counter to grab the to-go cup of coffee that Ford is filling up for her. She thanks him and turns to rush back out but I stop her as she walks past our table.

"Hey," I say, stopping her before she can leave. "Where's Mira?"

"Oh, she's sick this morning. I feel so bad. She probably caught what I had," Saffron says, looking sad.

I push to my feet, and she steps back, staring at me with wide eyes. Foster and Xavier don't look surprised as I grab my wallet and throw down some bills.

"I'll see you later," I tell them, and they wave as I head for the door.

I hop in my truck and head down the two blocks to Mira's apartment. The lights are off when I look up at the windows, and worry starts to gnaw at me as I hop out of my truck and hurry over to the door.

I ring the buzzer and wait impatiently. Finally, the intercom crackles, and I lean closer.

"Hello?" She croaks.

"Mira, it's me. Let me in," I growl into the intercom.

"I'm fine, Townes. I just need to rest."

The intercom crackles like she turned it off, and I hit the button again.

"Go away," she sighs when she answers again.

"Not a chance. I'm not going anywhere. Let me up or I'm just going to stand here all day and ring the buzzer."

"You can't order me around," she snaps, sounding more like herself.

"Wanna bet?" I snap.

The intercom remains silent, and I take a deep breath, trying to calm down.

"Mira, please let me in," I relent.

I would beg her for anything. I would get on my knees

and grovel for her to just look at me. I am clearly wrapped around her finger, and she doesn't even seem to realize it.

She sighs loud and long, but then the door buzzes and I push inside and take the stairs two at a time up to her door. She's leaning against the doorframe, looking pale and tired but still so beautiful.

"What are your symptoms?" I ask, already reaching to feel her forehead.

"I'm just tired and have a runny nose," she says, trying to push my hand away.

"What do you need?" I ask.

"Nothing. I just need to go back to bed," she insists.

"Give me your keys," I demand, and she glares up at me. "What? No."

"Give me your keys and you can go back to bed."

She groans but reaches over and grabs her keys. She drops them into my hand, and I smile at her.

"Get some rest."

She closes the door in my face, and I turn and jog back downstairs and over to my truck. The Wolf Valley Market isn't far, and I head there to grab her some things. I try to think about what would make me feel better. I've never taken care of anyone or had anyone take care of me, so I feel woefully unprepared in this moment.

I head down the first aisle and grab Mira some medicine, shower steamers, some Vitamin C gummies, and Kleenex. I pass by the produce and decide to make her soup too. I pull up a chicken noodle soup recipe and grab everything listed under the ingredients there. Before I head to the checkout, I grab some Gatorade and juices.

I pay and load all of the bags into my truck and then make the short drive back to Mira's apartment. She's asleep when I carry everything inside, so I line the medicine and everything else on the counter and then I get to work making the soup.

It's just after noon when she comes out of the bedroom, looking half asleep.

"I got you some things," I say, nodding towards the medicine and Kleenex.

"Thanks."

"And I made you some soup."

"You didn't have to do that," she insists, and I frown at her.

"I know. I wanted to. Now sit down. You need to eat."

She looks away from me, and I dig through her cabinets until I find her bowls and grab two. I ladle the soup into the bowls and pass her one. She hands me a spoon and we sit together on her couch, side by side, to eat.

We eat in silence, and I take Mira's bowl when she's done.

"Thanks again. I'm just going to go back to bed," she tells me.

"Okay. I'll be here."

"You can leave," she tries to argue, but I just shake my head.

"You should drink something. Do you need anything else?"

She heads over to the fridge and grabs a Gatorade, chugging half of it in one big gulp. She plops back down on the couch next to me and wraps herself up in the blanket that's draped over the back of the couch.

She doesn't say anything as she turns the TV on, leans her head back against the couch, and flips through the channels until she lands on some cooking show. She yawns, and I settle in next to her and pretend to watch the show when really I'm watching her.

We spend the rest of the day on her couch. Mira sleeps on and off. I keep passing her juice and Gatorade and set an alarm on my phone so that I can remember to give her medicine every six hours. We finish up the soup for dinner and then Mira puts a movie on and promptly falls asleep next to me.

At one point, her head falls onto my shoulder and I smile down at her sleeping form. I pull the blanket tighter around her and lie down next to her on the edge of the couch so that she can't roll off.

Then I turn the TV off and start to drift off too. Even though I have a crick in my neck from the couch armrest and my feet are hanging off the other end of the couch, it's still the best night's sleep of my entire life, all because I'm sleeping next to the woman of my dreams.

THREE

Mira

I WAKE up the next morning, my face smashed against Towne's chest. His arms are locked around me, holding me in place, and I take a moment to appreciate his strong, warm body pressed up against mine.

I peek up at him and see that he's still fast asleep, his slow, even breathing blowing the loose hair at my temples.

I hate to wake him up, but I really need to go to the bathroom. I try to wiggle out of his hold, but he only holds me tighter.

"Townes," I whisper, squirming against him a bit.

He blinks his eyes open and smiles down at me. His smile is so bright and open that I stop moving and just stare at him.

"Morning," he grumbles, burying his face in my neck.

His stubble tickles my skin, and I rub against him.

"Ah, morning," I say, my voice coming out low and breathy.

His hands grip my hips, and he tugs me against him. I can feel his erection digging into my stomach, and I gasp at the size and hardness that I feel.

"I... uh, I'm feeling better," I blurt, and Townes freezes against me.

I can feel his eyelashes brush against my neck as he blinks, seeming to wake up more. Then he clears his throat and pulls away from me slightly.

"That's good."

He sits up, and I scramble to sit up too. Then I stand and clear my throat.

"Thanks for taking care of me yesterday," I tell him, feeling shy all of a sudden.

"Anytime. I'll get out of your hair, but you should take it easy today," he says, and I nod.

I walk him over to the door and smile as he pauses.

"You know, if you really want to thank me, you could go out to dinner with me tonight."

I blink, freezing. I'm not sure how to respond. On the one hand, I want to go out with him, but is that a good idea? I'm still trying to figure out who I am, still trying to find my freedom and my place in this world. Townes could mess all of that up.

"I have work tonight at Wet and Wild," I tell him, and he nods.

"We'll go out tomorrow then."

I'm a little surprised that he's pushing this. He hasn't made a move on me in the months that I've known him. I wonder what's changed in the last twenty-four hours. Maybe he's just finally worked up the nerve to ask me out. Maybe this is the first opening that he's had with me.

"Alright," I say, trying to hide the excitement that I feel about going out on my very first date.

I never had the chance to date in high school, and once I moved out of my mom's house, I was too busy trying to survive and make ends meet to think about dating. Besides, I wanted to be alone. I wanted to explore and finally live my life. It's not like any guys were asking me out anyway.

"Tomorrow then. I'll pick you up at six."

I nod, not trusting my voice at that moment, and he smiles and then heads down the stairs. I watch him go and then turn back to my empty apartment. At some point last night, he did the dishes, and they're drying in the rack by the sink. My medicine and Kleenex and everything else that he bought for me are on the counter by my bedroom.

I head into the bedroom and then into the shower, washing off the sleep and sickness from my skin. I think about Townes, about how he surprised me by showing up yesterday.

Maybe it should have though. He's consistently been there for me, and I've never once asked him to be there for me. He's a good guy, someone that I trust. I would say that we're almost friends.

I just hope that tomorrow's date doesn't mess all of that up.

I finish my shower and get ready to go to work. I overslept this morning, and I need to be at the bookstore in an hour. I still need breakfast, so I head over to the Nosh Diner and grab a breakfast sandwich and coffee to go.

I pass by Xavier as I leave, and he smiles slightly at me as he holds the door open for me.

"Thanks," I say, and he just grunts in response.

I can see why the two of them are best friends. They're so alike. He must be grabbing them a late breakfast or something. Xavier and Townes own their own consulting firm.

They work in cyber security, and from what I've heard, they spend a lot of time staring at computer screens.

I hurry down the block and into Shelf Indulgence, waving at Saffron and her sister, Ginger, as I set my things down behind the front counter.

"Hey! How are you feeling?" Saffron asks me.

"A lot better. I was just kind of cold and run down yesterday, so it wasn't too serious."

"Good," Ginger says, sounding relieved.

"You would have thought it was with the way that Townes ran off when I told him that you weren't feeling well yesterday," Saffron says with a laugh.

"He what?" I ask, and she giggles.

"I went into Nosh to grab a coffee before I opened yesterday, and he stopped me and asked about you. I told him that you weren't working because you weren't feeling well, and he ran out of there like his butt was on fire," she tells me.

"Oh," I respond, not sure what else to say to that.

"He's so into you," Ginger says with a grin, and I smile weakly.

"I don't know about that."

"Oh, trust me, he is," Saffron says.

"I would love to have a big, strong, sexy man who followed me around like a puppy dog," Ginger adds, and jealousy spikes inside of me.

"What did you want me to work on today?" I ask, hoping to change the subject.

"I just need to finish up inventory and scan in those new books," Saffron says, and I nod and hurry back to the counter to get to work.

I can feel my friends' eyes on me as I go, but I ignore

them. I need to figure out how I feel about Townes before I start adding in other people's opinions.

I try to push thoughts of Townes out of my head as I grab the first book and get to work.

FOUR

Townes

"WHERE ARE YOU TAKING HER?" Xavier asks me, his voice sounding far away, and I know he must have put me on speakerphone.

"We're going over to Rosewood. She likes Mediterranean food, and there's supposed to be a good restaurant there."

"How do you know that she likes Mediterranean food?" He asks.

"She's always looking at recipes on her phone from that region."

"Stalker."

"Like you didn't know everything about Olive before you two started dating," I challenge him, and he doesn't respond.

"Good luck tonight," he tells me sincerely.

Xavier and I have been best friends since boot camp. We were both in the military together, but when Xavier got shot on our last deployment, we decided to get out. I followed him back to Wolf Valley since I didn't know where else to go.

I've never really had a home or a supportive family. Xavier and this place are the closest that I've ever gotten to either of those things. Until I met Mira, that is. Now, wherever she is feels like home.

"Thanks. I'll talk to you tomorrow," I say.

"See you."

We both hang up, and I take one last look at myself in the mirror, smoothing my hands over my button-down shirt and brush my dark hair back off my forehead. It's time for me to go pick her up, and I smile as I grab my keys and head out the door.

I bought a cabin a few miles from downtown Wolf Valley when we moved back here. It's a few miles away from Xavier's place and only ten minutes from Mira's apartment.

When I park outside of Mira's place, she's already out front, and I hurry to jump out of my Jeep and open the door for her.

"I would have come up to get you," I tell her with a smile as she heads my way.

"Oh, I had to drop something off at the bookstore for Saffron. I was just walking back and saw your Jeep so I waited."

I close her door, jog around to the driver's side, and climb behind the wheel. I smile over at her, taking her in. She's wearing a pair of dark, tight blue jeans and a maroon sweater. It's still chilly out today, and I wonder if she's warm enough. I reach over and crank up the heat as I pull away from the curb.

"You look beautiful," I tell her as we drive out of town and towards Rosewood.

"Thanks. I wasn't sure what we were doing or how dressed up I should be."

"You're perfect," I assure her.

I make the turn towards Rosewood and she stares with wide eyes out the window.

"Where are we going?" She asks, staring at the passing scenery.

"I found this restaurant in Rosewood that I think you'll like."

"I've never been to Rosewood," she mentions, and I smile.

I like the thought of showing her around and experiencing something for the first time with her.

"It's a lot like Wolf Valley. A small town, but it's a little bigger than Wolf Valley. We can look around if you'd like," I offer.

"Maybe."

The sun is already starting to set as we drive down the main street, and I decide to do a pass so that she can see all of the shops before I head back towards Pasha, the Mediterranean restaurant.

"I love Greek food!" Mira says as soon as she sees me park outside of the restaurant.

"I know," I say before I can think better of it.

She frowns over at me and I scramble to think of an excuse, but I don't want to lie to her. I'm all in with Mira. Maybe it's about time that she knows that.

"I've seen you looking at a lot of recipes on your phone," I admit, and she blinks.

"Oh."

I climb out of the Jeep and go around to her side to open

her door for her. She smiles at me distractedly, her eyes looking at Pasha and the shops on either side of it.

I place my hand on the small of her back and lead her over to the door and inside. It feels so good to be touching Mira like this, so natural, so I decide to leave my hand there as we head to the hostess and check in.

"Right this way," she says, and we follow her towards a table in the back of the restaurant.

The place is just as nice as it looked in the pictures online. There are plants hanging down and covering the back wall where the bar is. Murals of the ocean and beaches cover the other three walls, and I slow my pace when I see Mira staring wide-eyed at the paintings.

We reach the table, and I pull out Mira's chair for her, then sit down across from her. The hostess hands us our menus and Mira smiles her thanks at her as she heads back up front.

"Have you ever been to Greece?" I ask her, and she laughs like the idea is crazy.

"I wish!"

I file that information away for later, already imagining taking her there.

Maybe for our honeymoon...

"Is that your dream vacation?" I ask, and she nods.

"I'd love to go there, but there's so many places I'd like to see someday."

"Do you like traveling?"

"I don't know. I haven't done much of it."

"Really? Your family didn't go on vacations when you were younger?"

"No."

Her smile falls and her voice turns sharper. I'm guessing

that her family or her childhood are sore subjects for her. Looks like we have that in common.

"Yeah, me either," I tell her.

"Really?" She asks, seeming surprised.

"Really. My family... we're not close. I haven't talked to them since I joined the military."

"I'm not close to mine either. It was just my mom and me growing up. I haven't talked to her since I moved out."

"Hi there, and welcome to Pasha," our waiter says as he stops next to our table.

I hurry to open my menu and scan the list of drinks.

"Can I get you two something to drink and maybe an appetizer?" He asks us.

"I'll just have water," I order.

"Me too," Mira orders.

"Would you like any appetizers?" He asks.

I look at Mira, and she scans the menu.

"What looks good to you?" She asks me, and I shrug.

"Get whatever you want. What do you recommend?" I ask the waiter.

"I love the hummus and pita and the Spanakopita," he tells us.

"That sounds good. Let's try that," Mira says.

"Sounds good."

The waiter nods, writing down our order as he turns to head back to the kitchen. We both glance at our menus, and I decide on the chicken gyro. Mira takes longer to study the menu, biting her lip as she tries to decide what to order.

"What brought you to Wolf Valley?" I ask her when she closes the menu.

"It was cheap," she says with a self-conscious laugh. "I was living in California before, and it was just getting to be too expensive. When I was laid off from my job there, I knew that I needed to make a change."

The waiter comes back with our drinks and appetizers. He pulls out his notepad and we both order. As soon as he's gone, we both dig into the appetizers.

"What about you?" She asks as she takes a bite of Spanakopita.

"Xavier was from here, and I wanted to stay close to him."

"He's your best friend."

"More like a brother at this point," I admit, and she smiles.

"That's nice. I was an only child and it could be lonely."

"Same. I used to wish for a brother or sister. When I got older, I was kind of glad that it was just me. Having a sibling would have tied me to that family more. Unless they were willing to leave too."

"I know. I was the same way," she says.

We finish the appetizers and our food is dropped off a minute later. The conversation turns to lighter subjects, and I learn that she loves salty food over sweets, her favorite color is green, she loves the cold more than the heat, and she's always wanted a house with a fireplace and a dog or two.

All of that information has been filed away, and I'm determined to give her all of those things. We'll live in a green house that's always cold, has at least two fireplaces and a kitchen that is stocked full of salty snacks, and has a whole pack of dogs running around.

"Did you save room for dessert?" The waiter asks as he clears our plates.

"Oh, no," Mira says, rubbing her stomach. "I'm stuffed."

"We'll take the baklava cheesecake to go then," I say, and she smiles at me.

"You got it," the waiter says.

He drops off the check as he heads to grab our dessert, and I pay, shaking my head when Mira tries to give me some money.

"It's my treat."

She looks like she wants to argue, but the waiter is back with our to-go dessert, and I stand, offering her my hand as we get ready to leave.

I lead her back outside and over to my Jeep. I open the door for her and then pass her the dessert.

"Did you want to try to check out any of the shops?" I ask her, and she shakes her head.

"I think a lot of them are closing. Maybe another time," she says, and I smile.

"Planning another date already?" I ask her, and she smirks.

"No, I was going to go by myself," she sasses.

"Liar. We'll come again soon," I promise her.

I close her door, climb behind the wheel, and make the short drive back to Wolf Valley. The streets are nearly deserted as I park outside of Mira's apartment and hop out to walk her upstairs.

Mira seems more relaxed with me as we climb up to her apartment. I'm hoping that's a good sign because I'm about to ask her out on another date, and I desperately want her to say yes.

"Thanks for dinner," she tells me, and I smile.

"Anytime. In fact, why don't we do this again sometime?"

A pink flush covers her cheeks and she smiles up at me.

"Okay, that sounds like fun."

I want to fist bump and cheer, but I'm afraid that would scare her off so I refrain and just grin down at her.

"Tomorrow?"

"I have work. I'm free on Friday, though."

"Friday then."

She smiles up at me, and my heart starts to race as I lean down towards her. She licks her lips and I close the gap between us and press my mouth against hers.

Her lips are soft and firm beneath mine, and she sighs as her head tilts, giving me better access to her mouth. I lick the seam of her lips, and she gasps, opening for me.

She tastes like Greek spices, and I reach up, cupping her face in my hands. Her tongue flicks against mine shyly, and I swear that I nearly come in my pants.

A door slams beneath us, and Mira jumps, pulling back from me. Her eyes are wide and hazy looking as she stares up at me. Her lips are red and swollen from mine, and all that I can think about is kissing her again.

"Night," she whispers, stepping back from me, and I clear my throat.

"Good night, Mira."

I wait while she unlocks the door and heads inside before I turn and jog back outside to my Jeep. I've got another date lined up with my dream girl and my lips are still buzzing from our first kiss.

Things are finally looking up for me.

I smile the whole way home.

FIVE

Mira

I SMILE as I brush out my hair. I've been doing that a lot lately. Ever since my date with Townes the other night. He's been stopping by work the last two days and bringing me food on my breaks. It's kind of been like a little date. I've been living for those stolen moments with him.

I've been learning so much about him. It's kind of crazy how much we have in common. We both didn't have the best childhoods and neither of us talks to our families now.

Tonight, we're going on another real date. He wouldn't tell me what he had planned for us, but I'm sure that I'm going to love it. Townes seems to hang on my every word, and he remembers everything that I so much as mention. He seems to know all of my likes and dislikes already.

I kind of love that he's been paying so much attention to me. He seems to file away everything that I've ever said that I like or dislike. I love being with him. He makes me laugh and smile more than anyone else. I just wish that he wasn't so bossy sometimes.

I'm not even sure if bossy is the right word. He just takes charge of situations and tells me that we're doing something rather than asking. I know that I'm probably just being sensitive and that getting ordered around just reminds me of my mom, but I still can't seem to shake the annoyance everytime he does it.

I finish getting ready and just in time because Townes knocks on my door as I'm tugging my shoes on.

I opted to dress up a bit more tonight and put on the one and only dress that I own and the only pair of high heels as well. The dress fits a little tighter than I remember, but Townes seems to love my curves, and I think that they're shown off nicely in this dress.

The black material hugs my breasts and is snug around my waist and hips. It ends just above my knees and I smooth the material down as I head to answer the door.

"Hey -eh," Townes says as I open the door.

His eyes widen as he takes me in and then he just stares at me, his mouth hanging open slightly. His reaction is a major ego boost for me and I stand straighter, more confidently.

"Hey," I greet him, taking him in.

He's wearing jeans and a flannel shirt. His muscles fill out the shirt and make him look like a lumberjack. A sexy one.

"You look..." he starts, trailing off as his eyes travel down my body again.

"Good?" I supply, and he nods, his eyes locked on my hips, then my legs, and then back up to my face.

"Gorgeous," he says, his voice deep with heat.

"Thanks," I say, and I can feel my cheeks heating with a blush.

I grab my purse and pull my door shut behind me, locking it and dropping my keys into my bag.

"Where are we going tonight?" I ask him, and he takes my hand and helps me down the stairs.

"I thought that I would cook for you tonight. If that sounds good to you?"

"Sounds perfect."

He helps me into his Jeep and I try to contain my excitement at the thought of being alone with Townes. I've never seen his place, and I try to imagine what it looks like. Townes is kind of a grumpy, no-frills guy, so I bet that it's a typical bachelor pad with just a leather couch and a big TV.

He pulls up outside of a cabin that's surprisingly bigger than I expected. It's surrounded by forests, but still looks warm and inviting. He parks and hurries to open my door while I look around.

"Here, careful. There might be some ice there," he says as he takes my hand and helps me out of the car.

We hurry through the cold wind and inside. I freeze as soon as the door closes behind us.

His house is nothing like I expected. There's a leather couch and flatscreen TV, sure, but there's also throw pillows and rugs. There are a few pictures on the mantle of Xavier, Townes, and a few other soldiers.

"Come on, I'll show you around."

I take off my coat, and he tosses it over an armchair as we head down the hallway. He opens the first door, and I peek in, spotting an office.

"This is where I work. Right down here is a bathroom and then the kitchen."

He leads me into a large kitchen that looks like a chef's

dream. There's a fancy looking oven and stone, marble countertops, and dark wood cabinets. Everything is gleaming and looks brand new, and I wonder how much time he spends in the kitchen.

"What are you making for us tonight?" I ask him as he heads over to the shiny fridge.

"I thought that we could have spaghetti."

"Sounds good. Can I help with anything?"

"No, I've got it. Can I get you something to drink?"

"Sure."

"Wine? Water?"

"Wine, please."

He nods and grabs a bottle of white wine.

"Is this alright?"

"I don't know much about wine, but I'm sure it will be good."

He pours us each a glass and I take a sip, savoring the sweet taste. Townes moves around the kitchen, filling a pot with water and turning on the stove. He grabs a box of spaghetti and a jar of sauce. I watch as he pulls a loaf of garlic bread out of the freezer and opens that.

"Do you cook often?" I ask him, and he nods.

"Yeah. I had to learn how to at a young age if I wanted to eat," he tells me, and I nod.

"I wish that I was better at it. My mom, she had a lot of... mental health problems," I hedge. "She didn't like me touching things in our house. If I did, we'd have to wash them three times."

"Why three times?" He asks with a frown, and I shrug.

"She has undiagnosed OCD. She did a lot of things three times. She was also a huge germaphobe and was terrified of the outside world. I had to go to school and then straight home. When I got home, I'd shower and change my clothes. Then we'd clean."

"Sounds hard," he says softly, and I nod.

"It was. It was stifling and so restrictive."

"I'm sorry, Mira."

"I tried to get her help," I tell him, and he looks at me with sad eyes. "But she didn't want it. Said that there was nothing wrong with her."

"Maybe she'll realize she's wrong one day," he offers, and I give him a sad smile.

"I doubt it."

We're silent for a moment as the water starts to boil behind him.

"My parents were drug addicts. I tried to get them help too, but it never worked. In order to get better, they'd have to want that, and they never did."

"I'm so sorry, Townes."

He nods, opening the box of spaghetti and fiddling with the cardboard.

"I can't fix them, and the sad truth is that I'm better off without them. Happier."

"Good."

He smiles slightly, and I smile back.

"I'm happier without her too."

We share a smile, and he goes back to cooking.

"I like your house," I tell him, and he grins over his shoulder at me.

"Thanks. I need to finish the tour later."

"After dinner," I say, and he nods.

I watch him move around the kitchen, and I can feel my core clenching as he stirs the spaghetti and bends to grab a baking tray for the garlic bread. There's something so sexy about seeing him cook for me.

I take another sip of wine before I stand and move to his side.

"Here, let me help with that," I say, grabbing the jar of spaghetti sauce.

"No, I've got it," he says, trying to take the jar back from me.

The only problem is that I had already opened the lid, and when he grabs it, I end up holding the lid as the spaghetti sauce spills all over my dress, shoes, and the floor between us.

"Shit, Mira! I'm so sorry," Townes apologizes as he sets the jar aside and reaches for some paper towels.

"It was an accident," I say, taking the paper towels and trying to wipe up the sauce.

"That's going to stain. Let me wash it for you. You can take a shower and borrow some of my clothes," he tells me.

"That would be good, thanks."

I follow him upstairs and down the hallway to his room. As soon as I step inside, I freeze.

"Are you painting in here?" I ask him as I spot the half-finished walls.

"Oh, yeah. I just... thought that it needed a change."

I stare at the freshly painted green walls and try not to read too much into it.

He leads me into the bathroom and sets clean towels on the vanity.

"I'll throw your clothes in the wash once you're done. Just let me know if you need anything," he says, and I nod.

"Sure, thanks."

He nods and leaves the bathroom and I take a deep breath, step out of my shoes and pull off my dress. I try to rinse off the sauce in the sink and then leave the dress to dry on the counter.

I turn the shower on and try not to think about the fact that I'm about to be naked in Townes' house.

The water pressure is amazing, and I moan as I let the warm water wash over me. I grab his body wash and scrub off the spaghetti sauce from my legs and feet. I rub the soap over my breasts and bite my lip as a wave of lust slams into me at his scent on me.

I shut the water off, trying to get my libido under control as I wrap a towel around my body. I dry off, but as the cotton rubs against my heated skin, I find myself having a naughty thought.

I could walk out to Townes in just his towel. I wonder what he would do? Would he make a move on me? Do I want him to?

Yes.

The answer is there so fast and I feel alive for the first time in my life. I want him.

I roll my shoulders back and take a deep, steadying breath as I walk out of the bathroom in just a towel.

I'm heading towards the door when it opens, and Townes freezes in the doorway, his eyes locked on me.

He clears his throat, tearing his eyes away from my still-damp legs to look me in the eyes.

"Sorry, I just realized that I never set out clothes for you," he says, and I smile.

"That's okay. I don't mind."

I take a step toward him, trying to show him that I want him, and I smile when I see Townes swallow hard, his eyes dropping back to my towel-covered curves.

My heart races and an awareness skitters along my skin. I can feel it.

Something big is about to happen.

SIX

Townes

I'VE HAD dreams like this a lot since I first met Mira.

Maybe that's why I don't react right away as she walks towards me, dripping wet and wearing only my towel. It isn't until she reaches out, her fingers brushing against my arm tentatively, that I snap out of my daze and realize this isn't a dream.

This is really happening.

Fucking finally.

I reach for her, pulling her into my arms and flush against my body. She lets out a little gasp and I smile as I cup her jaw and tilt her face up towards mine. Her green eyes meet mine and then flutter shut as I dip my head and claim her lips with mine.

Her lips and skin are still damp from her shower, and her hair drips water onto my arms as I pull her closer to me. All I can think about is if she's this wet for me between her thighs.

Her lips are soft but firm against mine, and I slip my hands into her hair, holding her in place as our lips meet over and over again. I feel like I'm in a daze or maybe a dream when she finally pulls away.

"You're too tall," she says with a laugh as she drops back down onto her feet.

I hadn't even realized that I had pulled her up onto her tiptoes when I was kissing her. I wrap my arm tighter around her waist and lift her up off the ground.

She gasps, her arms wrapping around me as she clings to me.

"Now wrap your legs around my waist," I order, and she blushes.

"Then the towel will come undone," she whispers, and I give her a wicked grin.

"Uh-huh, and I'll be able to see all of those sexy curves. Isn't that what you wanted? I know damn sure that it's what I want."

Her cheeks flush, but she does as I say and wraps her thick thighs around my waist. She presses fully against me, and I nearly come just from feeling all of her curves pressed against me.

Sure enough, the towel knot loosens and comes undone, falling to the ground.

I hold her eyes for a beat, and it feels like neither of us is breathing. Then my eyes dip down, and I groan at what I see.

I suddenly regret holding her because it means that I can't touch her the way that I want to.

"I'm going to need to get those tits in my mouth," I tell her as I start walking toward my bed.

Mira's grip on me tightens, and I smirk as I realize that she likes my dirty mouth.

I lay her down, and in the next instant, I'm cupping the soft mounds of her breasts in my hands. They fit perfectly, and I roll the stiff peaks of her nipples between my thumbs and forefingers until she gasps and arches into my touch.

"That feels so-oh good," she gasps, and I grin.

"We're just getting started."

My head dips and I lick one nipple and then the other, alternating until I hear her breathing pick up. She's panting, her body restless beneath me, and I know that I'm driving us both crazy.

I give her a kiss right between her tits and drop to my knees at the edge of the bed. Her eyes are half-lidded as I grab her thighs, but they fly open as I tug her to the edge of the bed.

"Townes!" She cries, and I give her a devilish smirk as I wrap my hands around her thighs and bury my face between her legs.

"Oh!" She screams at the first lick.

I moan, her sweet flavor exploding over my taste buds. Just like that, I'm instantly addicted.

I bury my face deeper in her soft folds and eat her like a starving man. My tongue licks over her clit, and her thighs spasm around my head. When I do it again, her legs clamp down around my head. When I do it a third time, she comes against my mouth.

"Townes!" She screams, and my cock demands attention behind the zipper of my jeans.

"Fuck, I love hearing you scream my name like that," I tell her, my thumb moving to her core.

I find her clit and start to rub lazy circles over the sensitive pearl.

"Please," she begs, and I smile.

"I've got you," I promise her.

I push a finger inside of her, surprised at just how tight she is.

Could she be...?

"Are you a virgin?" I blurt out, and her blushing cheeks give me my answer.

"Um, yes," she says softly.

"Shit, Mira. Are we going too fast?" I ask, already pulling away from her.

"No! Don't stop. I want this."

I study her for a moment, but she seems sincere. My heart jumps in my chest as I realize that she must like me as much as I do her. She wouldn't be giving me this honor otherwise.

"I have no idea what I did to deserve you, but I swear that I'll never stop doing it."

She smiles slightly, and I push a finger back inside of her, determined to loosen her up some before I try to make love to her.

Her hips start to move as I slowly slide my finger in and out of her snug channel. Soon, I'm adding a second finger and then a third. It only takes a few pumps before she's coming again, and I can't take it anymore.

I kiss her clit and then stand and start tearing at my clothes. She watches me with half-lidded eyes until I strip off my jeans and boxers. Then her eyes widen and lock on my hard-on.

"I'll go slow," I promise, and she nods.

I climb onto the bed next to her and then move us both to the middle of the mattress.

Her hands cling to my biceps, and I know that I need to help her relax, so I lean forward and cup her face with one hand, pulling her mouth towards mine. Our lips meet, and she opens for me right away, letting me slip my tongue into her mouth. I wonder if she can taste herself on my lips.

Her tongue flicks against the tip of mine, and I growl, my hand sliding around to the back of her head, and I hold her in place as our tongues battle together.

"Townes," she moans against my lips, and my fingers tighten in her hair.

Her hands move cautiously down my chest and stomach. I grab them before she can wrap her fingers around my cock.

She blinks, frowning at me as I grit my teeth.

"Don't you want me to..." she asks, trailing off.

"God, yes. Right now, though, I need to be inside you. You can explore me later," I promise her.

She nods, and I move her under me. Her thighs spread in invitation, and I have to remind myself that this isn't a dream as I line my cock up with her tight opening.

Our eyes meet as I push in an inch, and she lets out a shaky breath.

"Good?" I ask her, praying that it is.

"Uh huh," she moans, her hips shifting under me, pushing me in a little more.

Her green eyes are dark now and filled with lust as she watches me. I push in another inch and bump up against her virginity.

"Fuck," I hiss.

She's moaning beneath me, which has to be a good sign, but I'm hanging on by a thread here and hearing her moan for me, feeling her tits rubbing against my chest; it's all too much. I'm going to come before I can even fuck her properly.

Make this good for her! I scold myself, and I grit my teeth as I thrust forward and pop her cherry.

She inhales sharply as I fill her fully, and I study her, praying that I didn't hurt her. She blinks up at me, her mouth falling open.

"I'm so... full," she gasps as I start to move tentatively inside of her.

"Is it too much?" I ask her.

Please say no, please say no, please say no.

"No, it feels good," she says.

Thank God.

I start to move more then, pulling almost all of the way out before I slide back in. I do that over and over again, letting her get used to the size and feel of me. Soon, she's rocking her hips in sync with my thrusts.

Having my dream girl beneath me is the hottest thing that I've ever seen in my life. Hearing her soft sighs and moans is driving me wild, and I know that I won't be able to last much longer.

I lean back on my heels so that I can rub her clit. The change in angle has her eyes lighting up, and I start to fuck her harder as my own orgasm starts to brew inside of me.

"Townes! Oh-ohh God!" She cries as her pussy clamps down around me.

I grit my teeth, determined to get her off before I come.

I press more firmly on her clit as I pound into her, and she screams my name as she comes. Feeling her juices coat my cock has me following her over the edge, and I choke out her name as I come with her.

"Oh," she whispers as we both catch our breaths, and I laugh as I collapse on the mattress next to her.

"Oh?" I ask her, and she giggles.

"Yeah, oh."

"Hmm, you're hurting my ego here. I think I'm going to need a redo so I can try for a better reaction than oh," I tell her, and she gives me a little smirk.

"Well, I *guess* that you can have one more chance," she says, and I grin as I pull her against me.

"Challenge accepted," I whisper a second before my lips land on hers.

SEVEN

Mira

WHEN I FIRST OPEN MY eyes, I'm so confused. This isn't my apartment, and why am I so warm? Then I feel Townes' arms tighten around me and last night comes rushing back to me.

He had made love to me twice before we finally left bed and went downstairs to eat. It was midnight by the time the spaghetti was ready, and we had laughed and talked while we ate, then headed right back up to bed to make love again.

I must have passed out after that. It's bright outside, and I wonder what time it is as I try to wiggle my way out from beneath Townes' arms.

"Where are you going?" He mumbles sleepily, and I look over my shoulder to see his eyes still closed.

"To the bathroom," I whisper, and he grumbles but lets me go.

I scoot off the bed and head into the bathroom. It feels so strange to walk around naked like this. My body is sore, and I notice a few bruises and red marks from his hands and mouth on my hips and breasts.

I go to the bathroom and study my reflection as I wash my hands. I guess I thought that I would feel different after I had lost my virginity, but I still feel like me. I run my fingers through my brown hair, trying to untangle some of the knots.

I head back to the bedroom where Townes is sitting in bed. He smiles when he sees me and crooks a finger at me, silently telling me to come back to bed.

"I need to get home," I tell him as I head back towards him.

"It's still early," he argues.

"It's almost nine," I say with a laugh.

He glares at the alarm clock on his bedside table, and I wrap my arms around his neck.

"I really do need to go. I have a long to-do list today."

"Alright. Will I see you tonight? I can make us dinner again."

"Maybe. Let me see how today goes."

He looks like he wants to argue with me, to demand an answer right here and now, but he bites his tongue and leans forward and kisses me instead.

I pull back before he can deepen it, and he growls, trying to pull me back towards him.

"The faster I leave and get everything done, the faster I can come back," I remind him, and he sighs but lets me go.

"Fine. Go do what you have to. Or better yet, you could let me come and help," he offers.

"Don't you have work?"

"Probably," he admits, and I laugh.

"Go do that. I'll see you later."

I grab the dress from last night that we never managed to wash off his dresser, but he stops me.

"You can borrow something from me."

"It's fine. I'm just going home, and then I'll change there."

"Here," he says like I didn't say anything. "You can wear this."

He passes me a shirt and sweatpants, and part of me wants to argue with him, but what does it matter in the end?

"Thanks," I mumble as I get dressed and follow him downstairs.

"Just going to your apartment?" He asks me as we head outside to his Jeep. "Or do you want to stop for breakfast?"

"No, just my apartment."

"Are you sure? You have to eat," he says, and annoyance prickles at my skin.

"I'm sure."

He starts the Jeep and we head towards my apartment in silence. His words stick with me, and it isn't until he's dropped me off and I'm standing in my apartment that it hits me why.

He's bossing me around just like my mom used to. He acts like he knows better than me, like what he wants is more important.

I look down at the clothes that I didn't even want to borrow and frown. Was I warmer in them? Yes, but I had said that I didn't need to wear his stuff. Then, I just let him bulldoze me.

I'm mad at myself for not standing up to him, but I'm also mad at Townes for bossing me around.

My phone buzzes and I pull it out, scowling when I see that it's from Townes.

. . .

TOWNES: I'm at Nosh. I'll pick you up something to eat and drop it off in a bit.

Mira: That's okay. I have stuff here.

Townes: It's no problem. See you soon.

I WANT TO SCREAM, but I settle for gritting my teeth and tossing my phone onto the counter. I pace back and forth around my small living room.

It's been almost two years since I left my mom's house, and I'm sure that the anniversary is bringing up old feelings too, but I can't shake the annoyance and anger I'm feeling about Townes's behavior.

I head into my room to shower and get changed, hoping that helps calm me down. It does. For a bit.

"Hey, breakfast is here," Townes says as I'm drying my hair.

I scream, ducking away from him in shock.

"Shit! You scared the crap out of me," I tell him, my hand covering my racing heart.

"You shouldn't leave your door unlocked," he tells me, and I grind my teeth together.

"Got it. Thanks for breakfast."

"Anytime."

He leans forward, kisses me, and then smiles as he turns and heads out of my apartment. I wait until he's gone before I grab the nearest pillow and scream into it.

This is all too much too fast. I mean, I was just starting to really stand on my own two feet, and now it feels like I'm suffocating. I know I'm probably just overwhelmed, but I can't shake the feeling that maybe jumping into a relationship right now isn't the best idea.

I mean, I was trying to find my freedom and myself, and

instead, it feels like I just tied myself down with a grumpy, bossy man.

Did I mess up? Did I just trade one overbearing dictator for another?

Townes cares about me, and I know that he isn't my mother, but it's hard not to make the comparison or to wonder.

I lock my front door and drag my hands down my face as I wonder what the heck I should do now.

EIGHT

Townes

"GOING TO SEE YOUR GIRL?" Ford asks as he bags up my to go order.

"Yeah, I'm bringing her dinner."

He nods, his eyes sliding over to where Cameron, one of the waitresses who works for him, is talking to a customer.

"I'm happy for you," he says quietly, and I smile.

"Thanks. When are you going to make your move?" I ask, nodding in Cameron's direction.

"Soon," he says, and there's a determined light in his eyes.

I know that feeling. Watching Xavier fall in love with Olive and seeing how happy they are now made me want that with Mira all the more. I'm sure that it's the same for Ford. He's had to watch his twin brother, Foster, finally get his girl, and now his closest friends are all settling down too. I'm glad that he's finally going to go for it with Cameron.

Ford passes me the bag of food, and I wave as I grab it

and head out to my Jeep. Mira is working at Wet and Wild tonight, but we've been eating in my Jeep behind the building to try to stay warm. Plus, it gives us enough privacy to make out a little bit.

I park in our usual spot and leave the Jeep running so that it's warm when Mira comes out. I grab my phone and send Mira a text to let her know that I'm outside, and then I wait for my girl.

These moments with her are the brightest spots in my day. I wake up looking forward to seeing her later. I spend all day counting down the hours until I can see her again.

The back door opens, and I sit up straighter, greedy for my first sight of her. She's wearing jeans and the black Wet and Wild work shirt and pulling on her jacket as she heads over toward my Jeep.

I hop out and smile as she looks at me. She smiles back, but it's not as bright as usual, and I pause as I reach to open the passenger door for her.

"How's work going?" I ask her, wondering if something happened tonight.

"Pretty good. We had two bachelorette parties come in, so it's been busy."

"That's good. I got you a burger and fries from Nosh," I say, and she smiles weakly.

I close the door, hurry over to the driver's side, and climb in next to her. She's opening the take-out bag and hands me the first container before she pulls out the second.

"Thanks for dinner," she says, and even her voice is subdued tonight.

"Is everything okay?" I ask her, starting to get worried.

"Yeah, I'm just tired. It's been a long day," she says.

She does look a little tired and I try to let the nagging feeling go as we both dig into our burgers and fries.

She finishes her food quickly and leans back in her seat, letting her head rest against the seat as she closes her eyes. I toss our trash back in the bag and turn to face her more.

"Are you working tomorrow?" I ask her, and she shakes her head.

"No, I have tomorrow and the next day off."

"Are we just going to be hanging out at home then? I can go to the store tonight and grab some snacks and food so we don't have to leave the house at all."

"That sounds amazing... but I need to get some things done around my apartment tomorrow."

"Tomorrow night then," I try, and she chews on her bottom lip and looks out the window.

"Maybe. I'll let you know."

My stomach cramps, and I realize that she's pulling back from me.

I try not to panic. After all, she could really need to do stuff at her apartment, or maybe she just wants to sleep in her own bed and decompress.

"Sure," I say, and I can hear the disappointment in my voice.

"I should get back in there. Thanks again for dinner."

"Anytime."

She reaches for her door handle and I frown and stop her.

"I'll get your door," I tell her, and she sighs, seeming frustrated as she sits back and waits for me.

I hurry to get out and get her door for her. She hops out and avoids my eyes as she brushes past me.

"I'll talk to you later?" I ask, and she nods.

"Yeah," she says softly, and I want to reach out and grab her.

I want to make her face me, to demand that she tell me

what's wrong so I can fix it. I know that would only make her close up more though so I squeeze my fingers into my palms and stand still.

"Night, Townes," she says before she heads inside, and I swallow, trying to dislodge the rock in my throat.

"Good night, Mira."

The door closes behind her, and I stand there in the cold for another minute, praying that she'll come back out and tell me that this was all some kind of terrible joke.

She doesn't though, and I shiver as the wind blows my hair across my forehead. I hurry back to the driver's side and shift into drive.

I head towards Xavier's house, but when I pull up outside, his truck is gone, and I know he must be out with Olive. I turn around and head back towards town, trying to figure out where to go now.

I wind up at the Wolf Valley Market and decide to get groceries on the off chance that Mira comes over to stay this weekend.

I park and head inside, grabbing a cart and wandering aimlessly up and down each aisle. I spot a familiar head of brown hair in the cereal aisle and smile as I head over to Ransom.

"Hey," I greet him, and he looks up, giving me a lazy smile.

"Hey, are you getting groceries for the week too?" He asks, looking at my mostly empty cart.

"More like the weekend, but I don't know what I want to eat really."

"Cereal is always a safe choice," he says, tossing two boxes of Cinnamon Toast Crunch into the cart.

"True," I say, grabbing a box for myself too.

"I'm surprised that you're here. I figured that you would

be out with your girlfriend," he says as we turn and head down the aisle.

"She has to work tonight."

"Hmm," he says, eyeing a box of oatmeal for a moment before he passes. "What are you doing for Valentine's Day?"

"Valentine's Day?" I ask in confusion, and he snorts.

"Yeah, you know, that holiday for people in love? They have it every year in February. This isn't ringing any bells?" He asks with a smirk, and I glare at him.

"It is... I just forgot. I've never celebrated it before," I tell him.

"Me either," he says with a shrug. "Though I might try to this year."

"Ah, with Ruby," I say, and he frowns.

"Am I really that obvious about it?" He grumbles more to himself, and I shrug.

"I should make reservations somewhere," I say, and he nods.

"Or plan some kind of romantic night in. What are you going to do for presents?" He asks me as we turn and head down the chip aisle.

"Candy and flowers, I guess. It seems like I should keep it classic."

"Sounds like a plan."

He tosses in a few bags of chips, and I grab some pretzels and popcorn since I know that Mira loves them.

We brainstorm other ideas for Valentine's Day as we finish shopping and head to checkout.

"I'll see you later," he says as we head out to our cars.

"See you."

We head in opposite directions, and I hurry to load all

of the groceries into my Jeep and push the cart back up to the market.

I drive by Wet and Wild on my way home and crane my neck to try to get a glimpse of Mira, but she must be in one of the aisles or in the back. I head home and unpack all of the groceries. Then I just stand in my kitchen.

Something feels off with Mira, but I can't figure out what could have caused that. We had fun on our last date. She's been normal when I bring her food at work. We've been texting like usual. Nothing seems off. Until tonight.

I try to convince myself that it's all in my head, but as I clean up the kitchen and get ready for bed, all I can think about is how I'm messing things up with Mira.

I pull out my phone and plug it into the charger next to my bed. There's no message from Mira, but she's probably just getting home. I decide to text her and click on her name.

TOWNES: Good night. I'll talk to you tomorrow. Sweet dreams.

I STARE AT THE SCREEN, waiting for the dots to pop up so that I know she's texting me back, but they never come.

I frown at the screen. She's usually so quick to text me back, and panic starts to set in once again.

I lay back in bed and stare at the ceiling. All I can think is that I'm not going to lose Mira. Not when I finally have her.

Sleep doesn't come for a very long time.

NINE

Mira

I'M LOST.

Not literally. I mean, I'm standing in the middle of Shelf Indulgence. No, I'm lost with what to do.

It's been three days since I last talked to Townes. I thought that time and space away from him would help me clear my head and figure out what to do. Instead, it's left me feeling even more torn.

It's been hard to ignore him. I've been avoiding his calls and texts, refusing to answer when he knocked on my apartment door yesterday. I know that my time is running out though. He knows I'm working today, so it's only a matter of time before he shows up here.

I clock in and force a smile to my lips as I greet Saffron and head over to the front counter to see what I need to stock today.

"Mira," Townes says behind me, and I jump, spinning to face him.

That was fast.

"Hey," I say awkwardly.

Looking at him hurts. He looks so worried and confused. I hate that I did this to him. I never wanted to hurt him, and now I'm afraid that I'm going to hurt us both.

"Can we talk?" He asks me, and I look around, hoping Saffron will save me.

"Go ahead, Mira! We're slow right now," she says with a smile.

I'm sure she thinks she's being helpful, so I smile back at her and then lead Townes over to a deserted corner of the store.

"What's up?" I ask, trying to sound nonchalant.

"What's up? You tell me?" He growls. "Why are you ignoring me? You haven't answered any of my texts or calls. I came by your place yesterday, and I know you were home."

"I must have been sleeping," I lie, and he narrows his eyes at me.

"You're lying."

I swallow hard, crossing my arms over my chest and looking away from him.

"What happened, Mira? I thought things were good between us, and then you started to ice me out. What did I do?"

His words break my heart, and I clear my throat, trying to remove the lump forming there.

"Nothing. You didn't do anything. It's me. Things are just moving really fast between us, and I'm not sure I'm ready for that."

"Fine, then say that. We can slow down."

"Can we? Ever since we started dating, you've seemed to have one speed. I mean, we've only been together for like a week and a half, and we spend all of our free time together."

"I like spending time with you," he says, sounding confused and hurt.

"I do, too, I just... I don't even know," I admit.

Tears burn the backs of my eyes and I try to blink them back.

"I'm scared, Townes," I whisper, and he tries to pull me into his arms, but I push him away.

"You've experienced so much. You've seen the world. I've seen a few towns in the surrounding two hundred miles."

"So, we'll travel more."

"It's not just that. It's me," I stress, the first tears falling onto my cheeks.

"Mira..."

"I don't think you realize how isolated and alone I was growing up. It was just my mom and me. No friends, no boyfriends, nothing. Then I came here and I made friends. I have two jobs that I love, my own apartment, and my own space. I'm in charge of my life and I love that freedom. I'm trying to figure out what I like and it was going well."

I stop, but I can see that he knows where I'm going.

"Until you met me," he says quietly, and I choke back a sob.

"Not just that. I like you. A lot. I just feel like I'm losing myself. I'm so scared to go back to where it's just me and one person. I want to have friends and a life, and I think I would give that all away for you already."

"I would never ask you to do that," he insists, and I swipe at the tears.

"Maybe not on purpose, but you have a habit of taking over or bulldozing me."

"How?"

"Insisting on me not helping you cook, demanding that you open my door for me," I list off.

"I was just trying to be a gentleman," he says, and I nod.

"I know, but it triggers me. It reminds me of my mom bossing me around. I don't mind you doing that stuff sometimes, but I want to be independent. It's important to me."

"Okay, I can back off."

I sigh. *He says that but what happens if he can't? Can I trust him to keep his word? What do I want to do here?*

"I just... I need space."

"Mira, please don't do this," he begs, and I squeeze my lips together, trying to fight off the fresh wave of tears.

"I have to."

"No, you don't. Don't do this. Please. I love you, Mira. I have since I first saw you. I can't lose you," he says, tears sparkling in his eyes.

His words and seeing him like this breaks me, and I sob, tears spilling onto my cheeks.

"I need time," I choke out before I brush past him and run into the back room.

The door closes behind me, and I lean back against the wall and cry.

"Mira? Are you okay?" Saffron asks gently, and I shake my head.

"No," I sob. "I'm pretty sure I just broke my heart and Townes'," I admit.

Her arms wrap around me, and I lean into her hold, letting her try to keep me together as my heart breaks more in my chest.

I don't even remember going home and I know that Saffron must have taken me and made sure that I made it back to my apartment alright. I must have fallen asleep at some point and I wake up to my phone buzzing on the nightstand next to me.

It's still dark out and my first thought is that it's Townes calling me. When I look at the screen though, I'm shocked to see my mom's name there instead.

I stare at it, debating what to do.

Why is she calling me? What could she possibly want? Could she be reaching out because she changed and wants to apologize?

I chew on my bottom lip, debating what to do for so long that the call goes to voicemail. My phone dings with an alert that I have a new voicemail, and I collapse back onto my mattress.

I'm still so raw after breaking up with Townes, and I just can't deal with my mom right now on top of all of that. I'll call her back later.

I close my eyes and try to go back to sleep, but I can't. My mind is racing, and with a sigh, I open my eyes and stare up at the ceiling until the sun starts to spread light around the room.

Finally, I feel strong enough to listen to her message and I grab my phone.

I don't realize that I've gotten my hopes up until I press play, and my mom's nasally voice screeches at me.

"Mira, you need to call me back. I need you to come home and help me. The landlord is raising the rent, and I'm not moving, so you need to come home and help with the bills. It's time for you to start being a good daughter and help your poor mother for once in your life. Call me back so that I know when to expect you."

The message ends, and I let out a deep breath as tears start to spill onto my cheeks.

She wants me to come home. To fix things for her. To help her, even though she's never done anything to help me.

She doesn't even miss me. She just needs me to make her life easier, and she's going to manipulate and boss me around until she gets what she wants.

I can't help but compare Townes and his version of ordering me around with my mom. Townes can be bossy, but he's always looking out for me, and I know that he has my best interests at heart, even if his highhandedness can be a bit annoying at times.

Was it unfair to lump the two of them together? Did I just mess up the best thing to ever happen to me?

I curl up in bed and debate that until the sun starts to set and my eyes are too tired to keep open.

TEN

Townes

SO, this is what it feels like to have a broken heart.

It fucking sucks.

It's even worse because everywhere I look, I see Valentine's Day decorations, and it only reminds me that all of the plans I had made for Mira and me this year won't be happening.

I'll be spending the holiday alone.

Again.

I've been trying to give Mira the space she asked for, but I swear to God, it's killing me. The first few days, I tried to pretend like everything was normal. I went into town and had breakfast at the diner with Xavier and my friends. Then Mira came in, and it felt like I got kicked in the stomach.

I drove to the market and saw her walking to work and almost crashed my car. The ache in my chest took hours to fade after that so I just stopped leaving my house. It seemed safer that way.

A VERY GRUMPY VALENTINE'S DAY   61

It hasn't been easier though. I can still smell Mira on my sheets, and I haven't had the heart to wash them yet.

Today is Valentine's Day, and I don't know what to do with myself. The flowers and chocolates I got for Mira are sitting on my kitchen counter. The reservations that I made at the steakhouse in Rosewood have been canceled.

I can't even go out with Xavier to distract myself because he's spending tonight with Olive.

I'm not sure how much more of this I can take. I can feel myself splintering with each passing day. It's a slow death, and I hate it.

I'm a fighter. It's what got me out of my parents' house and away from them. It's why I joined the Army and then became a Ranger. It might not be what Mira wants right now, but I can't just sit around waiting for her. I'm going to fight for her. At least one more time.

I grab my keys, flowers, and chocolates and march out the door. I know that she had tonight off of work, so I head towards her apartment. The lights are on when I park, and I take a deep breath, jog over to the door, and hit the buzzer for her place.

She buzzes me in right away, and I take the stairs two at a time up to her door.

"It was like fifteen dollars, right?" She asks, counting the cash in her hand.

"What?" I ask her, and her head snaps up.

Her eyes meet mine and I take her in. She looks sad and I wonder if maybe she's been missing me.

"Townes... I wasn't; I thought that you were the pizza delivery."

"Oh."

We stare at each other for a moment, and I thrust the flowers and chocolates at her.

"Happy Valentine's Day," I tell her, and she blinks, taking the gifts slowly.

"Oh," she says as her phone starts to buzz on the counter behind her. "Sorry, I should get that."

She turns and grabs her phone, answering it without looking at the screen.

"Hello?" She says, and I can tell that something is wrong from the way that she tenses.

Her back is ramrod straight, and her fingers clench around the bouquet of flowers and box of chocolates.

"I know, Mom. I got your message. I've just been busy. I was going to call you back though and –"

It's her mom?

I thought that they didn't talk. What could she possibly want now? Is that why Mira pushed me away? Did something happen?

I take a step towards her, and she turns, staring blankly at the wall next to me. Tears are starting to form in her eyes, and I can't stand the sight of them.

"Mom, I can't," she chokes out as the first tears fall onto her face.

That's my breaking point, and I step towards her, grabbing the phone and bringing it to my ear.

"She'll call you back if she wants to talk to you," I tell her mom firmly.

She starts to protest loudly, but I hang up and stare down at my girl.

As soon as I end the call, panic sets in. Did I just overstep? Is she going to be pissed at me?

"I'm sorry," I blurt, and she blinks, wiping at the tears.

"Are you?"

I hesitate, and she huffs out a laugh.

"Not really," I admit, deciding to go with honesty. "I fucking hate seeing you upset."

She nods, and I study her, trying to decide how she feels about me being here, but I can't quite read the expression on her face.

"Why are you here?" She asks, and I take a deep breath and launch into my prepared speech.

"I know that you asked for space and time," I start, and her eyes meet mine. "I tried to stay away, but fuck, Mira. It hurts."

Her eyes start to get shiny with more tears, and I hurry on.

"I love you, Mira. I can't be away from you. I need you in my life... so I promise to be whatever you want me to be. I'll never open a door or boss you around. I'll let you be independent. We'll travel anywhere that you want. We'll go at your pace. I'll do whatever you want, be whatever you want. I just need you."

A tear spills onto her cheek, and I hold my breath, waiting to see what she says. It feels like the silence stretches for hours, but I know that it's probably only a few seconds before she breaks it.

"I thought that you were like my mom," she admits, and the breath leaves my lungs in a whoosh.

"I don't mean to be," I rush to tell her, and she shakes her head.

"You're not. Not really. You can be bossy with me, but you do it from a place of love. You want what's best for me."

"I do," I promise her.

"My mom has called me a few times the last few days," she admits. "That was the first time that I've answered, but she's left a couple of messages and each one is her demanding that I do something for her. She doesn't care about me or what I want or need. All she can think about is herself and her own needs and wants."

I want to pull her into my arms and tell her how much I love her, but I can see that she needs to say her peace so I remain silent and still.

"I still want to have more independence, but...I missed you," she says softly, and my knees almost give out in relief.

I brace my hand on the doorframe, and she smiles shyly at me.

"I missed you too. So much," I tell her.

"I trust you. I know that you'll work to give me what I want, what I need," she says, and I nod.

"I would do anything for you," I tell her, and she smiles softly.

She takes a step toward me, and I can't hold back any longer. I cup her face in my hands and kiss her. All of the emotions that I've felt over the last couple of days are poured into the kiss. The pain and longing, the need and love, it's all there.

She gasps, and I slip my tongue into her mouth to tease hers. She tastes like chocolate and whipped cream, and I know that she must be drinking hot chocolate.

The wrapper on the flowers crunches as I step closer to her, and I pause, taking the flowers and chocolates from her and setting them on the table by the front door. Then I grab her and drag her body against mine.

"Townes," she sighs as my lips claim hers once again, and I moan.

"I love you, Mira," I whisper against her mouth.

"I love you too."

My heart feels like it's going to burst in my chest. This is the best moment of my life.

"Sorry to interrupt," comes a voice behind me, and I growl as I break the kiss and turn around.

An amused looking teen is there holding a pizza box, and I grab my wallet, hand him two twenties and grab the pizza from him.

"Have a good night," he says cheerfully.

I turn back to Mira, passing her the pizza, and she tries to hide her grin behind her hand.

"Are you hungry?" She asks, and I nod.

We head inside, and I kick the door closed behind us. She grabs the flowers and chocolates and sets everything down in the kitchen.

"Happy Valentine's Day," I tell her as she opens the chocolates and pops one in her mouth.

"Thank you."

She chews, and I grab two plates from the cabinet and set them next to the pizza.

"Listen, I want to be with you, but I think we still need to talk."

"Okay," I agree, and we take a seat at the counter.

"I like when you take care of me or show that you are thinking of me, but I want to take care of myself too. I want space to grow and explore."

"Whatever you want, Mira. I'll give it to you."

"What about you?" She asks, and I shake my head.

"I just want you to be safe, healthy, and happy. As long as you are, then I'm good."

She smiles at me as she grabs a slice of pizza, and I smile back as I grab my own slice.

This isn't what I envisioned for our Valentine's Day, but as long as I'm with Mira, I'm happy.

"I didn't get you a gift," she tells me as we're cleaning up, and I shrug.

"That's fine. I don't need anything," I assure her.

"I think that I have something else in mind," she says, her voice going low and husky, and my dick stands at attention.

When she runs her hand low over my back, I turn and follow her back towards her bedroom.

ELEVEN

Mira

I DIDN'T QUITE REALIZE how much I missed being with Townes like this until he's pulling my clothes off. Our skin brushes against each other, and I sigh, enjoying the feel of his hot, hard body against mine.

Our clothes are in a pile at our feet, and I smile as he lifts me in his arms easily and carries me over to the bed.

"I missed you so much," he tells me, and I nod.

"I missed you too."

"Now tell me that you love me," he says, then catches himself. "Shit, I'm sorry, Mira. I swear that I'm trying."

"No, it's alright. I kind of like when you're in charge when we're in the bedroom," I admit and he smirks down at me.

"Good," he whispers against the shell of my ear. "Now say it."

"I love you."

His body seems to sag in relief at my words and a thrill

goes through me as I realize the power that I have over him. Townes might like taking control, but he would do anything I asked of him if it made me happy.

That's the difference between my mother and him. My mom couldn't get past her OCD and what she wanted. I needed friends and to have a normal childhood where I wasn't afraid all of the time. She never was willing to work to give me that.

Townes kisses my neck and thoughts of my mother and the past disappear as I get lost in him. He lays me down in the center of my twin-size bed and grumbles a bit as he tries to get comfortable on it next to me.

"Please let me buy you a bigger bed," he begs. "Or better yet, you can just move in with me."

"I like my bed."

He sighs, then moves so that he's above me, caging me in with his arms. My core clenches as I feel his weight on me, and I wrap my arms around his neck, pulling him down until his lips meet mine.

His mouth moves against mine in a slow, decadent kiss. I get lost in him, my hands running over his body everywhere I can reach. I run my hands down his sides, then up his back, over his chest and arms. I can feel his cock harden further between my legs, and I start to grow restless beneath him, my hips lifting so that his length rubs him right where I need him most.

I wrap my legs around his waist, and he laughs against my skin.

"So eager. I need to get you ready for me," he tells me as I continue to rub against him.

"Oh, trust me, I'm more than ready," I assure him.

His dick rubs through my folds, and we both groan at the contact. I arch against him, and he kisses down to my breasts, taking one nipple into his mouth to tease between his teeth.

"Townes," I moan, and he bites down softly on the sensitive nub.

He switches to my other breast, giving it the same attention, and I let my eyes close as we move together.

We're teasing each other, driving both of us closer and closer to the edge. I'm so close to coming and he's not even inside of me yet.

"Please," I beg, and he growls against the swell of my breast.

"Fuck, Mira. You drive me crazy," he groans as he sits back on his heels.

I watch him greedily as he fists his cock and guides the tip to my entrance. We both hold our breaths as he starts to sink into me.

"Townes!" I gasp as he bottoms out inside of me.

"Fuck, I love hearing you say my name like that."

"Make me do it again then," I challenge him, and he grins as he braces his hands on either side of my head and starts to move inside of me.

His lips find mine, and my hands slide over his back, pulling him closer. I want to feel his weight on me. I want to feel every inch of him against me, in me.

We're both so on edge after not being together in a few days, and I know that this first time isn't going to last very long. Already, Townes is starting to lose control.

He starts to pound into me, over and over again, relentlessly. His thrusts push me up the bed little by little. Townes growls, and I force my eyes open to look at him.

"You need a bigger bed," he growls as he shifts his arm to hold me in place, never once slowing his pace inside of me.

I moan, my core clenching around him. I think it's the fact that he's looking out for me and what I need, even when he's equally lost in pleasure, that does it for me.

I'm close. So close.

"Fuck, Mira. Give it to me. Come all over my cock," he orders, and I let go with a cry as I do what he says and come hard.

He grunts and finds his own release, his pace slowing until he stops. We're both breathing hard, and I smile as I look into his blue eyes. His hair is damp and sticking to his forehead, but he's never looked sexier to me.

"Bigger bed," he tells me as he pulls out and tries to get comfortable next to me.

"Oh, I don't know. I kind of like being so close to you."

"We can do that in a king-size bed, too," he points out.

"Alright," I give in, and he lets out a whoop behind me.

"We can go pick one out tomorrow... if you want," he hurries to add, and I smile as I bury my face in his chest.

"If I'm getting a new bed, then there's something that I've always wanted to try with this one," I tell him, and he raises a brow.

"What's that?"

"Fuck me until we break the bedframe."

"Holy shit, I love you," he says, staring at me with wide eyes.

I grin, wrapping my arms around his neck.

"I love you too."

"Now, let's see about making your dream come true," he says as he rolls me under him once again.

It takes a couple of times, but he does make it come true.

Just like I knew he would.

TWELVE

Townes

FIVE YEARS LATER...

"ARE YOU READY FOR TONIGHT?" Xavier asks me as we finish up work.

"Yeah, I've got it all planned out," I tell him with a grin. "What about you?"

"Olive wants to stay in, so we're just going to make dinner together and watch a movie."

"Sounds fun."

"Should be," he says as he gathers up his things and pulls on his jacket.

"Have fun," he says with a wave as he heads out.

I close the door behind him and then hurry into the kitchen to check on dinner.

Today is Valentine's Day, and I can't wait to have some alone time with my wife. Don't get me wrong, I love my son more than anything, but it's been too long since Mira and I were able to really connect, just the two of us.

Mira and I have been married for four years. We actually got married a year after we started dating, or, I guess, a year and one month since we got married in March. We found out that we were expecting just a few weeks after we got back from our honeymoon, and our son, Noah, was born at the end of January.

We've been a little family of three for the last three years and just recently started trying for baby number two. Mira wanted to wait to make sure we had the hang of this parenting thing before we had any more kids.

I know she was worried that she might be like her mother was with her, but that couldn't be farther from the truth. She's so loving and compassionate. She's never afraid to make a mess with Noah. Seeing the two of them together is so touching. You can see the love between them in every moment, and I know she'll be an equally amazing mother to any other kids we might have.

Mira is still working part-time at Wet and Wild and Shelf Indulgence. She likes hanging out with her friends and making her own money, and I know having that independence is important to her.

She's working at Shelf Indulgence today and took Noah with her. I had offered to watch him here, but he was being extra clingy with her today. Saffron and the rest of the Baker sisters all love him, and they never mind when she brings them into work, though she doesn't usually take him to Wet and Wild.

I glance at the clock as I peek into the oven to check on dinner. I still have at least an hour until Mira and Noah are home and I smile as I turn to get started on our dessert for tonight.

The front door opens, and I freeze, frowning in confusion until I hear Mira call out for me.

"Townes, can you give me a hand?"

I head down the hall to greet her, and my steps quicken when I see Noah looking miserable, standing in all of his winter gear.

"What's wrong, buddy?" I ask him as I kneel to help him take his jacket and boots off.

"He threw up at the bookstore," Mira tells me, and I look up, noticing that she looks a little pale, too.

"How are you feeling?" I ask her as I put his boots and coat away.

"A little nauseous," she admits, and I move to help her take her coat off.

"I'll get Noah. Why don't you go lay down," I encourage her, and she nods, trudging upstairs.

"Do you want something to drink?" I ask my son, and he shakes his head.

"Okay, buddy, let's get you into the bath and then we'll see how you're feeling."

He holds his hands up, and I pick him up and carry him upstairs and into the bathroom. I set him next to the tub as I bend over and get his bath ready. The water starts to fill up the tub, and I pull off Noah's clothes.

His eyes are drooping already, and I know he probably just ate something that didn't agree with him and just needs rest. I hurry to clean him up and get him into clean pajamas. I tuck him in, and he's out before I'm even out of his room.

I pull the door closed a bit, and that's when I hear Mira throwing up in our bathroom. I run into our room and then into the bathroom.

Mira is bent over the toilet, throwing up, and I rush to

gather her hair and pull it out of the way. I rub her back as she throws up again.

"I can run to the store and grab Gatorade or Saltines," I offer, and she wipes her mouth and flushes the toilet. "I didn't hear about any bug going around town."

"It's fine. I'm fine," she says, leaning back against the wall.

"You're not. What do you need, Mira?" I ask her, crouching to look her in the eye.

"Help me stand up," she says, and I grab her hand and pull her to her feet.

I help her over to the bed, and she reaches into her bedside drawer and pulls out a box.

"Happy Valentine's Day," she tells me, and I frown.

"Mira, we can do gifts later. I need to run to the store for you before they close," I argue, and she shakes her head.

"I'm fine. Open the box."

"You're not," I snap, and she smiles.

"Open the box," she says more firmly, and I sit down next to her and take the lid off the box.

I freeze when I see what's inside.

"You're pregnant?" I whisper, and when I turn to look at her, she's grinning at me.

"Yeah. I found out yesterday morning. I have another Valentine's Day gift for you, too, but it's downstairs."

"This is all that I need. You, Noah, and this little peanut," I say, tears stinging the back of my eyes.

"I love you, Townes."

"I love you too, Mira. So much. You, Noah, and our little bean," I say, leaning over and kissing her stomach gently before I scoot closer to her and kiss her too.

"I made us dinner," I whisper against her lips, and she pulls back, covering her mouth like she might throw up.

"Is it the smell? Is it on me?" I ask.

I've been cooking all day, so I'm sure I smell like the Beef Wellington I prepared.

Mira nods, and I back away from her, stripping off my clothes and tossing them in the hamper, then moving the hamper out of the room.

Mira follows me into the bathroom, and I grin at her over my shoulder as I turn on the shower.

"What a weird way to get me to take my clothes off," I joke, and she laughs.

"I'm sneaky like that."

I test the water temperature, and when I turn around, Mira is stripping off her clothes too. I smile softly, holding out my hand to her as we both step into the shower and under the spray.

My hands run over her body, and I kiss her softly as we take turns washing each other. My cock responds to her touch and the sight of her naked body, but I can see that my wife is tired. She can barely keep her eyes open, so I turn off the water and wrap her up in a towel.

She dries off and I lift her into my arms and carry her back to our bed. I tuck her in and kiss her forehead as her eyes droop.

"Do you need anything?" I whisper, and she shakes her head.

"Just sleep," she mumbles, and I nod.

"Get some rest."

She nods, and I kiss her forehead again.

"Happy Valentine's Day," I whisper, and she smiles sleepily up at me.

"Happy Valentine's Day. Sorry that I ruined your plans."

"You couldn't ruin anything, Mira. You gave me the best Valentine's Day yet," I say.

She smiles, her eyes closing, and I tuck her in tighter before I tiptoe out of the room to put dinner away and clean up downstairs.

It isn't how I had planned for tonight to go, but I have my wife, son, and another on the way, so I can't be too disappointed.

I turn off the lights and smile to myself as I head upstairs to my wife.

***

Looking for more Wolf Valley holiday books? Check out Xavier and Olive's story or read the rest of the Wolf Valley: A Very Grumpy Holiday series!

Don't miss the other Grumpy books! Check out A Very Grumpy Best Friend and the other Wolf Valley Grumps here!

A VERY GRUMPY HALLOWEEN

*

It's just a fling... right?

Maple:

I need a break.

I've spent this last year working hard to get my business off the ground and to settle into my new apartment and town.

All work and no play, though, has made me a dull girl.

Now, I'm looking to change that, and I know just how to do it.

With Ryder Murray.

Ryder

When Maple Baker propositions me, I know that this is my chance.

I've had my eye on the bubbly redhead since she first moved to town, but she's never given me a second look.

Now she is, and I'm not about to let her look away.

She thinks that we're a fling, just friends with benefits.

I'm about to show her that we're forever.

ONE

Maple

I SMILE to myself as I walk to work, taking a deep breath of the crisp fall air. Fall is my favorite season, and Halloween is my favorite holiday. It has been ever since I was a little girl. I used to dress up every year, sometimes even throw parties for my friends once we got too old for trick or treating, but that was before. Before my parents died, before I moved to Wolf Valley with my sisters, before I started my shop.

Maybe I should have a party this year, I think to myself as I head down the street.

It's been too long since I've had some fun. I used to go out with friends and hang out with my sisters. I was in a book club and a craft circle. I used to be social, but lately, not so much.

The last year has been busy, filled with a move, settling into my new apartment, and opening my shop, Wet and Wild. My days have been filled with making sure that my store gets off the ground and is a success. It wasn't easy at first, but things have been going great for the last six months. I finally feel like I'm at a point where I can take a break. Now I just need to figure out what I want to do on my break.

Maybe a vacation? Although I don't really have the staff for that right now.

It's just me, my youngest sister, Ginger, and our friend, Lilou. Both Ginger and Lilou are part-time, and while I know they can handle things for a day or two, I'm not sure I'm at a point where I could leave for a week or two.

I weigh my options as I head into the shop, smiling at Lilou behind the counter.

"Hey, how's it going?" I ask her.

"Good. We've been busy," she says with a smile.

Hiring Lilou has been the best decision since opening this place. It gives me a chance to take a break and do all the little tasks that need to be done, and it's made us closer. It's nice to have friends besides my sisters, and she's a great friend to have. Plus, she's an awesome employee.

I set my things down behind the counter, getting settled as Lilou helps a customer check out. The door opens and in walks one of my other sisters, Olive. She's the eldest of us and runs the bakery right next door. She usually stops by after she closes, and I smile as I spot the bakery box in her hands.

"How's it going?" She says, and I smile.

"Pretty good. For me?" I ask as she hands it to me.

"Yeah, you and Lilou."

Olive is an amazing baker. She's great in the kitchen, period. She got that from our mom.

A pang hits me as I think about our parents. They've been gone for a few years now, but the ache hasn't gone away. I doubt that it ever will. My sisters and I had left our old house behind, deciding that we needed a change of scenery. Olive was the one who suggested Wolf Valley and when she declared that she was going to open up her own bakery, we all were inspired.

Olive owns the bakery Masterbeaters, I own Wet and Wild, and Saffron runs the bookstore Shelf Indulgence. Ginger hasn't settled on a single business yet, so she floats between them, helping out where she can. It's worked out well for all of us, and we've found a new home here. Still, though, my heart can't help but hurt for the one that we left.

"Have Saffron or Ginger stopped by?" Olive asks me, naming our other two sisters.

"Not that I know of. I just got in myself."

"Must be nice," she sighs, and I grin.

"If you want to sleep in, then you're in the wrong profession," I tease her.

"True, but now I get to go home and spend the rest of the night with my sexy man," she says, talking about her new husband, Xavier.

Olive and Xavier met when we first moved to town. They lived across the street from each other, and Olive was smitten from the moment that she saw him. He was, too, though he didn't think he was good enough for her and tried to fight his feelings. He should've known better. Once Olive sets her mind to something, she always gets it.

"Tell him I said hi."

"I will," she promises as she leans against the counter.

"Have you talked to Vera yet?" She asks, naming one of our friends in town.

"No, why? Is she alright?"

"Yeah, she's fine. She's decided to throw a Halloween

party this year. She mentioned a costume contest and some games," she says, giving me a knowing smile.

Halloween costume party? That's just what I need for my break, I think.

It's well known in my family just how much I love Halloween and dressing up and I smile at the thought of getting to do it this year and hang out with all of our friends.

"I haven't seen her yet," I say, and Olive nods.

"I'm sure she'll be by soon, or maybe she'll text you."

"Text who?" Lilou asks as she joins us at the counter.

"We're talking about Vera's Halloween party," Olive says.

"Oh! Yeah, she was by a little bit ago. Told me to give you this," she says, passing me an invitation.

I open it, smiling at the ghosts and bats on the card.

"Are you going too?" I ask Lilou, and she smiles.

"Maybe. If my boss will give me time off."

"Of course," I tell her. "Maybe we'll close early that day so we can all go."

"Yay! I already told her that Xavier and I would go. It should be a lot of fun!" Olive says with a wide grin, and I smile.

Fun. The word seems so foreign.

I frown at that thought, wondering when I became so sad and bitter.

When was the last time that I had any fun?

It's been nothing but work, errands, and sleep for me for the last year as I tried to get this place off the ground. I know that I threw myself into work to try to distract myself from my grief. Not that it worked. I would go home after work and think about my parents. I would be stocking here at the shop or driving through town and randomly think of them.

The ache in my chest has lessened in the last year, but I doubt that it will ever truly go away.

I shake my head, trying to shake off the gloomy thoughts as I focus on my sister and friend.

"We'll all go together," I say, offering Olive and Lilou a smile. "Maybe we can do a group costume!"

We debate ideas for a bit before Olive's phone rings, and she waves goodbye as she heads home to her man. Lilou and I get to work then, and I smile as I restock some shelves.

My sister is right I am due for some fun, I think as I look up, my eyes locking on him.

Ryder Murray.

His friendly blue eyes twinkle as he smiles at me, and I swallow hard, offering him a weak smile back.

I can feel my face blushing and I reach up, tucking a strand of hair behind my ear.

Ryder Murray likes me. He's even asked me out a few times, but I've never accepted. Mainly because of Wet and Wild and all of the work here, but also because I thought that he would get bored of me. I mean, the man looks like a freaking model, with his dark hair and piercing blue eyes, and I well... don't. Not unless we were talking about a plus-size model.

The two of us seem like polar opposites. He's not really much of a talker, and he seems more like a loner who prefers to be by himself. Whereas I like having people around and being social. Still, there's something about him that calls to me.

I watch his tall frame as he continues down the sidewalk, and suddenly, I know exactly how I'm going to have some fun.

TWO

Ryder

MAPLE BAKER.

God, she's perfect.

That same thought hits me every time I see her, every time I even think about her. She is too, or at least she's perfect for me.

Too bad she can't seem to see that.

I've tried for the past year to get close to her. Ever since she moved to town, she's kept me at arm's reach. Sometimes, I think that she can feel this thing between us, too. There's a certain glint in her eyes, a pink blush staining her cheeks that proves to me that she's not so immune to me, but she has yet to admit it or take me up on any of my offers to take her out.

Granted, I've only worked up the courage to ask her out a few times. Still, getting rejected by your dream girl isn't fun, and I've been trying to figure out a plan to convince her to give me a chance.

So far, I've come up with nothing.

I sigh as I pop the cap on another beer bottle and set it down on the crowded bar in front of Nolan. He's been a semi-regular in this place ever since he moved to town. I thought at first that he was here to hit on the girls who were always making eyes at him, but then I noticed that he never so much as glanced in their direction. My new theory is that he's just lonely and hangs out here to get out of his place.

I get that. It was part of the reason why I started working here. I knew that it would be too loud for me to be forced to make small talk, and that works in my favor. I'm not great at talking to new people, or really people in general.

"Need anything else?" I ask him and he grunts out a no.

I move on to the next customer, and my mind drifts back to Maple.

When I first heard that they were opening a sex shop downtown, I was surprised and curious. That's what made me walk by on their grand opening, and it was then that I saw her.

She was smiling at a group of women and talking animatedly. She was gorgeous with bright green eyes that reminded me of Christmas and dark auburn hair. Another girl had walked over and joined her. I would later learn that there were four new sisters in town, but I had only ever really paid attention to Maple.

There was just something about her that clicked with me right away. Before I had even said a word to her, I knew that she was meant to be mine.

I had gone into the store the next day when it wasn't as busy and introduced myself. She had blushed up at me, and I thought that my happily ever after was within reach.

When I had asked her out though, she had turned me down and then gone to help a customer.

Ever since, I've tried to talk to her every time that I see her. I try to get her to open up a bit to me, but it's been hard.

I set down a round of shots onto a tray and nod at Sally, the waitress, who hefts it into the air and heads towards a nearby table.

I sigh as I grab a rag and wipe down the bar top. I've been working at Murphy's Bar ever since I came back to town after graduation. It was a good way to earn money, and it meant that my days were free to take on clients. I'm a freelance web designer, so I spend my days doing that. My business has been taking off for the last eighteen months, and I'm almost to a point where I think I'll be able to quit working at the bar. Not that I mind. It's a pretty easy, laid-back job.

I've been doing odd jobs since I was a teen. At first, it was just to get out of the house and away from my parents and their arguing. Then it became about making my own money to save for college and my future.

I knew that I didn't want to move back home after I went to college, so I worked hard and saved every penny that I could to make that happen. In the end, it didn't matter. My parents divorced my freshman year and both moved away. My mom threw herself into work, and we barely talk. My dad has a new, young girlfriend every other week and prefers to forget that he has a son, so we don't really talk either.

It used to hurt that they weren't interested in me and never seemed to care about me, but I've grown used to it over the years.

Or I mostly have, I guess.

As I grab another beer, I wonder what it would be like to have a big, close-knit family like Maple's.

As if my eyes are drawn to her, I glance up and stare as the door opens and Maple walks into the bar. She's been in once or twice in the last year, but always with her sisters or friends. Tonight, though, it looks like she's alone.

She glances around nervously, and I tense.

Is she meeting someone? Is she on a date?

I glare out at the crowd, trying to decipher who she could be meeting, but no one stands out. When I look back at her, she's looking at the bar, and my eyes snap to Nolan, the only guy sitting at it.

"Did you ask out Maple?" I growl at Nolan, and he snorts.

"No, why would I do that when everyone knows that you're in love with her?"

"She's here," I grumble, and he stares at me like I'm insane.

"And you're mad about that because...?"

"She's too good for this place. What if she's here on a date?"

"Then I'll cause a scene, and you'll drag the guy out back and scare him off," he says, and I smile.

I knew I liked this guy.

I set another beer down in front of him and grin.

"On the house."

He shakes his head at me, and I look back at my girl.

Maple is staring right at me, and my heart takes off like a shot as I hold her gaze.

"Shit. She's coming over here," I whisper, and Nolan rolls his eyes.

"Jesus, I can see now why you're still single," he says, and I flip him off without looking at him.

I can't seem to pull my eyes away from Maple. I watch as she takes a deep breath and then heads my way. The gentle sway of her hips is mesmerizing, and my mouth waters at the sight of all of her curves. She walks right towards me, and by the time she reaches the bar, my hands are sweaty, and my heart is beating out of control in my chest.

I stand up straighter as she leans over the bar slightly.

"When are you off?" She asks me, and I almost pinch myself to check that I'm not dreaming.

"Uh..." I say eloquently as I glance at my watch. "Two more hours."

She nods, and I bite my tongue before I can ask what's happening here and ruin the moment.

"Do you want to sleep with me?" She blurts, and my knees give out.

I catch myself on the bar before I can make a total fool of myself by knocking myself unconscious and stare at her in shock.

"Yes!"

"Smooth," I hear Nolan groan, and I cringe inwardly.

I have no idea what's happening here, but I don't want to stop it. For some reason, Maple finally seems to be on the same page as me and I don't want to do anything to change it.

Maple nods once and then backs up a step.

"Tonight, then. After you get off."

She reaches into her purse and passes me a slip of paper. I glance down at her address and almost tell her that I don't need this. I've known where Maple lived since she moved to town. I bite my tongue, though, and just nod.

"See you soon," she says, and then she turns and disappears into the crowd.

I watch her go until she leaves the bar and then look over at Nolan.

"What the fuck was that?" He asks me, echoing my own thoughts.

"I have no idea."

But I'm going to find out.

THREE

Maple

I HAD BEEN SO excited when I first walked into the bar and approached Ryder. It felt like my old confident self, but now that I'm back home, I'm panicking.

Why did I think this was a good idea? I think as I pour myself a glass of wine and take a healthy swig.

I wanted to have some fun and Ryder seemed like exactly the kind of fun that I needed. I remind myself as I take another drink for courage.

I've already picked up my entire apartment, not that it took long. I live in a little one-bedroom place above a hardware store in the middle of downtown. The place is tiny, but it suits me just fine. I don't need a lot to be happy. Just a good book, a cozy blanket, and some snacks.

I drain my glass of wine and grab the bottle, pouring some more into my cup as I pace around my kitchen. I still have half an hour until Ryder gets off work and comes here, and I'm not sure what to do with myself. I can't keep pacing around, though.

I finish off my second glass of wine and head to my bedroom. I start to rummage through my dresser drawer, looking through my lingerie for something to wear.

I've always loved lingerie. It makes me feel sexy and powerful. That's part of why I opened Wet and Wild. I wanted to help other women feel that way, too.

My fingers find a red silk babydoll dress, and I pull it out, smiling as I hold it up against my body. I know that this is the one. I bought it months ago, but I've never had an opportunity to wear it.

That's actually the case for all of my lingerie and toys. It's a bit embarrassing, but I'm a twenty-four-year-old virgin. A twenty-four-year-old virgin who also owns an adult toy store.

My parents were always sex-positive. They were always open with sex, letting us know that it was a natural thing. They never expected me to wait until marriage, but I knew that I didn't want to lose my virginity to just anyone. I wanted what they had.

True love.

I've never been interested in anyone before, not until Ryder. I know that's why I approached him tonight. I'm sick of being a virgin. I want to use the toys that I have in my shop with someone. I want to stop feeling like a fraud when I help customers out with things around the store. I want to finally be with a man.

I see the time on my alarm clock and strip in a hurry, pulling on the dress and checking that it's in place in the mirror hanging over my closet door. The red silk of the cups pushes up my breasts, and the fabric hanging down hugs my curves, giving me a perfect hourglass shape. I smile as I look at myself and then do a little twirl, giggling as I stumble into my bed.

Okay, I might be a little tipsy...

A knock sounds at the front door, and I take a deep breath as I make my way down the short hallway and over to answer it. I trip over my own feet a few times, and my head spins as I make my way.

I paste on a smile, cocking my hip in what I hope is a seductive pose as I pull the door open and look up into Ryder's blue eyes.

"Heyyy," I say with a giggle.

I step aside to let him in, and he reaches for me, his hand landing on my hip to steady me as he comes into my apartment.

"Hey, you look... amazing," he says, swallowing hard.

"Can I get you a drink?" I ask, and I'm proud of myself for sounding coherent this time.

"I'm okay."

I nod, grabbing my empty wine glass and the bottle. I pour the last of it into my cup and then make my way to the couch. He follows suit and sits next to me. There's too much room between us, and I take another sip as I scoot closer.

I wonder if he can tell that I'm nervous.

"I don't normally drink this much," I blurt out, and he smiles.

"I know."

"Is it obvious that I'm a lightweight?" I ask with a giggle, and he grins.

"Yeah, a bit. I'm not much of a drinker either," he tells me.

"But you work in a bar!"

"Maybe that's why then. I'm around alcohol all the time, so it's lost all of its appeal," he suggests, and I snort.

"Not for me. I'm around lingerie and sex toys all day long, and sex is all that I think about."

His mouth drops open, and I sway towards him.

"What about you? Do you think about sex too?" I whisper, and he swallows hard.

"More and more," he whispers, and I finish off my wine, dropping the glass down on the coffee table a little too hard.

Ryder reaches over and saves it before it can fall off of the table, and I blink.

"Whoops!"

"Why did you drink tonight?" He asks me, and I lick my lips.

"I was nervous," I admit, and he smiles softly.

"Me too. We don't have to do anything. I mean, I wasn't planning on sleeping with you tonight anyway."

I frown at his words.

"Then why did you agree to come here?"

"Well, in case it isn't obvious, I'm into you, Maple. I have been since you got to town, and I didn't want to turn you down because I was afraid that you might never ask again."

"So, you were just going to come and let me down easy?" I ask him, hurt starting to pop the giddy bubbles in my bloodstream from the wine.

I grab the blanket off of the back of the couch and pull it around myself. Suddenly, the lingerie isn't making me feel sexy or confident. Just embarrassed.

"No! I just thought that I could ask you out or that we could talk and get to know each other more. I don't just want one night with you, Maple."

He looks like he wants to say more, but he bites his tongue and just watches me, studying my reaction. I wish that I hadn't gotten drunk so that I could do a better job of hiding my feelings. I feel vulnerable and exposed right now, but I find that I'm not that upset by it. I trust Ryder not to hurt me.

"Alright," I say finally, and he blinks.

"Alright, what?"

"Alright, treat this like our first date. Tell me about yourself."

He seems surprised by my words, but he does as I ask.

"Well, I was born and raised here. I moved away for college, but I've been back for a little over a year now. I actually came back to town right before you moved here."

"Do you like it here?" I ask, and he nods.

"It's home. It's always been home. I love the people and the small-town way of life."

"Me too," I whisper, and he smiles. "So, is being a bartender the dream then?"

"No," he says with a laugh. "I'm a web designer. Things have been going pretty good the last few months, but I kept working at the bar because it was something to do. It filled the nights and brought in some extra cash."

I nod and he shifts, his body angling towards mine more.

"What about you? Was the dream to always own a sex shop?"

"No," I say with a snort. "I didn't know what I wanted to do, but our parents died, and Olive wanted to move, and the rest of us followed her. We came here, and Olive opened her bakery, and Saffron started the bookstore, and well, I needed something to do. I've always liked lingerie. It makes me feel sexy, and I just... landed on that," I finish.

He nods, his eyes dark and filled with heat.

He wants me.

That's the only thought in my drunken mind as I stare at him.

"What about Halloween?" I blurt out, trying to ignore the way that my body reacts to the lust in his eyes.

"What about it?"

"It's coming up next week," I inform him, and he nods.

"Yeah."

He doesn't seem as excited about the holiday as I am, and I frown.

"You don't like Halloween? You don't dress up? Hang out with friends? Go to a party? Pass out candy?"

"Not really. I haven't celebrated since before I left for college. Probably not since I was a little kid," he tells me almost apologetically.

"You can come with me to a party this year! We can pick out costumes together!"

"Do we have to dress up?" He asks, and my enthusiasm wanes.

"No, you don't have to," I say quietly.

My eyes start to feel heavy, and I smother a yawn as I lean back against the soft couch cushions.

"You don't have to go to the party," I murmur sleepily.

"I want to."

I nod, my eyes starting to drift shut.

"You don't have to stay."

"I want to do that too," I hear him say before sleep pulls me under.

FOUR

Ryder

"OH MY GOD," Maple groans next to me, and I blink my eyes open, watching as her hands come up to scrub at her face.

I smile as she stretches and sighs.

"Good morning to you, too," I say, my voice sounding rough with sleep.

She gasps, her big green eyes widening as she spots me in bed next to her. A second later her whole face turns as red as her hair.

"Oh my god!" She yelps.

I watch in amusement as she buries her whole head under her pillow. I'm guessing that she regrets drinking so much last night, and I scoot closer to her as I lift the corner of her pillow to peek down at her.

"Is this how you wake up every morning or..." I trail off, and she groans.

I laugh, and she pops her head out, giving me a sheepish look.

"I'm so sorry about last night," she starts, and I tense, wondering if she regrets getting drunk, oversharing, or inviting me over altogether.

"I had fun," I tell her honestly, and she looks at me like I'm insane.

"Your idea of a good time is watching someone embarrass themselves?" She grumbles, and I laugh.

"You didn't embarrass yourself. You were adorable. It was nice getting to see you with your walls down for a bit."

"I don't have walls," she protests, and I snort.

"You have walls and a whole damn moat."

She sighs, pulling herself up in bed until she's sitting, and I follow suit.

"I don't mean to have walls," she says softly, and I nod.

"I know."

We share a look, and I wait to see what she'll do next.

Does she want me to leave? Should I ask her out now?

The blanket sits down, and I see that damn lingerie. I was hard as soon as the door swung open last night, and my erection didn't go away until I was falling asleep next to her in bed.

I had carried her to her room after she fell asleep on the couch and tucked her in, but then she had reached for me and pulled me closer. I had laid down next to her on top of the covers, but sometime during the night, I guess I found my way under them with her.

Her breasts are spilling out over the top of the red silk, and I bite back a groan, shifting away from her in the bed.

I had never planned on sleeping with her last night, but when she answered the door and I saw that she was tipsy and on her way to drunk, I knew that it was definitely not going to happen. I meant what I said last night. I want Maple for more than one night. I want her forever.

"I'm sorry again about last night. I mean, I invited you over for sex, bored you with all of my ramblings, and then fell asleep on you," she says, her cheeks heating with a blush.

"No apology necessary. I wasn't bored, and like I said last night, I never intended on sleeping with you last night. I just wanted to spend time with you."

"Still, let me at least make you breakfast," she insists, crawling out of bed.

Her cheeks heat even more when she realizes that she's just wearing the babydoll lingerie.

"Sure, I'll just... head out there."

I climb out of bed and head out to her kitchen to wait for her. I grab her wine glass from last night and start to clean up. I toss the empty wine bottle and then wash the glass, leaving it to dry in the sink.

"You didn't have to do that," she tells me as she joins me in the kitchen.

She's changed into black yoga pants that mold to her thick thighs and a knitted white sweater. She looks sexy and reserved, just like always.

"It's no bother. Why don't you let me take you out for breakfast? I know that you have to get to work soon."

She seems surprised as she glances at the clock and then nods.

"Yeah, grabbing breakfast would be better."

We both put our shoes on and then I hold the door open for her as we head out onto the street. We head over to the Nosh Diner, and I wave at Ford, the owner, as we head to a booth in the back.

"Hey there!" Cameron greets us.

"Morning," Maple says with a warm smile.

The Baker sisters made a lot of friends when they moved to town. I'm not surprised. It's hard not to like them.

Ford comes over and wraps his arm around Cameron's waist, pulling her in and dropping a kiss on her cheek.

"Take your break soon?" He asks, and she nods.

"Yeah, I'll meet you in your office," she says with a smirk.

Maple's face is a light shade of pink as she watches her friends flirt in front of us, and I smile at her.

"What can I get you two?" Cameron asks as Ford heads back behind the counter and disappears into his office.

"I'll have the pancakes," Maple orders, and I nod.

"Same, with a side of bacon, please."

Cameron nods and heads back to put our orders in, and I turn to face my girl.

"How are you feeling?" I ask her.

"Hungover," she says with a little laugh, and I grin.

"I bet. You'll have to drink lots today," I tell her as Cameron sets two glasses of water and two cups of coffee down in front of us.

I reach over and add two creamers and three sugars to Maple's cup and she blinks, seeming surprised.

"I've been paying attention," I tell her, and she nods.

"I can see that you have."

She looks like she doesn't know how to feel about that. I give her a moment to process it, grabbing my own coffee and taking a sip.

"Have dinner with me tonight," I say, and she chokes on her coffee.

"I... I," she stutters, her green eyes wide and locked on mine.

I bite back a smile as she swallows a drink of coffee and then she straightens in her seat and nods.

"Alright. Dinner."

"It's a date," I say as Cameron drops off her food.

"I'm headed on break now, but here's the check when you're ready."

"Thanks," I say, grabbing the check before Maple can try and pay for breakfast.

She gives me a look, and I just give her a wide smile in return. She rolls her eyes, but I can see the beginnings of a smile at the edge of her lips.

We both dig in, and I nudge the plate of bacon closer to her. She smiles sweetly as she takes a piece and bites into it.

I ask her about what she has to do today and listen as she tells me about a shipment that's coming in for work.

"And we're decorating for Halloween a bit more. I ordered more decorations, and they came in last night."

"Sounds like fun."

She eyes me dubiously, and I wonder what that's about.

"You hate Halloween," she says, and I shake my head.

"I don't hate it."

"You don't celebrate it," she argues, and I shrug.

"I never wanted to, I guess."

She raises a brow at me, and I shake my head.

"I like it," I tell her.

I don't think that she believes me, though.

We finish eating, and I pay the bill and offer her my hand as we stand and head for the door. As she slips her small hand in mine, tingles race up my arm, leaving goose-bumps in their wake. I pray that she doesn't notice them.

"I'll wake you to the shop," I tell her, and she shakes her head.

"You don't have to do that."

"I want to."

She doesn't argue after that, and we walk to Wet and Wild in companionable silence.

"Thanks for breakfast," she says as we stop outside the doors.

"Anytime. I'll pick you up for our date at six," I tell her, and she nods, her cheeks turning pink as I smile down at her.

"Until tonight," I whisper, leaning down and brushing a kiss against her cheek.

I hear her sharp inhale as my lips brush against her soft skin, and I smile as I pull back and head down the street.

Now, I just need to nail this first date and win my dream girl.

FIVE

Maple

TONIGHT.

I'm going out on a date tonight.

With Ryder.

My mind has been racing since he left me at Wet and Wild earlier today. Part of me still can't believe that I'm going out on my first-ever date tonight. I can't help but wonder if maybe he only asked me out because he's trying to get lucky since I kind of fell asleep on him last night before we could get to that part.

I wince as I remember it.

"What's that look for?" Saffron asks as she peers at me from above the book in her hand.

"Just remembering something," I mumble, and her eyebrows raise.

"Remembering what? Your last dental appointment," she jokes.

"I wish."

"What could be that bad?" She asks as the front door opens and our youngest sister, Ginger, walks in.

"What's bad?" She asks as she hops up on the other chair behind the counter.

"My dating life," I tell them, and they both snort.

"*What* dating life?" Ginger asks, and I sigh.

"I asked Ryder out last night."

"What!?!" Ginger asks, leaning forward with excitement. Saffron just looks surprised.

"Yeah..."

"How did it go?" Saffron asks, and I sigh again, louder this time.

"Terrible. Or, well, not so bad considering that I got drunk and fell asleep on the guy that I had invited over for sex."

"How is that not so bad?" Ginger cries, and I can't help but laugh.

"Okay, yeah, it was pretty bad," I admit.

"I hope that you didn't like the guy," Saffron mumbles, and my smile drops.

"I do," I tell them quietly.

"Then we'll help you figure out a way to salvage this," Ginger says, and Saffron nods, closing her book.

My sisters and I have always been close, and I love that even though they have no experience with dating or guys, they're willing to drop what they're doing to help me out with my boy troubles.

"He actually asked me out for tonight," I tell them, and they both squeal.

"Really! He must be half in love with you then!" Ginger exclaims and I can feel my cheeks start to blush.

"Hey, sorry I'm late!" Lilou calls as she hurries in.

"No worries," I assure her.

"We're talking about Maple's love life," Ginger tells her with a saucy smirk and Lilou's gaze swings to mine in surprise.

"Ryder?" She guesses, and I nod.

"I knew it! He's always making eyes at you," she says, and I laugh when she does her imitation of it.

"I, I don't think that I've ever seen him look at me like that," I say with a laugh, and she giggles as the door opens and Milo comes in.

Lilou is ducking behind the counter to put her purse and coat away so she doesn't see him, and I bite my bottom lip as I wait to see her reaction.

"I wish that a guy would look at me like that," she tells me, and Milo frowns.

"Darling, I'll look at you any way that you want me to."

Lilou stands up so fast that she almost tips over, and Saffron reaches out to steady her as she gapes at Milo.

"What are you doing in here?" She asks him, and he grins.

"I thought that you might like to point out a few of the things that you like," he says and her face flames bright red.

"No thanks. Maple, I'll be in the back doing inventory," she says before she turns and practically sprints towards the back room.

Milo sighs, and I roll my eyes.

"Was your intention to scare her off?" I ask him, and he frowns.

"No, but I don't know how to get through to her. I've tried giving her space, tried just talking to her, but it's like as soon as I get close to her, she startles and takes off."

"You should ask Ryder for some tips," Ginger says, giving me a wicked grin.

I roll my eyes again and get back to stocking. I see Milo leave, and a moment later, I see him stop Ryder and say something. I watch them from beneath my lashes until Ryder opens the door.

"Are you here to get stuff for tonight?" I ask him, and he laughs.

"Nope. Hey, why did Milo just ask me to show him how I look at you?" He asks, leaning on the shelf above me.

Ginger and Saffron both giggle until Nolan walks in. Then Saffron shoves her book into her purse and stands.

"I'm headed home. I'll see you guys tomorrow," she says, and I wave bye.

"I'll walk you," Nolan tells her, and she ducks her head.

"I need to start charging people for coming in here and flirting with my employees," I mumble, and Ryder snorts.

"You'd be a millionaire in no time," he agrees as we watch them leave.

I make a mental note to interrogate Saffron about what's going on between her and Nolan the next time that I see her.

"Are you here to cancel tonight?" I ask him as I stand, and he looks bewildered.

"Fuck no! Why? Did something come up?"

"No, I just didn't expect to see you again so soon."

"Oh, I just wanted to ask if you had any allergies or a preference on where you wanted to go tonight for dinner. I would text you, but I don't have your number."

He pulls out his phone, and I rattle off my number for him.

"No allergies, and I'm good with whatever," I tell him.

He smiles, and I can practically see his brain turning as he makes plans.

"Okay, I'll see you in a few hours then."

"See you."

He gives me a heated look before he heads out, and I let out a dreamy sigh as I watch him go.

"It looks like he isn't the only one who has it bad," Ginger remarks, and I clear my throat.

"Why don't you go tell Lilou that the coast is clear?"

"You got it, boss."

I ignore her and try to get lost in work for a few hours. I manage to put out a lot of new inventory before it's time for me to head home and get ready for my date.

"Do you guys need anything else before I leave?" I ask them, but they both shake their heads.

"Have fun tonight! Call me if you need anything," Ginger says, and I smile, giving her a quick hug before I grab my thing and head for the door.

"I'll see you both tomorrow!" I call before I head out.

The walk back to my apartment is quick, and I smile as I pass all of the shops on the way and admire their Halloween decorations. Something about the cute little ghosts and bats taped to the windows brightens my spirits. I grin as I head up the stairs to my place.

I don't have long before Ryder will be, so I hurry through a shower and then pull on a pair of jeans and my favorite knit sweater. I'm not sure where we're going for dinner, so hopefully, this will work for whatever restaurant we go to.

I pull my hair back and braid it so that it hangs over one of my shoulders and then apply some mascara and lip gloss. I'm just pulling on my boots when Ryder knocks on the door.

"Hey," I say as I answer it. My eyes widen as I take in the bouquet in his hands.

It's Halloween-themed, with orange and black roses. There's even a little pumpkin and bat on a stick in the bunch, and I grin as I take them from him.

"Thank you so much! I love them."

"I thought you might," he says with a pleased smile.

"Let me just put them in some water."

"Take your time."

I usher him in and then go to find a vase. I don't get many flowers, so it takes me a minute to find something that will work and fill it with water.

"Thanks again. They're beautiful."

He nods, and I grab my purse and follow him out of my place. I lock the door behind us, and he takes my hand as we head downstairs.

His truck is parked right out front, and he leads me over to it, opening the passenger door for me. I smile slightly as I climb inside.

I feel comfortable around Ryder, but that doesn't mean that I'm not nervous to be going on my first date. Things that I never thought of before keep popping into my head. Thoughts like, what do I do with my hands? What do we talk about? Am I dressed appropriately? Am I breathing too loud?

That last one is because I can feel myself starting to panic as Ryder climbs behind the wheel and starts the truck up.

"Ready? Hey! Are you okay?" He asks me, turning to me in concern.

His hand lands on my knee and his thumb rubs circles there. I can feel his heat through my jeans, and I shiver.

"It's okay. You're okay, Maple."

I suck in a deep breath and nod.

"Are you not feeling alright? We don't have to do this tonight. There's no rush. No pressure."

I snort at that, and he cocks his head.

"No pressure? You're not nervous? Cause I'm kind of freaking out," I admit, and he smiles at that.

"I'm nervous," he tells me. "I don't want to mess this up. I don't want to pressure you to do anything that you're not ready for. I don't want to push you away."

I take a deeper, calmer breath this time and nod.

"This is my first date," I whisper, and he nods.

"It's mine too," he whispers back, and I blink.

"How is that possible?" I blurt out, and he laughs.

"Well, it's probably the same reason why you haven't been out with anyone before."

"Social anxiety, being overweight, and a lack of interest in the opposite sex," I say, listing my reasons, and he frowns.

"You're not overweight."

I snort again, and he frowns harder.

"You're not, Maple. I love your body and all of your curves."

"Alright, well, other men haven't."

"They do," he grumbles darkly, glaring out the truck windows like he's about to see a line of men all ogling my body.

"It doesn't matter. No one has ever caught my eye before," I tell him and his gaze swings to me.

"Until me," he says matter-of-factly, and I turn my head to buckle my seatbelt so that he doesn't notice the blush on my face.

My stomach growls and Ryder shifts the truck into drive, and we take off.

"Where are we going?" I ask him as we cruise down Main Street.

"How do you feel about steak?"

"Love it."

"Good. I thought that we would go to Palmer's Steakhouse."

"What were we going to do if I hated steak?"

"Well, there's Mancini's or Toasty Buns."

"Well, for the record, I love pizza. It's my absolute favorite food."

"Want to go to Mancini's instead?"

"No, it's alright."

"What do you get on your pizza?" He asks as we pull into the Palmers parking lot.

"Pepperoni and mushroom. What about you?"

"Well, my favorite food is tacos, but for pizza, I'm good with pretty much anything. Pepperoni is my favorite, though."

We park, and Ryder climbs out and hurries to open my door. He offers me his hand, and I smile as I slip my palm against his.

"Have you been here before?" He asks me as we head up to the door.

"Yeah, we came here once a few months ago for Ginger's birthday and had a great time."

We head inside and I look around at the place. Palmer's is pretty much the only upscale place in Wolf Valley. They also have the best steaks.

Candles are in the center of each table, their tiny flames casting shadows around the place. The restaurant isn't very big and only holds about twenty tables, which makes it feel more intimate.

We're shown to our table, and I pick up my menu, scanning it as I try to get my bearings. So far, the date seems to be going well.

"Have you ever been here?" I ask him, trying to get the conversation going again.

"Yeah, a couple of times when I was growing up."

"Oh, that's right. I keep forgetting that you were born and raised here. Was this your favorite place to go when you were growing up?"

"No, I always liked King's Tacos best. This was where we went for fancier occasions. The meals were usually... tense," he finishes.

"How so?"

"My parents, they didn't really like, well, they didn't really like each other that much."

"Oh."

"Yeah, I mean, they're divorced now and seem happier, I guess. I don't really talk to either of them."

"I'm sorry. That seems rough."

"It's honestly better without having them in my life."

"Hey there. Welcome to Palmers. Can I get you two something to drink?" Our waiter asks, interrupting us.

"Just a water for me," I say, and Ryder nods.

"Me too."

He nods and heads off to get our drinks and I scan the menu, deciding on a sirloin for dinner.

"Have you and your sisters always been close?" He asks, and I grin.

"Oh, yeah. Well, I mean, we had the usual fights growing up, but I always knew that they had my back. It was kind of nice having three built-in friends everywhere that I went."

"That sounds nice."

"Do you wish that you had siblings?" I ask him, and he shrugs.

"Maybe sometimes. I've always been more of a loner, though, so I'm not sure."

The waiter comes back with our water, and we both order a sirloin and some sides. The conversation flows smoothly after that. I tell him about family vacations, more about my sisters, our family dog, and growing up in Oregon. He tells me about living in Wolf Valley and more about his business. By the time Ryder pays the check, and we head out to his truck, I'm feeling more relaxed around him than I am with anyone else who's not related to me.

We make the short drive back to my apartment, and Ryder parks out front. I'm about to invite him in, when I pause. I like Ryder and I don't want him to think that this is just a fling to me. I won't tell him, not when this is all so new, but I think that he could be the one for me.

He's the first man that I've ever been interested in. He's the first one to make me feel sexy and wanted and at ease.

"I'll walk you up," he says, and I smile.

He opens my door for me and holds my hand as we walk up the stairs to my apartment. As we reach the top of the stairs, I fumble for my keys, my heart pounding in my chest. Ryder is standing so close, his warmth radiating against my side, and I can't help but feel the weight of the moment.

I turn to face him, a soft smile tugging at my lips, but before I can say anything, Ryder reaches out, brushing a strand of hair that has fallen loose from my braid behind my ear.

"Tonight was fun," he says, his voice low and soft, making my heart flutter.

"It was," I agree, my voice barely a whisper as I stare up

into his eyes. They're warm and intense, filled with something that makes me feel like I'm the only person in the world.

He takes a small step closer, and my breath hitches. His hand lingers on my cheek, his thumb brushing lightly over my skin as his gaze drops to my lips. I can feel the tension building between us, electric and undeniable.

"Maple," he murmurs, his voice thick with emotion.

He leans down, closing the distance between us, and my heart skips a beat. For a moment, all I can do is stare at him as his lips hover over mine. Slowly, Ryder leans down, his lips brushing against mine in the softest, most tender kiss. It feels like everything I've been waiting for— gentle but filled with so much promise.

His hand moves to cup the back of my neck, deepening the kiss just enough to make my knees weak, but he keeps it slow and patient, like he's savoring the moment as much as I am. It feels like he doesn't want this kiss to end, which is lucky because neither do I.

My hands fist in his shirt, and I cling to him as his mouth moves over mine. His lips are so soft and firm against mine and I find myself leaning into him more. His grip on me tightens, and I love the feel of his hard body against mine.

When we finally pull apart, we're both breathing a little heavier. Our foreheads resting against each other as I try to catch my breath. Ryder's thumb traces my jawline as he whispers,

"I've wanted to do that all night. A lot longer than just tonight."

I can't help but smile, my heart soaring as I look into his eyes.

"Me too," I admit, my voice soft but certain.

He grins and drops one more kiss on my lips before he steps back.

"We should do this again sometime," he says, and I nod. "Night, Maple. Sweet dreams."

I smile as I let myself into my apartment and lock the door behind me. I smile as I get ready for bed and even as I slip under the covers, and as I drift off to sleep, I smile as I dream of Ryder.

SIX

Ryder

IT'S late as I walk down the street towards Wet and Wild. I know that Maple is closing tonight and I want to catch her before she can head home. I think that our date the other night went well, and we've been texting since, but it's not the same as actually seeing her and being with her.

I've spent every day for the past nine months thinking about Maple and wishing that I was with her. Now that I've been out with her— now that I've kissed her, all of those feelings are so much stronger. I need to see her for my day to feel complete, for me to feel right.

Most of the other stores on the block are closed, their windows dark, and doors locked up tight. Wet and Wild is the only one that's still all lit up, but as I get closer, I see the lights start to turn off one by one.

I see Maple behind the counter, gathering her purse and I smile as I knock on the front door. Her head snaps up, and our gazes lock. I grin at her, and she smiles, looking happy to see me too.

She unlocks the front door, and I step inside the dark shop.

"Hey, I'm glad that I caught you."

"What are you doing here? Were you working at the bar? Did you just get off?" She asks.

"No, I just wanted to see you."

Maple tries to hide it, but I can see her smile before she ducks her head.

"I missed you," I tell her, taking a step closer to her and wrapping my arms around her waist.

"I missed you too," she admits, and my heart beats hard in my chest.

I've wanted Maple for so long, since the day that I first saw her, and it feels like maybe she's finally starting to want me, too.

"Are you hungry? I thought that I could make you dinner," I tell her as my hands rub up and down her back, pulling her closer with each caress.

"You cook?" She asks skeptically, and I laugh.

"I do. It's one of my secret talents."

"What are your other secret talents?"

I smirk as I lean down closer to her.

"Wouldn't you like to know," I whisper in her ear, and she shivers.

I see her swallow hard, and I fight a grin as I pull back and take her hand.

"How does grilled chicken and some roasted vegetables sound to you?" I ask her as I lead her out the door.

"Delicious," she says as she locks the door behind us and drops the keys in her purse.

I take her hand and lead her over to my truck.

"Did you drive today?" I ask her, and she shakes her head.

"No, it was nice out, so I walked."

"You can't be walking home in the dark."

She rolls her eyes, and I grit my teeth. I know that I could tell her not to, that it isn't safe, but I doubt that will stop her. I'll just have to make sure that I'm here to walk her home every night. It's a good thing that I already put my two weeks' notice in at the bar, so I'll be free to spend my nights with my girl.

I start the truck, and we make the short drive over to my place. I park out front and jump out, rushing around to open Maple's door before she can beat me to it. I hold my hand out to her to help her out of the truck and lead her inside.

I spent most of today cleaning my place so it's clean when we walk in. I have all of the ingredients for dinner, and I lead Maple into the kitchen and pull out a chair for her.

"Have a seat. Can I get you something to drink?"

"Um, just water is fine. Do you want me to help with anything?"

"No, I've got it. You relax. How was work?" I ask her as I fill a glass with water and hand it to her.

"It was good. We were pretty busy, actually. We had two bachelorette parties come through, and some older ladies in town stopped in, too."

"Is it weird seeing people that you know buy sex toys?" I ask her as I preheat the oven.

"Not really. Maybe it's because I don't really know that many people that well here. Or, I don't know, I guess that I was just raised to believe that sex was normal and natural and to not judge people."

"That's a good point."

I start cutting up the vegetables and tossing them in olive oil and spices before I slide the tray into the oven.

"I just need to go start the grill," I say, excusing myself.

I head out to the deck and start the grill. Once it's hot enough, I put the chicken on the grill and head back inside to Maple.

Maple is sitting at the kitchen table, watching me with a soft smile as I walk back in. Something about seeing her here, in my home, makes everything feel right.

"You know, I never imagined you as someone who could cook," she teases, her eyes sparkling.

I laugh as I grab a bottle of olive oil to brush on the chicken. "I've got a few tricks up my sleeve."

"I'm starting to believe that," she says, her tone light but her gaze lingering on me in a way that makes my heart race.

As I move around the kitchen and outside, flipping the chicken and checking on the vegetables, I keep stealing glances at her. She looks so comfortable here, so at ease, and it makes me want to keep her here as long as possible. Finally, the food is done, and I plate everything, bringing it over to the table.

"Dinner is served," I say, setting the plates down.

"This looks amazing," she says, her voice filled with genuine surprise as she digs in. "And it tastes even better."

I smile, watching her enjoy the meal.

"What do you usually like to eat?" I ask her as I dig in.

"I usually just make sandwiches or some kind of frozen meal. Olive is the one who likes cooking, and she was always around to cook for us growing up. I guess I was spoiled."

"I can teach you a few things. Or you're always welcome over here when you're hungry."

"I might just take you up on that," she says as she eats another piece of chicken.

When the meal is over and the plates are cleared, there's a comfortable silence that settles between us, the kind that feels intimate, like we don't need to fill it with words.

I stand by the counter, watching her as she finishes her water. The dim light of the kitchen casts a warm glow around her, making her look even more beautiful, if that's even possible.

Without thinking, I move towards her, taking her hand and pulling her gently out of the chair. She stands up slowly, her eyes widening just a little as I guide her closer.

"Maple," I murmur, my voice thick with emotion.

She looks up at me, her breath catching, and for a moment, neither of us says anything. The only sound in the room is the soft hum of the refrigerator, and all I can focus on is the way her hand feels in mine, the way her lips part slightly as she stares up at me.

I can't wait any longer. I cup her face with both hands and bring my lips down to hers. The kiss starts slow and soft, like before, but this time, there's a hunger behind it. She melts into me, her hands sliding up my chest and around my neck as I pull her closer, deepening the kiss.

Her body presses against mine, and I can feel her heart racing in time with mine. The kitchen around us fades, and all I can think about is how right this feels—her in my arms, her lips on mine.

When we finally break apart, both of us are breathing hard. She looks up at me with those wide green eyes, and I smile softly.

There's something in her eyes, a glint of lust, and I swallow hard as I stare down at her.

"Maple," I whisper, and she licks her lips.

"I want you," she whispers, and my grip on her tightens.

I'm about to ask her if she's sure and assure her that I'm not in any rush, but before I can, Maple takes a step back and pulls off her shirt.

My mouth drops open as I take her in.

"Fuck me," I whisper, and she laughs.

"Alright," she agrees cheekily, and my cock presses hard against the zipper of my jeans as I stare down at her.

SEVEN

Maple

I PRESS myself closer to Ryder, loving the feel of his body against mine, of his erection pressing into the soft curve of my stomach.

My confidence flares inside of me, and I trail my fingers down his chest as I lean into him more.

"Want to show me where your bedroom is?" I whisper up at him huskily, and he nods.

A second later, I'm over his shoulder, and I laugh as Ryder takes off down the hallway to his bedroom. I try to take in his house a little more as we go, and I realize that there's not much to look at. There aren't many decorations or personal touches. It hits me that there's not even a pumpkin or anything fall or Halloween-related in sight.

He hasn't brought up the Halloween party, I think, as we head into his room. My stomach sinks, but I try to push away that thought as Ryder sets me down next to the bed.

"So, this is your room," I say, looking around at the giant king-size bed and dark blue comforter.

His room is like the rest of the house. It's bare, with just the essentials.

"When did you move in?" I ask him, and he blinks at the change of subject.

"Like a year and a half ago," he says gruffly, and I nod.

"Are you a minimalist or something?" I ask, and he frowns, looking around his room.

"No, why?"

"Never mind."

I step into him, my body heating as I look up into his dark eyes and see nothing but lust in them. He wants me, and that's a heady feeling.

My fingers trail down his chest until I reach the bottom of his shirt, and I smirk at him as I start to tug it up. He takes over once I get to mid-chest, and I step back, taking him in. His gorgeous, tanned skin was on full display. He has muscles that I didn't even know existed, and my mouth waters as I take in the v that leads down to his cock.

My hands reach for his jeans, wanting to see all of him, and he unsnaps the button and pushes them down for me.

"Your turn," he says, his voice low and filled with heat and longing.

I pull my shirt over my head, revealing the lacy bra that I picked out this morning. I push my yoga pants down and kick them to the side, then look at him. His eyes are locked on me, and I shiver when he licks his lips.

"We should have gone to my place. I have so much lingerie there," I whisper, and his eyes snap to mine.

"I want to see you in all of it, but you could be wearing a trash bag and still be every man's fantasy."

His eyes trail over my curves, and I believe him. He's

looking at me like I'm the best thing that he's ever seen in his life. I stand up a little straighter as I step closer to him, then my hands are on his chest, and I push him backward.

He blinks, his arms shooting out in surprise as he falls back onto the bed, and I giggle as I step between his legs. His black boxers are tight across his thick thighs, and I can see the bulge of his cock.

My hands trail up his thighs, and I see him tense as I reach the edge of his boxers.

"I haven't ever..." I start, and he nods.

"Me either," he admits, and I smile slightly.

I'm not surprised that Ryder is a virgin, too. He might be smoking hot, but he doesn't seem to love people that much. When he admitted that he had never been on a date before either, I figured that he was just as inexperienced as I was in all things romantic.

"I like that I'll be your first," I whisper as I drop to my knees, and his eyes widen.

"Only," he murmurs, and I want to ask him about that, but his hips shift, and my eyes are drawn to his cock.

I reach for his boxers and pull them down, my mouth dropping open when I see how big he is. My fingers wrap around it or try to.

"You're way bigger than any of my toys," I tell him, and he grunts, his cock jerking in my hold.

"Need you to stop talking if you want me to last," he tells me and I smirk.

"You don't want to hear about all of the toys that I have at home?" I ask him innocently, and his eyes screw shut tight.

"Maple," he groans, and my smirk widens.

"Want to know what my favorite one is?" I ask as I start to stroke his cock with my hand.

I lean forward, stealing a taste of him, and he shouts out a curse as my mouth wraps around the tip of him. The muscles in his thighs and stomach tense, and a rush zips through me as I notice the effect that I have on him.

"I have this lingerie set," I tell him as I let his cock out of my mouth with a pop.

He's breathing hard, his eyes heavy-lidded as he looks down at me.

"It's white with little cherries all over it. The material is sheer, so it doesn't really leave much to the imagination," I tell him, and he swallows hard. "I think that you would like it."

He nods, his chest rising and falling quicker as I jerk him off faster.

"Oh! Or I have this maid outfit. It has this cute little lace collar and knee-high stockings. I look pretty hot in that and my black high heels."

"Maple, fuck," he grits out, his dick swelling in my hand.

"I thought that I could be it for Halloween since I haven't bought a costume yet."

He groans, his head falling back on the bed, and I lean forward, licking a path up the underside of his cock. His hips jerk, and so I do it again before I wrap my lips around him and start to suck in time with my hand.

It doesn't take long, and then he's pulsing on my tongue. I swallow down his release, loving the salty taste.

I pull back, wiping my mouth with the back of my hand as he stares down at me.

"Fuck," he whispers, and I smirk at him.

"Whenever you're ready," I tell him, and he lunges for me, grabbing me and rolling me under him on the bed.

"Do you really have a maid costume?" He asks me, and I laugh.

"Uh-huh. I have two whole drawers of lingerie. I'll have to show you sometime."

"Yes," he agrees, and I can feel his cock hardening between us again already.

"Tell me about these toys," he orders as he starts to kiss down my neck.

"Well, I have the usual ones. Small vibrators, one that looks like a rose. Then there's just stuff that I was interested in trying."

"Like what?" He asks against my skin.

I feel his fingers slip underneath me, and a moment later, my bra loosens, the straps slipping down my arms as he pulls it off.

"Nipple clamps. Butt plugs. Um..." I trail off as his hands cup my breasts.

I'm distracted by his mouth and talented fingers, my sentence hanging in the air between us. I can feel his warm breath, and I arch in his hold, offering him more of me— all of me.

"We can play with all of that next time," he says, and I nod.

His lips wrap around one of my nipples, and I cry out as his tongue flicks over the sensitive peak. His fingers pinch my other nipple, and I cry out again, heat blazing through me. His teeth graze over my breast, and I shiver, my breath coming in short pants as he has his way with me. He switches breasts, and I arch against him, loving the feel of his skin on mine.

When his hands smooth down my sides, I look down at him and see him give me a devilish smirk as he starts to kiss his way down my body. His fingers hook in my thong, and he turns it down my legs, tossing it to the side before his hands wrap around my thighs, and he pulls my legs apart, spreading me wide.

He kneels between my legs, his eyes roaming over me, and while I would normally feel self-conscious, with Ryder, I just feel wanted and confident.

His shoulder nudges my thighs wider apart as he settles between them, and I hold my breath as he leans forward and buries his face between my legs.

"Ryder! Fuck!" I shout as his tongue finds my clit and starts to move over the little bundle of nerves.

My thighs snap shut around his head, and he moans as he licks me. I'm a trembling ball of need under him, powerless to do anything except let him have his way with me.

One thick finger rims my opening and then slowly starts to push into my tight channel, and I moan so loud that I'm pretty sure his neighbors hear me.

"Goddamn, Maple," he grits out.

My fingers twist in his sheets, and I hold on as his lips tease my clit and his finger moves in and out of me.

"Is this what you do with your toys?" He asks me, and I can only cry out his name as my orgasm starts to grow inside of me.

He adds another finger, and the sharp sting of pain sends me over the edge. I half scream, half sob his name as I come, and he licks up all of my release.

"Ryder," I mumble as I come back to Earth, and he prowls up my body.

"Mine," he growls, his lips claiming mine, and I wrap my arms around his neck, clinging to him.

His cock brushes against my drenched folds, and we both tense and look down as he nudges my opening. We watch together as he takes me, sinking one inch and then two inside of me.

"Ryder," I moan as he hits my virginity, and he says my name like a curse as he pops my cherry and claims me fully.

"So goddamn perfect," he groans as he bottoms out inside of me, and I nod, my nails biting into his arms as I hold onto him.

"Wrap those legs around me, Maple," he orders, and I do as he commands.

He starts to move then, and we both seem to be holding our breaths as he pulls out slowly and then sinks back into me just as slowly.

"Fuck, you're so tight and wet. The best damn thing that I've ever felt," he tells me, and I feel myself grow wetter at his dirty words.

I feel so full as he bottoms out inside of me again, and I swallow hard, my hips moving restlessly against his.

"Are you ready for more?" He asks.

"God, yes."

He grins down at me before he braces his arms on either side of my head and starts to pick up his pace. My hips rise, meeting each of his thrusts, and I cry out as the base of his cock presses against my clit.

"So...good," I say in between thrusts, and he grunts in agreement, his hand gripping my thighs and holding my leg in place as he starts to pound into me.

I can tell that I'm close again, and when he leans down, sucking one of my nipples into his mouth, I start to come.

"Fuck!" I cry out, my pussy clamping down around his length.

He curses against my skin, and a moment later, I feel him start to come inside of me.

"Shit," he says, rolling to the side before he can crush me.

He takes me with him, and I wind up sprawled across his chest, his cock still buried in me as we both try to catch our breaths.

He reaches up, his hands gentle as he pushes some of my hair away from my face.

"You good?" He asks me, and I giggle.

He frowns, and that just makes me laugh harder.

"So romantic," I tease him and he actually blushes.

"Sorry, I... was that alright for you?"

"Uh-huh," I assure him, still giggling.

I can feel his cock start to harden inside of me, and I raise an eyebrow as I stare down at him.

He shrugs, and I smile.

"Would you like to go to my place so I can show you my collection?" I ask him, and his hands grip my hips.

"Collection, huh? Yeah, that I have to see."

We grin at each other for a moment, and his hands slide down to my butt. He cups the smooth globes, giving me a squeeze, and my body reacts.

"Okay, we'll go... in a minute. There's something that I want to try first," I tell him, and he grins.

"Yeah? What's that?"

He listens attentively as I tell him exactly what I want him to do to me.

We don't make it to my place until much, much later.

EIGHT

Ryder

"I'M GOING to be honest with you; I don't even know what this does," I tell her as I hold up the little pink circle.

"It goes around your cock, and then when you're fucking me," she says, hitting a button that has the whole thing vibrating.

"Huh," I say with interest, and she laughs beside me. "You have the best damn job."

That has her laughing harder, a sound that I absolutely love. It's my favorite sound in the whole world.

I grin as I watch her. She's so beautiful.

We're lying in her bed, lingerie, and sex toys surrounding us. The floor littered with packing from said toys and our clothes.

"Shit! What time is it?" Maple asks, sitting up in bed and peering over at the alarm clock on the bedside table. "I have to be at work in half an hour."

She collapses back onto the mattress beside me and groans dramatically.

"I'm not sure that I can move," she says, and I scoot closer to her.

"I'll carry you around everywhere then. It's the least that I can do."

She smiles at me, and I fall even more in love with her at that moment. If I wasn't sure that she was the one for me before, I would know now.

"How about you start by carrying me into the shower?" She asks, and I nod.

"I can do that."

I stand and reach for her, lifting her easily into my arms. Her legs wrap around my waist, and I drop a kiss onto her lips as we head into the bathroom.

"I love how you manhandle me," she says as I set her down on the sink and turn the shower on.

"Well, I'm here to do that anytime you want."

She laughs, and I turn back to her, grabbing her again as we step into the shower. My cock is hard and rubbing between us, driving us both wild.

I make sure the water isn't hitting her in the face as I close the shower door behind us and look up at her. She pushes some of my hair off of my forehead and then leans down, her lips landing on mine.

She kisses me, her tongue tangling with mine as my hands mold her ass. Soon, she starts to rock against me, showing me that she wants more, and I shift her higher in my arms. Her hips angle, and we both groan as I sink into her.

I pin her back against the shower tiles as I start to thrust lazily in and out of her. This is how I want to wake up and start my day every day, and I wonder if I could convince Maple to move in with me or to let me move in with her.

Her phone starts to ring in the bedroom, but we both ignore it. Her hands cling to my shoulder, and she kisses me harder, her thighs squeezing my hips as her orgasm starts to grow inside of her.

"Ryder," she moans, her head tilting back against the shower tiles and I hum, my lips finding her damp skin as I kiss a trail up her neck.

My teeth nip at her earlobe, and she shudders in my hold. My pace is starting to grow erratic as my own orgasm grows bigger and bigger. I know that I need to get her off before I come, so I reach between us, my thumb finding her clit and rubbing over the sensitive little pearl until she's tensing against me.

She cries out my name and I amend my earlier statement.

That is my favorite sound.

I follow her over the edge, coming so hard that my legs feel weak. I let her slide down my body reluctantly, and she sighs as she leans against me.

I grab her shampoo and start to wash her hair.

"That feels good," she moans, and I clear my throat.

"If you keep moaning like that, you're really going to be late for work," I warn her, and she gasps.

"Shit! Gosh, I lose track of time around you."

She takes over and rinses her hair out. I watch as she grabs her body wash and scrubs her body, and then she hurries from the shower and back into the bedroom.

I rush through my own shower and join her just as she's pulling on her shoes.

"I have to go, but I'll see you later, right?" She asks, and I nod.

"Of course. I'll text you."

She smiles and leans up, kissing my cheek before she jogs from the room. I watch her go and then pull on my own clothes and try to make a plan.

I finally have Maple's attention and she's finally let down her walls around me. Now I need to figure out how to make her mine.

Permanently.

NINE

Maple

I WAS SO WRAPPED up in Ryder that I completely forgot that the Halloween party was tonight, and I never confirmed that he was coming with me. I went to text him around lunch, but then I stopped.

I don't know what happened between this morning and tonight, but I've been plagued with nothing but doubts all day. We were so happy and perfect together this morning and last night, but what is this to him? What am I to him?

I check the time for the third time in as many minutes, anxiety bubbling up in my chest. I should have left ten minutes ago if I wanted to make it back home, shower, and get ready for the Halloween party.

I've been distracted all day. I can't stop thinking about Ryder. The way he kissed me last night, the way he held me like I was the only thing in the world that mattered. It made me feel things, *real* things. That kiss wasn't just a casual fling. There was something more behind it—something I can't ignore anymore.

I'm falling for him.

I actually think that I've been in love with him for months now, but I was too afraid to let him all the way in, too afraid that he might leave me like my parents did. I know that fear is irrational, but I couldn't help it.

Then, once we started going out, I was helpless to stop loving him. Things have been moving so fast, though, that I know I can't tell him—not unless I want to scare him off.

I shake my head as I grab my purse and head for the door. No, *I've* already fallen for him. I'm in love with Ryder Murray, and I have no idea where his head is at. Does he feel the same, or is this just some fun for him? The thought that he might not be as invested as I am makes my stomach twist with worry and doubt.

I need to talk to him before the party. We need to define whatever this is. I can't go any further if I don't know where we stand.

I lock up Wet and Wild and start heading towards Ryder's place, my nerves on edge the entire way. The cool autumn air bites at my skin, but I barely feel it, lost in my own thoughts. I don't want to have this conversation, but I know I need to. The last thing I want is to be vulnerable with someone who isn't ready to give me their heart in return.

When I finally reach his house, my palms are sweating, and my heart is racing. I knock on the door, trying to calm myself down before I hyperventilate. Ryder opens the door almost immediately, a smile lighting up his face when he sees me.

"Hey," he says softly, stepping aside to let me in. "You're here early."

"Yeah, I—" I pause, not sure how to start this. I wring my hands together, avoiding his gaze. "I need to talk to you about something before I head home to get ready for the party."

Ryder's smile falters, and I can see the confusion in his eyes. "What's wrong? Did something happen?"

I take a deep breath, forcing myself to look at him. "I just... I need to know what this is. Between us."

His brows furrow and he takes a step toward me, his hands hovering near mine like he wants to reach out but isn't sure if he should. "Maple, what do you mean?"

"I mean..." I swallow hard, trying to get the words out. "I've been having a lot of feelings lately, and I just don't want to get hurt. I can't keep doing this with you. I need to know if this is serious for you or if it's just... fun."

Ryder blinks, his face falling slightly as he takes in my words. For a moment, he looks like I've punched him in the gut, and it only makes my heart race faster. *God, what if he's not as into me as I thought?*

"Wait, are you... are you breaking up with me?" Ryder asks, his voice strained.

I blink, caught off guard. "What? No! I'm not breaking up with you. I just... I don't even know if we're together, Ryder. I don't know what this is."

His shoulders relax, and he lets out a breath, running a hand through his dark hair. "You scared the hell out of me," he mutters, taking a step closer and grabbing my hands. "I thought you were about to tell me this was all over."

My heart does a funny little flip, but I hold firm. "I'm not breaking up with you, but I need to know where we stand. Because I'm starting to catch real feelings for you, Ryder. Like, *real* feelings. And I don't want to get my heart broken."

Ryder's eyes soften, and he pulls me closer, his hands resting on my waist. "Maple, I've had real feelings for you since the day I met you."

My breath catches in my throat as his words sink in. He stares down at me, his blue eyes so intense that I feel like I'm drowning in them.

"I love you," he says, his voice low and steady. "I've always loved you, Maple. Since the first time I walked by your shop, I knew you were it for me. You're the one I've been waiting for."

I blink up at him, my heart pounding so loudly that I'm sure he can hear it. "You... you love me?"

He nods, his grip on me tightening. "I love you. I've been trying to tell you for weeks, but I didn't want to scare you off. But I can't keep it to myself anymore. I'm all in, Maple."

Tears prick at the corners of my eyes, and I let out a shaky laugh. "Oh my god. I love you too."

The words come out in a rush, but they feel right. They feel true. I've been holding back, but now that they're out there, I realize how much I've been wanting to say them.

Ryder's face lights up, and before I can say anything else, he's kissing me. His lips crash against mine, and I gasp, wrapping my arms around his neck as he pulls me flush against his body. The kiss is deep, hungry, and filled with all the emotion we've been holding back for so long.

He backs me up against the wall, his hands roaming over my body like he can't get enough of me. I moan into his mouth, my fingers tangling in his hair as the heat between us intensifies.

"Wait," he mutters against my lips, pulling back just enough to look at me. "I have something for you."

I blink, dazed from the kiss. "What?"

He grins and steps back, heading toward the closet. He rummages around for a moment before pulling out a garment bag and holding it up with a proud smile.

"I bought this for tonight. I was planning on surprising you at the party."

I raise an eyebrow, curiosity piqued. "What is it?"

He unzips the bag, revealing a ridiculously detailed pirate costume—complete with a hat, eye patch, and boots. I can't help but burst out laughing.

"You're... you're going to wear that?" I ask between giggles.

Ryder grins. "I told you I don't usually dress up, but for you? I'd wear anything."

The sincerity in his voice makes my heart swell. He really would do anything for me.

"You're going to be the hottest pirate at the party," I tease, stepping closer and running my fingers over the costume. "You're really doing this for me?"

"I'd do anything for you," he says, his voice low and serious again. "I told you, Maple. I'm all in. I've been in love with you for longer than you know, and I'm not going anywhere. Ever."

His words send a shiver down my spine, and before I know it, I'm kissing him again.

This time, there's no hesitation, no holding back. I push him against the wall, my hands fumbling with the buttons on his shirt as his fingers slip under my sweater, caressing the skin of my back.

"Maple," he groans as I press my body against his, my hips grinding against his in a way that makes us both gasp.

"We don't have much time," I whisper, my voice shaky as I tug his shirt open. "I have to get ready for the party."

"Then we'll make it quick," he mutters, his voice rough with need.

Before I can respond, he's lifting me up, my legs wrapping around his waist as he carries me to the kitchen counter. He sets me down, his hands gripping my thighs as he kisses me like he can't get enough. His lips move down my neck, and I arch into him, my mind spinning with how fast everything is happening—but I don't care. I want him. I need him.

Our clothes come off in a blur of heat and desperation, and before I know it, he's inside me. The world tilts on its axis as we move together, fast and frantic, the need between us too intense to slow down.

"I love you," he whispers against my lips as we reach the edge together, his voice filled with emotion. "God, I love you so much, Maple."

"I love you too," I gasp, my fingers gripping his shoulders as waves of pleasure crash over me.

When it's over, we stay like that for a moment, tangled together, our breathing ragged and uneven. I rest my forehead against his, trying to catch my breath as my heart races from more than just the physical.

Ryder pulls back just enough to look at me, a satisfied grin on his face. "You're moving in with me."

I blink, still trying to process everything that just happened. "Wait, what?"

"You're moving in," he repeats, his tone leaving no room for argument. "I don't want you going back to that apartment anymore. You're mine, Maple. You belong here, with me."

I stare at him, my heart pounding in my chest. "Ryder, we can't just—"

"Yes, we can," he says, his voice firm but filled with love.

"We love each other, right? So why waste time? Move in with me. Let's start our life together."

My mind races, a whirlwind of thoughts and emotions spinning in every direction. Moving in together? It seems fast—too fast, really—but when I look into Ryder's eyes, filled with sincerity and love, I can't bring myself to argue.

"Are you serious?" I ask, my voice soft but unsteady. "I mean, we haven't even been dating for that long."

Ryder chuckles, brushing a strand of hair from my face. "We've been on two dates, Maple, and I can't wait to take you on a million more. I want to spend every moment we can together. I love you. And if you feel the same, there's no reason to keep waiting. I want you here with me."

I bite my lip, feeling a mix of excitement and nerves. It's such a big step. Moving in together feels monumental, like stepping off a cliff without knowing if there's a net to catch you. But the way he's looking at me, with those steady, honest eyes, makes me feel safe, like I've already fallen—and maybe he *is* the net.

"I don't even have that much stuff," I joke, trying to lighten the moment, but the truth is, I'm terrified. Terrified of making the wrong decision, of getting hurt, of losing what's already been built between us.

Ryder smiles, his thumb tracing over my bottom lip. "Then it'll be easy. Just a few boxes and your heart, and we'll be good to go."

His words make me laugh, the tension in my chest easing just a little. I think about my tiny apartment above the hardware store, the creaky floors, and the drafty windows. It's not much, and it never really felt like home—not the way being here with Ryder feels. There's something about being in his space, with him, that feels like everything I've been missing. Safety, warmth, belonging.

"Okay," I whisper, the word slipping out before I've even fully processed it. "Okay, I'll move in."

Ryder's face lights up, his grin so wide it's contagious. He pulls me in for another kiss, this one slower, deeper, like he's savoring the moment. When we finally pull apart, he rests his forehead against mine, his arms still wrapped securely around me.

"You have no idea how happy that makes me," he murmurs.

I smile, feeling the warmth of his breath against my skin. "I think I have a pretty good idea."

We stay like that for a moment longer, wrapped in each other's arms, and for the first time in a long time, I feel like everything is exactly where it's supposed to be. Ryder loves me, and I love him, and even though this is happening fast, it feels *right*.

"Alright," I say, pulling back slightly and glancing at the clock on the wall. "I really do need to get ready for the party."

Ryder groans playfully, pulling me back against him. "Do we *have* to go? I could think of plenty of reasons to stay right here."

I laugh, swatting at his chest. "Yes, we have to go. I've been so excited about it! I promise that you'll have fun."

He sighs dramatically, letting go of me but not before planting a quick kiss on my forehead. "Fine. But just so you know, I'm counting down the minutes until I can get you back here."

I roll my eyes, my cheeks flushing. "You're impossible."

"And you love it," he teases, grabbing the pirate costume off the counter and holding it up. "Are you sure you're ready for this?"

I grin, nodding. "I wouldn't miss it for the world."

He kisses me one more time, and I can't help but feel like this is the beginning of something new, something bigger than either of us expected. Ryder isn't just a fling, and this isn't just casual fun. This is real. He's real. And for the first time in forever, I'm not afraid to let myself fall.

"I'll see you at the party," I say, grabbing my purse and heading for the door, my heart still racing from everything that just happened.

Ryder watches me go, his eyes filled with so much love and affection that it makes me weak in the knees. "I'll be the one dressed as a pirate. Try not to swoon too much when you see me."

I laugh, shaking my head as I step outside and head down the street toward my apartment. The crisp fall air feels different now, lighter, like the weight that's been sitting on my chest for weeks has finally lifted.

I love him. I *really* love him. And he loves me.

As I walk back to my place, I can't stop smiling, my mind buzzing with thoughts of what the future might hold for us. Moving in together, building a life... it's all so new, so overwhelming, but it feels like the start of something amazing. Something that I can't wait to be a part of.

And tonight, at the Halloween party, we'll start the next chapter of whatever this is—together.

TEN

Ryder

FIVE YEARS LATER...

"READY TO GO?" Maple asks me as she comes downstairs.

"Yep."

I smile as I see her costume. We decided to do a family costume this year, and so Maple, our twins Rachel and Rowan, and I are all dressed up as jack-o-lanterns. All of our pumpkins are smiling and loose enough that it fits over our winter clothes. Maple bends down and fixes Rachel's hat before she lifts her into her arms. I take Rowan's hand as Maple gets Rachel buckled into their stroller.

The twins just turned three a few weeks ago, and they seem to have their mother's love for Halloween. We've already been to a kid's Halloween party and two Trunk or

Treats this week, but now that it's Halloween, we're taking them out to go trick or treating.

"Who is ready for some candy!" Maple says, and both kids cheer.

Rowan takes off, and I tighten my grip on his hand as we head out. We head down to Main Street, and I smile when I see Rachel's eyes start to grow heavy. She's been going through a growth spurt lately, and I'm not surprised that she's already falling asleep.

Maple turns and smiles back at me, and I grin. We've been married for close to four years now. We got married at the town hall here in Wolf Valley with our friends and families in attendance just one week after I proposed to her. Maple wanted a fall wedding, and I just wanted her to be my wife as soon as possible.

She moved in with me then, too, and I quit my bartending job and started spending more time hanging out with her at Wet and Wild. I ended up redoing her website along with Olive's and Saffron's, and now I manage all three.

Speaking of Wet and Wild, I've been helping out there, too. We've started selling products online, and it's always fun to help with stocking and setting aside any of the new toys or lingerie that we want to try.

We found out that we were expecting right after the wedding, but it was a shock to go to the appointment and learn that it was twins. I know that Maple was worried about taking care of two kids at once, but she's a natural. She's such a good mom, and she makes everything look so easy.

Her pregnancy was rough, so after the kids were born, we talked about it and decided that two was perfect for us. Besides, Rachel and Rowan can both be handfuls sometimes, and it can be exhausting just keeping up with them.

"Daddy!" Rowan says as we spot some kids up ahead.

We're meeting the rest of the Baker sisters and their families to go trick-or-treating, and I scan the crowds until I spot Xavier up ahead. He stands head and shoulders above the rest of the people, so it's easy to spot him.

"Over there," I call to Maple and she follows my finger until she spots him too.

We cross the street, and I jog ahead with Rowan, and he rushes to greet his cousins and friends.

"Hey, there you guys are," Olive greets us.

"Are we the first ones here?" Maple asks her, and Olive nods.

"Saffron just texted that she's running a little behind, and Ginger said that she forgot the kid's buckets and had to run back home. They should be here any minute."

I clap Xavier on the back, and he grins at me. He's wearing a piece of bread with peanut butter on it as his costume and I see that Olive has the matching jelly one.

"Nice costume," I tell him, and he smiles.

"Thanks. Olive picked it out."

Of course, she did. I don't know how a group of such bubbly, upbeat sisters all ended up married to such grumpy introverts, but they did.

"Hey, guys!" Townes says as he comes to join our group.

His wife, Mira, is by his side, holding the hand of their son, Noah.

"Noah!" Rachel says, wide awake now, and I smile as I move to unbuckle her from the stroller.

Rachel and Noah have been best friends since she was born, and Mira and Maple like to joke that maybe they'll end up together one day.

Ginger and Saffron both head our way a minute later, their husbands and kids in tow, and Maple heads to greet them. Cora and Huxley come downstairs, too, and Cora grins as she passes out candy to all of the kids.

"I wanted to be the first one to give you candy tonight," she tells them, and the kids are all excited.

"Ready to go?" Ginger asks the group, and the kids all scream yes. I grab Rachel and Rowan's hands as we start to make our way down the street.

Maple falls into step beside us, and I grin at her. I never thought that I would have this—a family, a big group of friends, people that I can count on. I never even knew that I wanted it—not until I met Maple.

She's given me a family and a community. She makes me so happy every day, and she makes me want to be a better man for her and our kids.

"What are you thinking about?" Maple asks me as we approach the first house.

"Just how lucky I am and how much I love you."

"Aww, I love you too," she tells me, reaching over and squeezing my hand. "And I'm the lucky one."

"Nu-uh," I argue, and she laughs.

"Alright, well, how about tonight we see if maybe we can both get lucky," she whispers and I laugh.

"It's a deal."

We share a smile, and I keep grinning for the rest of the night.

It's a very happy Halloween indeed.

Want more of Ryder and Maple? Then be sure

to check out this bonus scene of them at next year's Halloween party!

Looking for more Wolf Valley holiday books? Check out Xavier and Olive's story or read the rest of the Wolf Valley: A Very Grumpy Holiday series!

Don't miss the other Grumpy books! Check out A Very Grumpy Best Friend and the other Wolf Valley Grumps here!

A VERY GRUMPY THANKSGIVING

*

We just need to make it through Thanksgiving.

Saffron:

I made a mistake buying this house.

It needs work, more than I am capable of, and I can't afford to hire anyone.

I figure that I'm screwed... until my neighbor offers me a deal.

He'll do the renovations if I pretend to be his girlfriend for Thanksgiving with his family.

Nolan:

I can't do another family holiday where I'm being set up by everyone.

Which is why I made a deal with my new neighbor.

I thought that it would be simple.

We would eat, pretend to be in love with each other, and then go home.

There's just one problem.

The more time that I spend with my curvy fake girl-friend, the more I fall for her.

Now, I need to figure out how to make my fake girl-friend my real one.

ONE

Saffron

I'VE MADE A TERRIBLE MISTAKE.

That realization hits me as I stand on the sagging front porch of the house that I just bought. What was supposed to be my dream home now looks more like a cautionary tale, or maybe like I just got super into haunted houses and Halloween and forgot to take down all of the scary decorations after the holiday passed almost a month ago.

I sigh as I brush a strand of dark red hair away from my face and glance at the peeling paint on the porch columns. If I squint hard enough, I can still see the potential I had glimpsed when I first saw this place, but the reality is harder to ignore, especially when I'm standing in the middle of it.

I've always had this image of myself: shy, quiet, the girl who preferred the company of books over people. And for most of my life, that's exactly who I've been. But when I decided to move to Wolf Valley with my sisters after our parent's deaths, I thought that maybe, just maybe, I could start a new chapter. I'd move to a new town and get a new beginning. I could be whoever I wanted to be. It sounded so simple, so romantic, like something out of the novels that line the shelves of my bookstore, Shelf Indulgence.

When I first saw this house, I fell in love. It wasn't just the way the oak trees framed the front yard or the soft creaking of the porch under my feet. It was the promise of possibility. A house like this—old, charming, with just the right amount of wear and tear—it was begging to be brought back to life. I could picture myself fixing it up, spending weekends painting walls, replacing old fixtures, and maybe even learning how to lay new floors. I'd be a new version of myself here. I'd be handy, capable, and confident. I saw myself growing alongside the house, piece by piece, until it was mine in every way, until the new me felt like the right me.

What I hadn't factored into my daydream was just how much work a house like this would need orjust how terrible I am at home repairs.

Sure, I had a Pinterest board full of DIY projects and a box of tools that I barely knew how to use, but reality set in the moment I stepped inside. The leaky roof, the creaky floors, the wiring that sparked when I flipped certain switches... the house was a project, all right. And I had taken it on without enough money or experience to make it work.

Once again, I've romanticized my life and now I'm stuck dealing with the reality.

It's not that I don't love a challenge. I mean, I've spent the last year opening and running Shelf Indulgence, and if I can handle making a bookstore successful in a small town, I can handle this house. Right?

Only, the bookstore had its own sort of magic. Shelves

filled with stories of love, adventure, mystery. Things always worked out between those pages. This house? Not so much. I spent nearly all of my savings on buying the place, convinced that I could handle the renovations myself. Now that I'm realizing that I can't, I'm screwed cause what I didn't account for was just how expensive and time-consuming it would be to bring this place back to life.

I let out a sigh and pick up the ladder I dragged out of the shed earlier, leaning it against the side of the house. The gutters are clogged with leaves from last fall, another task that should have been dealt with months ago, long before I bought the place. This task feels like one that I can handle and I'm hoping that maybe if I'm successful with it, that my confidence will grow and I'll be able to tackle the next project.

Grabbing my gloves, I climb to the top of the ladder, my hands shaking slightly from both exertion and nerves. As I climb, each rung of the ladder seems more daunting than the last. The wind picks up, making the leaves in the trees rustle softly. I grip the ladder tighter as I reach the top, awkwardly leaning over to scoop out the debris. The ladder wobbles slightly under me, and my heart pounds in my chest. I shouldn't be doing this alone, but I don't exactly have a choice.

My sisters are all busy with their own business and they know about as much about home repair as I do, so they're not any help. I can't afford to hire anyone. My bank account is nearly empty after buying this place. All of my money went into the down payment, leaving me with barely enough to cover basic repairs, let alone hiring professionals to help.

I'm going to need to start saving up so that I can hire a contractor. I've bitten off more than I can chew here. The realization stings, but there's no denying it. I'm in over my head.

Speaking of over my head...

Heights have never been my thing, but I figured I wouldn't be up that high and that maybe it was time to face my fears. How hard could cleaning gutters be, anyway?

The answer comes in the form of the ladder wobbling beneath me. I grip the gutter tighter, my heart racing as I glance down at the ground, which suddenly seems a lot farther away than it did a moment ago. My foot slips, and for a split second, I think I'm going to fall.

Just as I'm about to lose my balance completely, strong hands grab my waist. The sudden contact sends a jolt through me, and I freeze, my breath catching in my throat. For a moment, I wonder if I'm imagining it, but then I hear a low, familiar voice.

"Are you trying to kill yourself, or are you just testing out the house's life insurance policy?"

I look down, and there he is—Nolan, my grumpy, stand-offish neighbor. He's the last person I expected to see today, but here he is, saving me from what would have undoubtedly been a trip to the emergency room. His hands remain firm on my waist as I try to steady myself on the ladder, and for a moment, I can't think of a single coherent thing to say.

From the moment I saw him, I couldn't help but imagine him as one of the heroes from my romance novels— tall, broad-shouldered, with a perpetual frown that made him look both intimidating and fascinating all at once. He's not the kind of man who strikes up casual conversations or waves from across the yard. No, Nolan is more the "stare from a distance and pretend you don't exist" type.

Despite his gruff demeanor, there's something about him that draws me in, something I can't quite put my finger on. Maybe it's the way he always seems so self-assured, so in control. Whatever it is, I've found myself daydreaming about him more than I care to admit.

And now, here he is, saving me like one of those very heroes I've read about a thousand times. Except this is real, and I'm not sure I know how to play the role of the damsel in distress.

His dark eyes meet mine, and I feel a warmth spread through me that has nothing to do with the crisp autumn air. Nolan and I have lived next to each other for a few weeks now, but I've barely exchanged more than a handful of words with him. He moved in around the same time I bought this house, and from day one, he's kept to himself. Distant is putting it mildly. He's the kind of guy who seems to prefer his own company, not one for small talk or neighborly chats. And yet, here he is, holding me steady on the ladder, like some sort of reluctant knight in shining armor.

I've spent more time than I'd like to admit wondering about him. There's something about his brooding demeanor that reminds me of the heroes from my romance novels, the ones who keep their hearts guarded but secretly harbor deep feelings. Sometimes, when I'm lost in my daydreams, I imagine Nolan as the hero, and I'm the heroine he's pining for. Of course, in real life, he's never shown any sign of interest.

Still, there's no denying that he's handsome. Ruggedly so, with dark hair that's always slightly tousled and a jawline that could probably cut through stone. And now, with his hands on me, I can feel the strength in his grip, the solidness of him.

"I—uh—thank you," I stammer, finally finding my voice.

Nolan releases his hold on me and steps back, crossing his arms over his broad chest. He's wearing a flannel shirt rolled up at the sleeves, exposing muscular forearms that only add to his whole grumpy lumberjack vibe. His expression is as unreadable as ever, but there's a flicker of something in his eyes. Concern, maybe? Or annoyance?

"You shouldn't be doing this alone," he says, his tone gruff.

I blink, taken aback. I've lived next to him for months, and this is the longest conversation we've ever had.

"It's just the gutters," I reply, trying to brush off the near-disaster.

"Yeah, and you almost fell off the roof."

"I wasn't on the roof!" I protest, though I know he's right. If he hadn't shown up, I probably would've been on my way to the hospital by now.

Nolan doesn't seem convinced.

"You shouldn't be up there alone," he says again, his tone gruff, as if he was scolding me.

"I, um... I'm fine," I manage, though the slight tremble in my voice probably gives me away. I wasn't fine. I was flustered, embarrassed, and way too aware of how close he was standing.

He folds his arms over his chest, his biceps straining against the fabric of his worn-out T-shirt. "Doesn't look like you've got this under control."

I bristled a little at that. Sure, I wasn't exactly *succeeding*, but I was trying. And maybe it wasn't going perfectly, but that didn't mean I was helpless.

"I've been handling it," I say, a bit more defensive than I intended.

His eyes flicker to the tools scattered around the yard and front porch, then back to me. "Uh-huh."

I exhale sharply and cross my arms, trying to regain some sense of dignity. "I'm just... I'm learning as I go."

His brow lifts, skepticism clear in his expression, but he doesn't argue. Instead, he shifts his weight and glances up at the roof. "That's dangerous. You should hire someone."

"I can't," I blurt, then immediately regret it. The last thing I wanted was to admit to him, of all people, that I was in way over my head. But there it was, out in the open.

His gaze softens slightly, though his expression remains unreadable. "You can't, or you won't?"

I sigh, feeling the weight of my situation settles back onto my shoulders. "I... I can't afford it," I admit quietly. "I spent everything on buying the house. I don't have anything left to hire help."

Nolan is silent for a moment, his eyes scanning my face as if he is weighing his next words carefully. When he finally speaks, his voice is a little less gruff, almost... concerned. "You can't do this all on your own, Saffron."

I blink, surprised he even remembers my name. We've had exactly two conversations before this, both of them awkward, and he'd always seemed more interested in keeping to himself than in getting to know me.

"I'll figure it out," I mumble, not meeting his gaze. I had to. I don't have a choice.

But the truth is, I was starting to realize I've bitten off more than I can chew. The house needs way more work than I'd anticipated, and I was only one person with very little DIY experience. The roof alone is a nightmare, not to mention the plumbing, the electrical issues, and the peeling paint. I'm overwhelmed, and no amount of internet tutorials is going to fix that.

Nolan shifts again, and I can feel his eyes on me, but I don't dare look up. It's bad enough that I'd nearly fallen off the roof in front of him. I don't need him seeing the cracks in my carefully built facade too.

"If you need help," he says after a long pause, "you should ask."

I blink, surprised by the offer. He doesn't strike me as the helpful type, at least not with how standoffish he's been since moving in. And yet, here he is, catching me before I fall and offering... what, exactly?

For a moment, neither of us says anything. The wind rustles the leaves in the trees, and I can hear the faint hum of traffic from the road in the distance. I expect Nolan to walk away, to go back to whatever it is he does all day in his house. But instead, he surprises me.

"Thanks, but I'm okay," I say quickly, even though I know it's a lie.

He clears his throat, giving me a long, measured look before nodding once. "Suit yourself."

With that, he turns and walks back to his side of the yard, leaving me standing there, heart pounding, wondering if I've just made a huge mistake.

I watch him go, biting my lip as I imagine what it would be like if he were the hero in one of my books. The brooding, handsome neighbor, swooping in to save the day, and me—the damsel in distress, swept off her feet. But this isn't a story. It's real life. And in real life, grumpy neighbors don't just offer to fix your roof and sweep you off your feet.

Right?

I sigh and look up at the house again, trying to let go of my romantic daydreams about my grumpy neighbor and get back to work.

TWO

Nolan

SHE FELT SO damn perfect in my arms.

That's the first thought that hit me as I caught her; her body pressed up against mine for just a few seconds longer than it should have been. I was almost afraid to let go. Afraid that the moment I do, she willdisappear like some daydream I've had a thousand times before, but no, Saffron is very real.

Warm. Soft.

Perfect.

I grunt, setting her down as gently as I can, though I try not to linger, pulling my hands away like her skin might burn me. Her cheeks flush pink, and she mumbles a thank you, avoiding my gaze like I'm some sort of grumpy ogre instead of just a man who doesn't know how the hell to talk to her.

That's the problem, though, isn't it? I've never known how to talk to women, and Saffron? She's in a whole different league. A class of her own. Someone like me has no business even standing next to someone like her, let alone catching her off a ladder, like some kind of hero.

Not that she's noticed me much. I've been in Wolf Valley for six months, but to her, I've just been the grumpy neighbor next door. Hell, she hardly even looked at me when she first moved in. She had her nose buried in one of those books she's always reading. It was probably some romance where the guy knew exactly what to say, what to do, and how to win the girl.

Not like me.

I moved to Wolf Valley for the quiet. A fresh start. I needed to get away from... well, from everything. The noise, the pressure. Life back home had felt too loud, too crowded. I figured a small town in the middle of nowhere would suit me just fine. I didn't need much, just some space, some solitude. But then Saffron bought the house next door.

I didn't know what to think when I first saw her, moving boxes into that rundown house like it was some grand palace instead of the money pit it is. She was smiling, bright-eyed, and full of hope, while I stood there watching, arms crossed like the brooding idiot I am. And when I found out she'd just opened a bookstore in town a few months prior? Well, that about did me in.

Saffron Baker isn't built for this place. Not for that house, not for the mess she's gotten herself into. I could see it clear as day. She's delicate, fragile, like some kind of dream you're scared to touch because you might ruin it. And me? I'm a bull in a China shop, always have been. At close to six and a half feet tall, I've always towered over everyone and felt so out of place no matter where I was.

She thanks me again, her voice soft, and I grunt, nodding as I look away. "You should be more careful," I manage, though it comes out harsher than I intend. She doesn't need a lecture, but my nerves are shot, and I can't get my thoughts straight with her standing so close. She stares up at me, biting her lip, and the blush on her cheeks deepens.

"What?" I ask, trying to sound normal, but failing miserably.

Her eyes widen, and she looks away quickly, flustered. "Nothing," she stutters, and I can tell she's lying. She's thinking something, but I'm not good at reading people, especially not women like Saffron. I want to ask her what's on her mind, but before I can, my phone rings, jarring me out of the moment.

I glance at the screen and groan inwardly. It's my mom. Of course, it's my mom.

"Uh, I've got to take this," I say, excusing myself awkwardly, grateful for the distraction but also regretting it immediately. Saffron gives me a small nod, her eyes dropping back to the tools scattered around the yard, and I turn away, answering the call as I walk back to my side of the fence.

"Hey, Ma."

"Nolan! About time you answered. I've been trying to reach you all week," she says, her voice full of that motherly concern I know all too well.

"Yeah, I've been busy," I lie, glancing back toward Saffron, who's already fiddling with something near the ladder, trying to clean up after her little roofing adventure.

"Well, I'm glad I caught you. I wanted to ask you if you were planning on coming home for Thanksgiving?"

I stiffen. Thanksgiving. Right. I'd been trying to avoid this conversation. My mom had been on a kick lately, always trying to set me up with someone from her church or one of her friends' daughters. It was getting exhausting making up excuses to avoid them.

"I don't know, Ma. I might be... busy," I say, not committing to anything. I can practically hear her narrowing her eyes at me through the phone.

"Busy? On Thanksgiving?"

I run a hand through my hair, glancing back at Saffron again. She's messing with a screwdriver now, completely oblivious to the fact that my stomach is in knots. "Yeah, actually. I might be spending it with my girlfriend," I blurt out without thinking. The moment the words leave my mouth, I want to smack myself.

Girlfriend? Really, Nolan?

My mom goes silent on the other end of the line, and I can already tell I've just opened a can of worms I won't be able to close.

"Girlfriend?" she asks, her voice pitched with excitement. "Why didn't you say anything earlier? Who is she?"

I glance back at Saffron again, and before I can stop myself, I answer, "Saffron."

"Saffron," my mom repeats, like she's tasting the name, savoring it. "Oh, I like that. Pretty name. So, when do we get to meet her?"

I inwardly curse myself again. This is getting out of hand. "I don't know, Ma. We're... still figuring things out," I hedge, trying to dig myself out of the hole I've just dug.

"Well, bring her with you! You can come before Thanksgiving or even after if that works better for you two. You know your father and I don't mind adjusting the schedule. Just let me know when you're coming."

I grimace, trying to keep my voice neutral. "Yeah, I'll... I'll talk to her about it."

"Good! I can't wait. You know, I've been waiting for you

to settle down, Nolan. You're not getting any younger, and I'd love to see you with someone special."

I want to groan, but I keep my mouth shut. "Right. Well, I've got to go, Ma. I'll talk to you later."

She chirps something cheerful in response before hanging up, and I'm left standing there, staring at my phone like it's personally betrayed me.

Great. Now I'm screwed.

I glance back toward Saffron, who's still cleaning up, completely unaware of the mess I've just created for both of us. How the hell am I supposed to explain to her that I just told my mom we're dating? She'll probably laugh in my face. Or worse, she'll think I'm a complete idiot.

I run a hand down my face, feeling the weight of my own stupidity settle over me like a heavy blanket. I've always been a man of few words, someone who prefers to keep things simple. But this? This is anything but simple.

Now, I've got to figure out how to convince Saffron to pretend to be my girlfriend for Thanksgiving.

Perfect. Just perfect.

THREE

Saffron

I LOVE mornings in the bookstore, the quiet before the rush of regulars who come in for their latest reads or to sip on coffee while browsing the shelves. Shelf Indulgence had become my little corner of the world, a safe space where I could escape into books and stories—where everything made sense.

But today, I can't seem to focus. My mind keeps drifting back to yesterday, to the feel of Nolan's hands on my waist, steadying me when I'd nearly fallen off the roof. His touch had been firm but surprisingly gentle. And for just a moment, as he caught me, I'd let myself imagine that I was the heroine in one of my novels, and Nolan was the brooding hero coming to my rescue.

But that's not real life, I remind myself. Nolan isn't some fictional knight in shining armor. He's just my grumpy neighbor, a man who barely speaks to me, let alone sees me the way I secretly wished he would.

I sigh, running my fingers along the spine of a book I was supposed to be shelving. The truth was, I had a stupid crush on him. I'd noticed him the moment he moved in next door, tall and brooding, with that jawline that looked like it belonged on the cover of one of my romance novels. But he hadn't noticed me—not really. Not until yesterday, anyway.

The bell above the door jingles, and I glance up, expecting to see one of my regulars, but when my eyes land on Nolan standing in the doorway, all thoughts of shelving books fly right out of my head.

"Nolan?" I blurt, my heart skipping a beat.

He never comes into the bookstore. In fact, I'd never seen him set foot in here before. I'd always figured he wasn't much of a reader.

He doesn't say anything at first, just stands there, looking around the store like he's searching for something. Or someone.

"Are you... looking for anything in particular?" I ask, my voice coming out a little higher than usual. I tried to steady my nerves, but it was hard when he was standing there, all serious and intense.

His gaze flicks to mine, and for a moment, I could have sworn the air between us shifted. "Yeah," he says slowly, his voice low and rough. "I'm looking for you."

My heart thuds in my chest.

Me? He couldn't possibly mean that the way it sounded.

It feels like something straight out of a romance novel, and I swallow hard, trying to rein in the flood of feelings threatening to overwhelm me.

"What... what do you mean?" I manage, my voice is a little shaky as I force myself to meet his eyes.

Nolan steps further into the store, his presence

suddenly filling the space in a way that makes it hard to breathe.

"I need to talk to you about something," he says, his tone serious, and I can tell by the look on his face that this isn't just a casual visit.

"Okay," I say slowly, setting down the book I'd been holding. "What's going on?"

He runs a hand through his dark hair, glancing toward the front door to make sure no one else is around before turning back to me. "I... I told my family that we're dating."

I blink, certain I haven't heard him right. "What? You what?"

"I told my mom we were dating," he repeats, rubbing the back of his neck, looking slightly uncomfortable. "It just... slipped out."

My heart sinks. Oh. So that was why he was here. This wasn't some romantic declaration. This was a mess.

"How does that just...slip out? Why would you do that?" I ask, feeling a knot of disappointment form in my chest.

I try to ignore that sinking feeling as I study him.

Nolan sighs, stepping closer to me, his eyes meeting mine. "Because my mom's been trying to set me up with half the town, and I just... panicked, okay? I told her I was seeing someone, and when she asked me who, the first name that popped into my head was yours."

I stare at him, trying to process what he was saying. "So... you lied."

"Yeah," he admits. "And now she expects me to bring you to Thanksgiving."

The room feels suddenly smaller like the walls are closing in.

Thanksgiving with Nolan's family? Pretending to be his girlfriend?

I open my mouth to say something, but no words came out.

"I know it's a lot," Nolan says quickly, his tone softer now. "But I'm here to make you a deal."

"A deal?" I echo, my mind racing.

He nods, his expression serious. "I've seen you trying to fix up that house, Saffron. You're going to hurt yourself—or worse—if you keep going at it alone."

I bristle a little, even though he isn't wrong. "I'm managing," I mumble, though we both know I'm not.

Nolan crosses his arms, his gaze steady. "Let me help. I'll fix the house, get it into shape so you don't kill yourself trying to do it. In exchange, you come to Thanksgiving with me. Just pretend to be my girlfriend for one day, and we'll call it even."

I stare at him, my mind spinning. This feels like something straight out of one of my romance books—a grumpy, brooding hero making a deal with the heroine, all in the name of convenience. But this wasn't a story. This was real life.

"Why me?" I ask quietly, my heart pounding. "You could have told your mom you were dating anyone. Why pick me?"

Nolan hesitates, his jaw tightening for a moment before he speaks. "Because... you're the only person I could think of. You're my neighbor. We see each other all the time. It just made sense."

I don't know what to say. Part of me wants to turn him down, to tell him this was ridiculous. But another part of me —an embarrassingly large part,is tempted. I need help with the house. That much was obvious. And spending more time with Nolan? I can't deny that the thought makes my heart flutter.

But can I really do this? Can I pretend to be his girl-friend and not let my feelings get in the way? I already have a crush on him, and the last thing I need is to fall for him even more. I'm not sure my heart could take it.

"I don't know," I say, biting my lip as I look away.

"I'm not asking for much, Saffron," Nolan says, his voice gentle. "Just one day. One Thanksgiving. In exchange, I'll fix up your house, and you won't have to worry about getting hurt trying to do it yourself."

It was tempting. So tempting. And the truth was, I needed help. The house was too much for me to handle alone, and I couldn't afford to hire anyone. Nolan's offer was a lifeline.

But what about my heart?

I swallow hard, trying to push down the rush of emotions swirling inside me. "Okay," I say finally, my voice soft. "It's a deal."

Nolan's blue eyes met mine, and for just a moment, I think I see something flicker in his expression—something deeper, something real. But then it's gone, replaced by the same stoic mask he always wears.

"Good," he says, nodding once. "I'll come by tomorrow and take a look at the house."

I nod, feeling a strange mix of anticipation and dread settle over me. "Okay."

As Nolan turns to leave, I watch him go, my heart still racing. This isn't a romance novel, I remind myself. This is just a deal—a simple arrangement.

Now, I just have to make sure I don't fall in love with him even more.

FOUR

Nolan

SHE SAID YES.

Even now, I still can't believe that she agreed to my crazy plan.

She must really need help with the house, I think as I head over to her place, my toolbox in one hand and water bottle in the other. I gingerly walk up the creaky front porch steps and knock on the door. Saffron's car is still parked out front, so I know that she's home.

She opens the door a minute later and I open my mouth, but no words come out.

I've been lying to myself all morning, telling myself that this arrangement is just mutually beneficial, that it's just a business deal, a transaction, but that's not true, and as I stare at Saffron, I can't deny the truth any longer.

I want her. I want her more than anything and I'm hoping that maybe she'll start to develop feelings for me too over the next few days. Maybe if I'm a good fake boyfriend, she'll want to make this thing real.

"Morning, I was just about to head out to work, so perfect timing," she says softly, opening the door wider and ushering me in.

I follow her into the old, rundown kitchen and set my things down on the counter as I look around. The house really does need a lot of work, and I start to make a mental list as I take it in. My eyebrows raise when I see the hammer sticking out of the wall in the kitchen, and she blushes.

"I, uh, I tried to do some repairs myself. It didn't exactly go as planned," she mumbles.

I bite back a smile and nod as I turn to survey the rest of the kitchen.

"Are you sure that you can handle all of this?" Saffron asks me quietly, looking skeptical, and I nod.

"Yeah."

She doesn't look convinced, so I elaborate.

"My dad owns a construction company, and I grew up working for him. I can handle all of this," I promise her.

She nods, looking relieved, and then passes me a paper. I look at it and see that she's made a list of things that need to be fixed.

"I don't have a ton of supplies here right now, but if you give me a list of what you need, I can go to the hardware store or lumber yard and pick it up today."

"Okay. I'll do a walk-through and see what I can start on now and what we'll need."

She nods, and we stand there for a moment, staring at each other. Saffron's face starts to turn pink and I would give everything that I have to know what she's thinking about right now.

Before I can ask her, though, she blinks and turns away from me.

"I should get to work, but you have my number. Let me know if you need anything."

I nod, and she nods back and then heads for the door. I watch her leave and then turn back to her place and take a deep breath. Her sweet strawberry scent lingers here. I breathe deeply, enjoying myself as I start to walk through the house room by room.

I make a list as I go, writing down tasks and supplies needed for it. I have enough materials to get started on some of the smaller tasks, so I spend my morning removing most of the small half-bath downstairs. The toilet and vanity are all outdated and need to be replaced, but we need to fix the floor boards first.

"Whoa, you got quite a bit done, huh?" Saffron asks as she comes up behind me in the bathroom.

She seems impressed as she studies the now demolished bathroom.

"A bit. You'll need to pick out new furniture and all that, but I need to replace some of the flooring first, so you have some time."

She nods, taking a tentative step closer as she looks around the small space.

"I should paint too," she murmurs, and I nod.

"I can do that."

"*I* can do that. You're already doing so much for me."

"I don't mind. It's part of the deal," I remind her, and she nods slowly.

She seems almost disappointed at the reminder of our deal and I wonder if that's a good sign or not.

"I brought lunch," she says, holding up the brown paper bag in her hand.

"You didn't have to do that."

"I wanted to," she says simply, and I smile as I follow her into the kitchen.

"Do you always come home for lunch?" I ask her as she starts to take the sandwiches out of the bag.

"No, not really. I have Ginger watching the store for me right now though. I wanted to see if you had that list of supplies for me, and I was going to run to the hardware store and wherever else."

"Yep."

I pass her the list I made earlier, and her eyebrows raise when she sees how long it is. She seems shocked at the length, and then I see it—worry. I know that she said she couldn't afford to hire someone, and I wonder briefly about her finances.

"I can call around and use some of my family's contacts to get you some good deals. If we buy it in bulk for all of the projects, then that will be cheaper, too."

She nods, looking a little relieved, and I feel like a hero for helping to lighten her load.

"Why aren't you working for your dad and his company?" she asks me as she passes me a sandwich.

"It just wasn't for me. I wanted to make my own way, so I left when I was eighteen and joined the military. The Air Force. Ironically, I was put into structures."

She blinks, looking confused, and I rush to clarify.

"Structures is a career field. They do repairs on the buildings and build stuff."

"So, you left and ended up doing the same thing," she says, and I nod.

"Yeah, and for less money."

"Do you regret it?" she asks, and I shake my head.

"No, it got me out of my small town. I got to see the world, make some friends, and spread my wings a bit."

"And then you got out," she guesses, and I nod.

"Yeah, I was deployed, and one night, there was an air strike. A bomb ended up landing on my building, and I was hurt pretty badly. I was airlifted to the base in Germany, and then a few weeks later, I was discharged and sent back home."

"And you came to Wolf Valley?"

"It seemed like a good place to settle down," I tell her, and she nods.

"What about you? What brought you to this small town?"

"My sisters," she says with a small smile. "My parents passed away, and it just got to be too hard to stay in our childhood home with all of the memories. Olive wanted a fresh start and it seemed like a good idea, so we all followed her here."

"Olive is the oldest?"

"Yeah, then Maple, then me, and then Ginger."

"You guys are close."

"Yeah, they're all my best friends. Do you have siblings?"

I nod, and she takes a big bite of her sandwich.

"Two younger sisters and a younger brother."

"Do they all look up to you?" she asks.

"I doubt it."

I take a bite of food, and she frowns.

"You're not close to them?"

"Not especially. I talk to them like once a month, see them on holidays, but that's it. They all are married with kids and are busy."

She nods, and we eat in silence for a minute.

"Do you want that?" she asks quietly, and I swallow.

"Want what?"

"A wife and kids. A real one," she stresses, and I smile slightly.

"Sure. With the right person."

Our eyes lock, and we stare at each other for a beat.

"What about you?" I ask her, and she looks away, gathering up the wrapper from her sandwich and the napkins.

"Yeah, I want that," she whispers.

I can hear the longing in her voice, and I vow right then and there to give her anything that she needs. I'll be whatever she needs, whatever she wants. I just need her to be mine.

"Let's go get your supplies," I say, my voice rough, and she nods.

I follow her to my truck, and a plan starts to form in my mind for making Saffron more than just my fake girlfriend.

FIVE

Saffron

FOR THE FIRST time in forever, I'm actually excited to go home for the day, and I know that it's all because Nolan will be there waiting for me. He got so much done yesterday, and surprisingly, shopping for supplies with him was fun. The total was a lot less than I was expecting, and I know that I have him to thank for that, too.

We left the lumberyard yesterday with a whole truckload of wood, and I was able to order a bunch of the bathroom fixtures, too. They won't be in for a few weeks, but Nolan says that's okay since it will take him time to fix the floor and paint.

It's so nice to see my vision of the house finally starting to come to life. It's also a huge relief to not have to worry about that project anymore. I trust Nolan, and I know that my house is in good hands with him.

"I got pizza!" I announce as I step inside my place.

Nolan sticks his head out of the bathroom, wiping sweat from his forehead with the back of his gloved hand.

"Pepperoni?" he asks, and I smile.

"Of course."

I had asked him about his favorite foods yesterday when we were driving around together. I figure that the least I can do is feed him. Our deal isn't really fair. He and I both have to be able to see that it's heavily in my favor. I mean, he's fixing up my whole house, and I'm going to one family holiday meal with him in return.

Why does he even need a fake girlfriend? I mean, Nolan is so handsome. I'm sure that he could convince anyone to go out with him. So, why me?

"You don't have to keep feeding me," he tells me as he heads into the kitchen and starts to clean up.

I watch the muscles in his back flex as he leans over the sink and washes his hands.

"I don't mind. I mean, we both have to eat. It will be nice to cook in the kitchen here once that's finished," I say, looking around the space.

"I'll work on that next."

"Oh, I didn't... I wasn't saying that to rush you or anything," I start, and he shakes his head.

"No, it will work out since the cabinets will be in before the bathroom stuff."

I nod and grab some paper plates, handing one to him.

"How was work?" he asks as we each grab a slice.

"It was good. Busy. We started up some book clubs, and they all came in today to pick out their next book of the month."

"That's a good idea."

"Thanks. It's helped with business. It was Ginger's idea, actually. She's amazing with all this marketing stuff."

"Does she own part of the bookstore?" he asks me, and I shake my head.

"Nope, it's just mine. She helps us all out with our shops. She's still trying to figure out what she wants to do with her life."

"How did you land on a bookstore?" he asks as he takes a big bite of his slice.

"I've always loved books. Out of all of us, I was the shyest. I was the quiet, nerdy sister who always had her face buried in a book, so opening my own bookstore was kind of a no-brainer."

He smiles slightly, and I grab a slice and add it to my plate.

"What about you? What will you do now that you're out of the military?"

"Well, I have some time to figure it out. I don't need much, and I get checks now that I'm medically discharged."

"You haven't been getting bored? Just staying home all of the time?" I ask him curiously, and he shrugs.

"A bit. Doing this has been helping," he says with a small smile, and I laugh.

"Well, I'm happy to help. If you ever feel bored after all of this, let me know and I'm sure that I could find something else for you to do."

I don't mean for that to come out so sexual, but it does. My cheeks flame and I know that they must be as red as my hair as I stare at Nolan. He's staring at me, his pizza slice halfway to his mouth. I can't tell if I'm waiting for him to say something or if I would rather that the ground opened up and swallowed me whole.

"I—" I start, but I'm saved by my phone ringing. "Oh, thank god," I mumble as I scramble to answer it. "Sorry, I should take this," I tell him, and he nods.

"Hello?" I answer as I head out to the front porch.

"Hi, I'm with Cellular Live, and I was calling to see if you would be interested in switching over your phone—"

I hang up and groan as I scrub my hands down my still-hot face. *I need to get it together,* I think as I head back inside. *Remember that this is just fake to him.*

"I was thinking, we should get our story straight," I tell him as I head back into the kitchen.

"Story?"

"Yeah, you know? Like what we're going to tell your family."

"Tell them about what?" he asks with a frown.

"Us? I'm sure that they'll have questions. My sisters would want to know where we met, what our first date was, who asked who out, that sort of thing."

"Oh. Right."

"What have you already told them?" I ask as I finish off my slice.

"Just that you're new to town too and that you're my neighbor."

"Okay, that's good. We can just stick as close to the truth as possible then so that it's easier to remember."

"Okay."

"We'll say that we met when I moved in, that you asked me out, and that our first date was at the Italian place in town. Sound good?"

"Sure."

My phone buzzes, and I look at the screen to see Ginger's name.

"I have to get back to the bookstore," I tell him. "I'll see you later."

He nods, and I stuff the pizza box in the fridge before I head back to my car and make the short drive into town.

Ginger was covering for me at the shop again today and I smile at her as I walk in and see her behind the counter.

"Hey, thanks for watching things here."

"No problem," she says with a wide smile. "How's your man?"

I roll my eyes at her question. My sisters know all about Nolan and me. I told them as soon as he asked me because I wanted to know if I was making a mistake. They assured me that it was a good idea, but now I'm having doubts.

The way that we talk, the way that he is around me, it all just feels so natural. With such a big family, it's easy to disappear, but Nolan makes me feel seen, truly seen, for the first time in forever. It's easy for me to forget that this is all fake, just some deal.

And that's dangerous.

"He's good. The bathroom and stuff is coming along really well."

"And? Has he declared his undying love for you yet?" she asks, and I snort.

"Nope."

She sighs, and I smile as I join her behind the counter.

"This isn't a romance book," I say, trying to remind both of us of that fact.

"I've seen the way that he looks at you. Plus, there has to be a reason why he asked you and not someone else."

"I think that he just lied and said he was dating me because I was there when his mom called. I don't think he sees me like that," I tell her.

"Hmm," she says as she twirls an envelope in her fingers.

"What's that?" I ask, desperate to change the subject.

"A note."

"From who?"

"I don't know."

I frown at her, and she smiles sheepishly.

"It's from a secret admirer," she admits, and I grin at her.

"What!? Why didn't you tell me when I first came in? How long has this been going on? Is that the first message? What does it say?" I ask her, and she ducks her head, a pink blush staining her cheeks.

"I've gotten a few before, but they've been more frequent for the last two months or so."

"Why didn't you tell us?"

"Honestly, I thought that it was a joke at first, or maybe given to the wrong person."

She passes me the note and I laugh.

"Ginger, it's addressed to you. How could it be to the wrong person?"

"I don't know! I just... didn't believe that it was for me."

I don't ask her why. I have a feeling that if it had been me, I wouldn't have believed it either. It seems Ginger and I both have some self-esteem issues that we need to work on.

"What are you going to do now that you know it is for you?"

"I don't know. The letters show up in random places, so I don't know if I should leave one in return somewhere. There's no guarantee that the right person would get it, you know?"

"Have you tried to figure out who it is?"

"Of course! But they're so random. One week I get two or three messages, the next one, then four. And they show up on different days, in different places. There's no way to spy and try to see who is leaving them."

"Hmm," I say as I ponder how to solve this mystery. "I can look out for it too. We should tell Maple and Olive too."

"Maybe," she says and I quirk a brow.

"You don't want to know?" I ask her and she shrugs.

"It's been nice. What if I hate the person who is leaving the notes? What if he's terrible and—"

"And the fantasy is ruined," I finish for her, and she nods. "I get it. Alright, I'll let you handle it."

"Thanks. Now, let's talk about you and your handyman."

"There's not much to say. He's working on the house, and we have our story figured out for when we see his family. A few more days and the deal is over."

"And how do you feel about that?" she asks me, and I sigh again.

"I don't know," I admit. "Scared? My feelings are already out of control for him, and I'm afraid that I'm going to get hurt when this is all over and done with. And then I have to live next door to him!"

"Tell him that it's not fake for you," she urges me.

"I'll look insane. Like a lovesick fool when I just agreed to fake dating him a few days ago."

"He likes you too."

"I can't risk it," I tell her, and she nods.

The bell over the door dings, and we both look up as a group of four older ladies come in. We both get to work, and I try to forget about Nolan and my growing feelings for him.

I don't succeed.

I know that this is only going to get worse. The more time that I spend with Nolan, the harder it is for me to separate what's fake and what's real.

As I close up for the night and start to head home, I realize one thing.

I'm in trouble, and I don't know how to stop from falling completely in love with Nolan. I'm not sure that I could stop it even if I wanted to. And that means one thing.

I'm screwed.

SIX

Nolan

"I'M NERVOUS. ARE YOU NERVOUS?" Saffron asks me as we pull up outside of my parent's place.

"I mean, now that you just told me that, yeah."

"You're not supposed to say that!" she scolds me. "You're supposed to tell me that I'm being silly and that everything is going to be fine, and they're going to love me and not to worry."

"Everything is going to be fine, and they're," I start to parrot back to her, and she scoffs and smacks my arm lightly.

Saffron has really started to warm up to me over the last few days. She's still quiet, but I can tell that she feels more comfortable in my presence, and that makes me unbelievably happy.

I laugh as I unbuckle and turn to her.

"Okay, for real, they're going to love you, and it's going

to be fine. We'll eat and then head home. It will be a piece of cake."

She takes a deep breath and nods, her fingers tightening around the pie that she brought for tonight. She still looks nervous, but it really is going to be fine. My mom is already half in love with her just based on the little information that I've already told her about Saffron.

"Let's do this."

We climb out of my truck and I frown up at the darkening sky. It's starting to snow, but it's light. As long as it stays that way, the roads should be good enough to drive back to Wolf Valley later.

My childhood home looks exactly as I remember it. I haven't been back in a while, not since I left for the Air Force. The house is a two-story ranch style, the outside decorated for fall with orange lights and pumpkins everywhere.

We head up to the front door, and I try to discreetly take a deep breath before I turn the knob and usher Saffron in ahead of me.

"Uncle Nolan!" Five little kids shriek as soon as I walk in the door.

"Hey, guys!" I greet my nieces and nephews.

They all start talking to me at once, and I smile as I crouch down and pull them into a tight hug one by one.

"Guys, this is my friend, Saffron. Saffron, these are my nieces and nephews. There's April, Andy, Ben, Samantha, and Troy."

They all stare up at her with big, curious eyes, and she smiles down at them.

"It's nice to meet you. Happy Thanksgiving," Saffron says sweetly.

"Nolan!" My mom yells as she barrels into the front room.

"Hey, ma. Happy Thanksgiving."

She beams at me as she wraps me up in a tight hug.

"My boy finally came home," she whispers, and I wince, feeling guilty that I've stayed away for so long.

I just didn't want to have to field all of my family's questions about why I was still single and how I was doing after leaving the military. I didn't want to talk about the accident or the aftermath. I couldn't answer their questions about what's next because I don't know what's next.

"And you must be Saffron!" My mom says as she turns to take in my girl.

"Hi, it's nice to meet you. I uh, I made a pie," Saffron says shyly, holding the pie out to my mom.

"You too, dear! Oh, it's so nice to meet you," my mom gushes. "Nolan hasn't told me much, so I'm so excited to get to know you better. Come and let me introduce you to everyone."

And just like that, I lose track of Saffron.

My mom drags Saffron around to meet all of my aunts and uncles. I try to keep track of her, but the house is so full that it's hard to get around.

"Hey, I met your girlfriend," my sister greets me, and I nod, scanning the room for a certain curvy redhead.

"Yeah? Where is she?"

"Kitchen. Surrounded by all of our aunts," Shelby tells me. "She's nice. How did you land her?"

"Luck," I grunt out, and she laughs.

"I believe it."

"Believe what?" Aaron, our youngest sibling, asks as he joins us in our corner of the living room.

"That Nolan lucked out with his new girlfriend," Shelby tells him.

"Oh yeah, she's great!" Aaron agrees. "My kids are already calling her Aunt Saffron. Or Aunt Saffy in the case of Samantha."

I laugh as I see Aaron's youngest clinging to Saffron's leg as she comes into the living room. Our eyes lock, and she smiles. She seems more at peace with my family than I feel, and a warm feeling starts to spread in my chest. I'm happy to see that everyone seems to love her right away, not that I can blame them. She's easy to love.

I'm the oldest of the three of us and the only one not married or settled down with kids yet. I'm also the only one who joined the military and left town.

"It's time to eat!" My Aunt Kathy calls, and everyone starts to head into the dining room and kitchen.

I find Saffron in the crowd and slip my hand into hers.

"Everything okay?" I whisper to her, and she nods.

"Everyone is so nice."

I squeeze her hand, and she leans into my arm a bit.

"Where are we sitting?" she asks me, and I look around.

"Aunt Saffy! Can you sit with me?" Samantha asks.

"You're at this table," Aaron tells his daughter as he leads her over to the kid's table in the kitchen.

Samantha pouts and Saffron looks upset.

"We'll sit close to their table," I whisper to her as I lead the way over to the far side of the adult's table.

"Hey, Nolan!" Mark, Shelby's husband, greets me. "How's it going?"

"Pretty good. How about you?" I ask him as I pull out a chair for Saffron.

We all sit down, and I turn to check in on Saffron. She's happy, busy talking to the kids at the table next to us.

"Your girl is lovely," My Aunt Sarah tells me, and I smile.

"How have you been?" I ask her.

We start to pass the food around the table, and I hold the bowl of mashed potatoes so that Saffron can grab some before I pass it to my sister-in-law.

"So, tell us how you two met!" My Aunt Kathy says, and I turn to Saffron.

"We're neighbors," she says with a small smile. "We met when I moved in next door to him."

"Are you from Wolf Valley?" My dad asks, and Saffron shakes her head.

"No, me and my sisters moved there about a year ago."

"Saffron opened up a bookstore in town," I tell my family.

"Oh, how exciting!" Aunt Kathy gushes.

The conversation focuses on Saffron, her bookstore, her family, her new house, and finally, our relationship.

"So, how long have you two been dating?" Shelby asks.

"A few weeks now," I tell them as I dig into the food.

We all dig in, and finally, the conversation changes to what everyone else has been up to. Everything seems to be going great. My mom and dad are thrilled that I'm with someone. Everyone seems to love Saffron, and it's great to see my family again.

Still, I can't help but be on guard. There's this nagging feeling in the back of my mind that keeps telling me that this is the end. Our deal is over after tonight, at least on her end. I'll just have to be around her all of the time as I fix her house, but I won't be able to hold her hand or pretend that we're together.

I try to focus on the meal, but every time that Saffron

laughs or looks at me with those soft eyes, I wonder if maybe it's possible to make this thing between us real.

Could it be possible that this isn't fake to her either?

SEVEN

Saffron

"THANK you so much for having me. Dinner was delicious and it was so nice to meet all of you," I tell Nolan's family as he holds my coat up for me to slip my arms into the sleeves.

"Oh, any time, dear!" Mrs. Wright tells me as she steps forward to wrap me up in a tight hug. "You're welcome back here anytime."

"Thanks," I whisper, and she smiles as she pulls back slightly.

"Thank you. It's nice to see my son so happy and I know that we have you to thank for that."

"I'll see you guys later," Nolan says as he hugs everyone good.

He takes my hand, and I smile, waving one more time as he pulls open the front door. I've liked getting to know his family, but I'm ready to head home and be alone to process all of my feelings.

Nolan pulls open the door, and a blast of snow and freezing cold air hits both of us, knocking me back a step.

"Whoa," I blurt out when I see how bad that weather has turned in the few hours that we were here.

A foot and a half of snow is now covering his truck, and more is still coming down.

"You can't drive home in that!" Mrs. Wright says, and I glance up at Nolan.

"Uh..." He says, blinking as he looks out at the weather.

"You'll stay the night. We insist. Right, honey?" Mrs. Wright says, nodding at her husband.

"Of course. I'll get the sheets for your old bed," he says, and I blink as he takes off down the hall.

"Nolan?"

"Um," he says, shutting the front door. "Maybe the snow will stop soon."

He pulls his phone out and we both frown when we see that it's supposed to snow for another few hours.

He looks at me, and I can see that he's nervous about my reaction.

"I...I guess we should stay."

"Yeah. We'll leave first thing in the morning," he assures me.

I nod and unzip my jacket. Mrs. Wright is clearly over the moon that we have to stay longer, and I smile at her as Nolan hangs my coat back up.

"Well, do you want to see my childhood bedroom?" he asks, and I can't help but smile at his obvious discomfort.

He looks so nervous, and now I'm curious about what it looks like. We were so busy all day that I didn't get a chance to tour the whole house.

He takes my hand and leads me down the hallway and into a bedroom. There are some old trophies on a shelf, some books, and a few trinkets. I smile as I walk around and look at all of it.

"Football?" I ask him as I look at the trophies.

"I wasn't very good," he says, and I smile.

"You have trophies so it kind of looks like you were," I point out.

"It was the team. Not me."

He's so modest and I kind of swoon as I move on to the little moose figurine.

"I made it when I was sixteen and went through my whittling phase," he explains, and I laugh.

"You make it sound like everyone has a whittling phase."

"Don't we?"

I turn to see him smiling at me, a twinkle in his eye, and my heart flutters in my chest so hard that, for a moment, I wonder if I'm having a heart attack.

My eyes stray to the full-size bed, and I swallow hard as I stare at it, knowing that soon, we'll both be sleeping in it.

"It's hard to imagine you fitting on that bed," I say, my voice coming out hoarse sounding.

"I didn't go through my growth spurt until I was eighteen."

I eye him, taking in his six-and-a-half-foot frame. My eyes trail over his muscles, and my mouth starts to water as I imagine his hard body pressed against mine.

"Saffron?" Nolan asks, and my eyes snap to his.

"Hmm?"

"Did you want to take a shower first? You can borrow some of my old clothes to sleep in."

"Sure."

He shows me to the ensuite bathroom and grabs me a

towel, some of his childhood sweatpants, and an old high school t-shirt.

"Your mom doesn't get rid of anything, huh?" I ask and he snorts.

"Nope. I haven't lived at home in years, and it still looks like it did when I was in high school."

"That's sweet," I say softly, and he smiles slightly.

"I'll let you take a shower. Let me know if you need anything else."

I nod, and he backs out of the bathroom, closing the door as he goes. I turn on the shower and try to ignore the way my body reacts as I use his body wash and shampoo. It's no use, though, and as I pull on his clothes, I'm more turned on than I've ever been in my life. My nipples are hard, poking against the thin material of his shirt. I fold my arms over my chest to try to hide them as I step back into the bedroom.

Nolan smiles as he stands and heads into the bathroom, and I try not to think about him naked and wet on the other side of the door. My core clenches and I start to grow wet as I listen to the shower running.

I press my thighs together to try to ease the ache as the water turns off. I try to act normally as the door opens and Nolan steps out, dressed in a pair of pajama pants just like mine, only his are a few inches too short.

I giggle, and he glares at me.

"Not a word."

"What? I think it's cute."

He tugs the pants down a bit, exposing an inch of his stomach, and my smile drops as I stare at that stretch of skin.

"I'll sleep on the floor," he tells me.

"Knock, knock!" His mom says, poking her head around

the door. "I brought some toothbrushes and toothpaste for you two."

"Thanks, mom."

"Thanks, Mrs. Wright."

"Of course. Do you two need anything else?"

"No, we're good."

"Okay, see you in the morning!"

"Night!" I call as she heads out, closing the door behind her as she goes.

Nolan passes me a toothbrush, and we head into the small bathroom. It's cramped as we stand shoulder-to-shoulder at the sink and brush our teeth. My eyes stray to him in the mirror and we both smile at each other, white toothbrush bubbles around our lips.

I spit and rinse my mouth out and then he does the same. He hits the light and we file back into the bedroom.

"You don't have to sleep on the floor," I tell him, and he turns to me.

"I don't mind."

"It won't be comfortable," I point out, and he shrugs.

"I want you to be comfortable."

"I'll be fine sharing with you."

He nods slowly, and I climb onto the bed. He hits the lights, and a moment later, the bed dips as he climbs in next to me.

"Good night," I whisper.

"Night, Saffron. Happy Thanksgiving."

"Happy Thanksgiving."

I close my eyes, trying to slow my racing heart as we lie in the dark next to each other. I can feel his heat, can hear his breathing next to me. I'm hyper-aware of him next to me in the dark.

I shift, trying to get comfortable, but it doesn't work.

Not when my body brushes against him, setting my whole body on fire.

"Saffron," he murmurs, and I can't take it anymore.

It's like I'm a bowstring being pulled tighter and tighter, and I'm ready to snap. I lean forward, my hands rubbing up his chest, and my heart races as I hear his sharp intake of breath. He tenses under my touch, and I lick my lips.

"Nolan." His name tastes like a promise on my tongue, and the intensity in his dark eyes makes my heart stumble in my chest.

He takes a step forward, just enough that I have to tilt my head back to hold his gaze. There's a charge between us, electric and unsteady, and it's pulling me closer, pulling both of us into something dangerous and delicious. I don't know who moves first, but suddenly we're right there, breathing the same air, so close I can feel the heat of him like a storm building.

His hand rises slowly, like he's giving me a chance to stop him. I don't. Instead, I lean into his touch, and when his fingers cup my jaw, I swear my bones melt under the warmth of his palm.

His warm breath fans my face, and we both pause, our eyes locking in the dim light from the moon outside.

"Saffron," he whispers, and my eyes flutter closed as his lips meet mine.

I instantly go up in flames. I press closer to him, until our bodies are tight against each other. I gasp as I feel his hard cock against my stomach. Part of me can't believe that he's turned on by me, but then my brain shuts off, and all I can do is get swept up in the passion between us.

We pull apart, both of us sucking in a breath. Our eyes lock, and my heart feels like it's going to beat out of my chest.

"Saffron," he whispers, like he's been holding my name in his mouth for too long, waiting for this exact moment to let it go.

I don't wait another second. I reach up, grab the front of his shirt, and yank him down to me. Our mouths collide in a kiss that's as wild as the storm outside, all heat and hunger and pent-up frustration. His lips are firm and demanding, and I match him, kiss for kiss, like I've been starved for him without even realizing it.

He groans low in his throat when I open my mouth under his, and the sound sends a thrill straight through me. His hand slides into my hair, tugging just enough to make me gasp, and he uses the moment to deepen the kiss, his tongue sweeping against mine in a way that makes my knees threaten to give out.

I clutch at his shoulders, desperate to stay anchored as everything inside me tilts, shifts, and catches fire. Nolan kisses me like he's trying to memorize every second, like he knows we've wasted too much time, and he's determined to make up for it now.

"Night, you two!" Nolan's dad calls through the door, and we jerk apart.

Nolan almost falls off the bed and I reach for him, both of us panting as we stare at each other.

"Night," I call back, my voice unsteady.

"Night, Dad," Nolan calls, sounding just as affected as I feel.

I clear my throat as I listen to his footsteps fade down the hall.

"We should get some sleep," I say, my voice hoarse, and he nods.

We settle under the covers, and I take a deep breath as I try to calm my racing heart enough so that I can fall asleep.

It takes a long, long time before sleep finally claims me.

EIGHT

Nolan

WHEN I WAKE up the next morning, Saffron is already out of bed. In fact, she's not even in the room anymore. Her clothes from yesterday are gone, and the pajamas that she wore to bed last night are folded on the dresser.

I sigh as I scrub my hands down my face and sit up in bed. My mind flashes back to that kiss last night. I'd never been cockblocked by my parents before since I never had a girlfriend before, and I do not recommend it. I had been so close to going all of the way with Saffron last night. I wanted to strip her naked, throw her legs over my shoulders, and eat her out until she screamed my name. Then I'd bury myself inside of her and make her scream my name all over again.

I guess it's a good thing that we didn't go all of the way. When I make love to Saffron, I want it to be romantic and not in my childhood bed, in my childhood bedroom, with my whole family sleeping right down the hall.

I get dressed and go to find my girl. She's in the kitchen, helping my mom make breakfast and laughing at something that Samantha is saying to her. My heart lodges in my throat, and I freeze as I stare at her.

She's perfect, and I want her. I want her so goddamn bad. I want her to be my real girlfriend, my real wife, the real center of my whole fucking world.

"Morning, honey!" My mom calls, and I blink, trying to clear the vision of Saffron in a wedding dress from my head.

"Morning," I rasp out.

Saffron blushes as she looks at me, and I know instantly that she's thinking about our kiss last night.

"How's the weather?" I ask.

"All clear! It's sunny and gorgeous out this morning," my mom says. "Well, besides the fact that it's about three degrees out."

Saffron laughs, and I smile as I move closer to her.

"Are you ready to head out?" I ask her, and my mom frowns.

"No way! You have to stay for breakfast."

I look at Saffron, and she nods.

"Alright. Let's eat," I relent.

As we sit down and start to eat, people are still waking up. Saffron and I both dig in, and we eat quickly. Samantha is talking Saffron's ears off, and I smile as I listen in on their conversation.

Once we finish eating, I clear our plates and go back to Saffron's side.

"Ready?" I ask her, and she nods.

I can tell that she's getting overstimulated from being around so many people. Saffron is like me and needs to recharge their social battery often.

"We're going to head out," I tell my mom and dad, and my mom pouts but nods.

"Thanks again for having me," Saffron says, stepping forward to hug my mom and then my dad goodbye.

"You're welcome anytime," my mom tells her, and my dad nods in agreement. "Oh! You have to come back for Christmas!"

"Yeah!" Samantha cheers, and Saffron smiles.

I can see the moment that she remembers our deal and that we won't be fake together by then. Her smile dims, and I swallow hard. My heart sinks because I want to spend every holiday with her and I'm not sure that's possible. Why did I make the deal for just one holiday? I should have said until the house was fixed and then dragged the projects out for years, until she was in love with me.

"Maybe," she says, and I nod.

"I'll talk to you guys later," I say as I step forward and hug my parents goodbye.

We make the rounds, saying goodbye to everyone, and then I help Saffron into her coat, and we head out to my truck. I help Saffron into the passenger seat and scrape off the windows while the truck heats up. Then we're hitting the road.

She's quiet as I maneuver us down the snowy streets.

"Everyone liked you," I say, trying to break the silence.

"Yeah, your family is great. The kids were so cute," she says, and I smile.

"Yeah, Samantha seemed to especially love you."

"She was so sweet."

"I'm glad that you had a good time."

"Me too," she says softly.

We drive in silence for a few minutes, and then she clears her throat.

"What excuse will you give them for Christmas?" she asks, and my stomach sinks.

"I... I don't know. I guess that you had plans with your family. It's the truth."

She nods, and we ride in silence for the rest of the way home. I was going to try to broach the subject of us together for real, but after her comment, I don't think that's a good idea.

I pull into my driveway and park, hurrying out to open her door for her and help her out.

"I can come over in a few to start on the house," I tell her and she blinks.

"You don't have to do that today. I'm sure that you have things to do."

"Nope, I'll be by in a bit."

She nods, and I watch as she walks over to her house and lets herself inside. I head into my own house and wonder what to do now as I close the door behind me and look at my empty place.

I change clothes and then grab my tools and head over to her house. I hesitate as I raise my hand to knock on the door and take a deep breath. I knock, and a second later, she pulls the door open and ushers me inside.

"It's freezing out! I was going to build a fire."

"I can do that," I offer, and she smiles.

"I should probably check first and make sure that it's safe to do it," she says with a laugh.

Her hair is damp, and she smells like strawberries and roses. I breathe deeply as I set my tools down and head over to the fireplace to see what we're working with. Surprisingly, the fireplace seems to be in great condition, and it takes me no time at all to start a fire.

"Thanks," she says, and I nod as I wipe my hands off on my jeans.

"What did you want me to start with first?" I ask her and she blinks as she stares at me.

I can't quite read her expression, not at first. We stare at each other, and she licks her lips, her green eyes darkening and filling with heat. My body reacts to that and I shift on my feet like a racer about to take off. My breath stalls in my lungs as I stare down at her.

I blink, and a second later, we're crashing together, the heat from last night flaring back to life between us as my lips move over hers.

She tastes like tea and honey, and I pull her closer against me. I don't want any space between us. Ever.

"You drive me crazy," I murmur, my voice low, like a confession wrapped in a promise.

My thumb strokes along her cheek, and I feel the pull between us. It's magnetic, inevitable.

"Nolan..." she whispers a second before our lips connect again.

The kiss deepens as her hands find the front of my shirt, curling into the fabric as if she needs something to anchor her. I tilt my head, deepening the kiss. My fingers tangle in her hair, and I tip her head back as I devour her.

The kiss turns urgent, like we're both afraid that the other will stop it before we're ready. Saffron melts into me, her lips molding to mine perfectly. My cock presses against her, and she moans as she rubs against it.

We break apart, both of us breathing hard. She stares up at me, her eyes a little wild and her hair coming loose from her ponytail. I love seeing her like this and knowing that I'm the only one who gets to muss her up and get her to lose control.

"Remember where my bedroom is from the tour?" she whispers against my mouth, and I grin.

"Uh-huh."

"Let's go."

I don't need to be told twice. I swoop her up into my arms and take off up the stairs and into her bedroom. She giggles, the sound like music to my ears as I lay her down on the bed and come down over her.

The bed is perfectly made and I grin, loving the idea that we're about to mess it up.

"I want you," she whispers, and I kiss her.

"I want you too. Fucking badly."

She smiles, seeming to grow more confident from my words, and her hands wrap around the back of my neck. She tugs me down, and our lips connect once again. She's so soft. All of her is soft, her lips, her skin, her curves.

Her hand tugs on my shirt, and I sit up, tugging it over my head and letting it drop to the floor. Saffron's eyes are on me, and I pause as she admires my chest. Her fingers tentatively run over my abs, and I'm thankful that I kept up with my workouts even after I left the military.

She licks her lips, and the restraint that I've been holding onto so tightly starts to fray.

"Need you. Naked. Now," I tell her and she tenses beneath me.

I frown. Did I read the signs wrong? I thought that she wanted me.

"We don't have to do anything that you don't want to, Saffron," I tell her, and she blushes.

"I want you," she says softly. "It's just...you look like that and I... don't."

Her blush heats her whole face, turning it almost as red as her hair.

"I love your body. I've been dreaming about these curves for so long," I tell her, my voice low and husky as I stare down at her body. "Can't you feel what you do to me?"

I press my erection against her, and her eyes go hazy with lust.

"I just... I've never done this before."

"Done what?" I ask, my brain still on the heated look in her eyes and how good she feels against me.

"Sex."

"Huh?"

That gets my attention, and I blink.

"How is that possible?" I ask her, and she looks away from me.

"Well, believe it or not, but guys weren't exactly lining up to sleep with the chubby bookworm."

"Why not?" I ask her, and she blinks.

"I...because...because I'm overweight and shy, and that's not what guys want."

"You're not overweight."

And that's exactly what this guy wants.

"I am."

"No," I argue.

"Like medically," she starts, and I press my hand over her mouth, cutting her off.

"I don't want to hear it. You're perfect. I don't like hearing you talk badly about yourself."

"Itsteemuf," she mumbles against my palm, and I shake my head.

"No. Perfect."

She rolls her eyes, but I can see the pleased look in their green depths. If she wants me to tell her how amazing I think she is, I can do that. I'll do that every damn day, all day long if she'll let me.

I can also show her.

"Perfect," I whisper again as I bow my head and kiss her neck.

She shivers and so I do it again.

"I love that you haven't been with anyone before," I whisper against her skin, and she frowns against my hand. "I'm a jealous bastard, and I wouldn't have been able to stand if there was another man out there who knew you that way."

My hand drops from her mouth as I reach for her shirt, and she arches against me, helping me pull it over her head. My eyes drop to her chest, and I groan.

"Fucking hell, Saffron."

She blushes, but I notice that the hands that were reaching to cover her have fallen back to the bed.

"God, I'm not going to last two seconds with you," I grumble as my lips hover over hers.

"Well, I guess that's one way to make my first time memorable," she says, and I snort.

She giggles, and I kiss her neck, trailing my lips down to her plump tits.

"Don't worry, baby. I'm going to make it memorable."

I'm going to make it so damn good for her that she never wants to sleep with anyone else. I'll make her fall just as hard for me as I have for her, and then we can be together. For real.

My hands cup her breasts, pushing them up until they start to spill over the cups of her bra. My mouth waters at the sight of her cherry-red nipples peeking over the edge of the satin cups, and I lick my lips as I lean forward and take one into my mouth.

"Oh!" she cries as my tongue rolls over the sensitive peek.

I reach under her, my fingers unhooking her bra, and I drag the straps down her arms and toss it to the side. My hands greedily cup her breasts, and I pinch one nipple between my fingers while I suck on the other one.

"Nolan!" she shouts, her hips writhing against mine.

My cock aches in my jeans, and I groan as she rubs against me. I need her, but I need to get her off first. Multiple times.

My hands release her tits, and I reach for her soft leggings, standing so that I can peel them off of her legs. Her white panties are next, and then she's laid out before me, completely naked.

I have to grit my teeth to stop from coming instantly. Her curves are perfect. She's so pale, with freckles scattered across her skin. I want to find each one and mark it with my hands and mouth.

My hands grip her thighs, and I pull her legs wide as I drop down to my knees at the edge of the bed.

"Nolan," she says, nerves clear in her voice.

"I'm going to make this good for you, Saf," I promise, and our eyes meet and lock.

She nods, and having her trust me means the world to me.

I push her thighs wider as my eyes lock on her pussy. She's already wet, and I almost come just from the sight of her arousal. She smells like honey as I lean forward and take my first lick up her center.

"Goddamn," I groan as her flavor bursts across my tongue.

"Nolan," she says, her voice shaky.

I glance up at her, checking to make sure that she's okay, and see her white-knuckling the comforter.

"More?" I ask, and she nods her head forcefully.

I grin and do as she says.

My thumbs spread her folds apart as I lean forward and bury my face between her legs. She cries out as my tongue licks over her clit, and I do it again and again, until she's trembling beneath me.

"Nolan!" she shouts as I suck her clit into my mouth, my tongue thrashing it, then rolling softly over that little pearl.

"Oh! Oh! Oh, my—" she cries, her thighs tensing on either side of my head.

I know that she's close, and I trail one thick finger down her core until I find her snug opening. My finger rims that tight hole, and Saffron's sucks in a deep breath, her whole body freezing as if she's balancing on the edge of a cliff. With one more flick of my tongue over her clit, she falls, and I'm right there to catch her.

"Nolan!" she screams, her voice ending on a sob as I push my finger into her slowly.

She's so tight, and I wiggle the digit slightly, trying to loosen her up a bit.

"Fuck!" she sobs, and I lick her clit lightly, drawing out her orgasm as I work my finger into her more.

"Nolan! Please," she sobs, and I look up at her body until our eyes meet.

I can feel her juices on my lips and chin, and she shivers as she stares down at me, her green eyes so dark.

"I want to try," she says, and I lick her clit again.

"Hmm?"

"I want to try to make you come," she says and I smirk.

"Saf, you keep looking at me like that and you're going to get your wish."

"I want to... use my mouth," she says, rising up on her elbows to look down at me.

I freeze, my finger still buried in her pussy, her juices coating my mouth and chin.

"I don't think that that's a good idea," I croak and she looks embarrassed.

"Oh."

"Shit, Saffron. You can suck me, baby, but hell, it's going to be embarrassing for me."

"Why?" She asks innocently.

"Because you're not even touching me, and I'm close to coming. You get anywhere near my cock, and I'm going to come so fast."

"I don't mind," she says, and I laugh.

She wiggles away from me, and my laugh cuts off. I frown, reaching for her hips to stop her, but she's faster.

She stands next to me, looking down at me, and I swallow hard.

"Why don't you let me fuck that pretty pussy a few times, and then you can suck my cock," I offer, and she shakes her head.

"Please, Nolan? Just for a minute."

I groan, pushing to my feet.

"You've gotta stop begging to suck my cock, Saf."

"You don't like it when I do that? You don't like dirty talk?" she asks, her voice dropping on the last two words.

She's so innocent. Fuck, I love her.

"I love it," I tell her, and she smiles.

"I can talk dirty," she says softly. "I've always been better with words."

I have no idea what to say back to that because I've never been good with words.

Saffron drops to her knees, and her hands reach for my jeans. She undoes the button, and I swear that I stop breathing as she tugs the zipper down and then pulls my jeans and boxers slowly down my legs.

I kick them to the side and close my eyes, taking a deep breath to try to control myself.

"You don't want to see me on my knees in front of you?" she asks breathlessly, and I screw my eyes shut.

"Fucking hell," I grumble, and then her hand wraps around my length, and my knees almost buckle.

"You're so big. I'm not sure that I'll be able to take all of you," she says, and I glance down at her, my mouth dropping open as I get my first look at Saffron kneeling before me, her little hand pumping my cock as she licks her lips and looks up at me.

She shuffles closer to me, her warm breath fanning over my sensitive skin, and I try to imagine hitting myself in the face with a hammer to stop from coming all over her pretty face.

"Saf," I start, but then she wraps those damn lips around my cock, and my mind blanks.

My breath comes out in a rush, and I almost drop to my knees as her tongue swirls around the tip. I catch myself on the headboard before I can crush her under me and suck in a sharp breath.

"Saffron," I say urgently, and she hums around my cock.

I see stars.

"Saf, baby, please."

She sucks so hard that her cheeks hollow out, and my eyes roll back in my head.

Fuck.

"Need you," I groan as I step away from her.

She blinks up at me, her lips wet and swollen, and I snap.

I reach down, scooping her up and dropping her in the

center of the bed. I crawl over her, kneeing her legs apart as I settle between them.

"Tell me that you're ready for me," I order, and she nods.

"I'm ready."

"Thank fuck," I grit out as my cock nudges against her opening.

We both tense as I start to push into her, and I grit my teeth as her wet heat surrounds me. I make it halfway inside of her and have to stop to regain my control.

"You feel so good," she moans, and I growl.

"Not helping."

"I want more."

"*Really* not helping," I stress.

"I want all of you," she says, her ankles coming up and locking around my waist.

"Fuck, Saffron."

"Exactly."

I thrust into her, giving both of us exactly what we need. She gasps, and I lean down, kissing her until her pussy stops trying to strangle my cock.

"I need you to move," she whispers against my lips, and I swallow hard as I do as she orders.

She feels so damn good, so hot and wet and tight. She really is perfect, and I want to tell her that, but all of my energy is being spent on not coming just yet.

"Oh! Oh my gosh, right there," she moans and I want to put my hand over her mouth again, but I'm using it to balance above her.

"God, I love your cock," she moans. "And your body."

Her hands run over my chest, her nails scraping lightly down my arms. She's driving me crazy. I've never been so turned on in my life.

"I never want you to stop fucking me," she tells me. "But I really want to feel you come in me."

"Fuck, Saffron!" I shout, and her hands grip my biceps, clinging to me as my pace starts to grow erratic and rough.

"Can I feel it?" she asks me innocently, and I curse under my breath. "I mean, you're fucking me raw so..."

She trails off, and I grit my teeth. She's right, though. I didn't even think about protection. I didn't want there to be anything between us, and I guess some part of me was hoping to knock her up and tie her to me forever.

"Saffron," I start, but I have no idea what I was going to say next.

"I want it. You wouldn't let me suck your cock and taste you that way, so coming in me is the least that you can do," she whispers, and I lean back on my heels, my cock pounding into her now.

"Please, Nolan?" she begs, and I nod.

My thumb finds her clit, and I rub it in times with my thrusts. She tightens around me, and I can tell that she's close. Two more thrusts, and she splinters apart around me, pulling me with her over the edge.

"Fuck!" I shout as I come deep inside of her.

"Oh! Nolan," she moans, her legs tightening around my hips.

I keep moving in her until I'm sure that her orgasm has passed. Then I promptly collapse on my side next to her.

"Whoa," she whispers, and I smile at her.

"Uh huh."

"Is it always like that?" she asks me sleepily, and I shake my head.

"No, or it never was for me. Although... I've only been with one person before. It was in high school, a decade ago, and it was quick and forgettable."

"What was her name?"

"I don't remember."

I can't remember any other girl but you, I want to say, but I'm worried that will come on too strong. After all, she still thinks that we were fake dating.

I need to fix that.

I catch my breath, and I know that I need to talk to her and tell her that this is real for me and that I don't want her to be my fake girlfriend. I need to tell her what she means to me.

I take a deep breath and turn to face her... only to realize that Saffron is fast asleep.

I try not to be too disappointed as I pull her into my arms and let my own eyes drift shut. As I drift to sleep, I vow to tell her that I love her tomorrow. Just as soon as I wake up.

NINE

Saffron

I TRY to get lost in books as I unpack the new boxes that came in, but my mind is still back in bed with Nolan.

This morning was anxiety-inducing. I wasn't sure if I should stay until he woke up and then I started thinking about his reaction to last night and getting freaked out that maybe he would wake up and regret sleeping with me. In the end, I panicked, got dressed, and bolted out of my house without waking him up.

It's been a few hours, and I haven't heard from him yet, which makes me even more concerned that he regrets our night together.

"Hey! How's it—Whoa! What's wrong?" Lilou asks, rushing over to my side.

"What?" I ask, blinking out of my spiraling panic.

"You look totally freaked out. What's wrong?" she asks as she tucks her purse behind the counter.

I take a deep breath and look around the shop before I lean closer to my friend.

"I slept with Nolan," I tell her.

"What!?" A voice shrieks by the front door, and my head snaps up, relaxing when I see my sisters, Maple and Olive, standing at the door.

"I, uh, I slept with Nolan last night," I tell them.

"You're fake boyfriend?" Maple asks at the same time that Olive says, "Your neighbor?"

"Yeah..."

"So, are you two officially together?" Lilou asks me.

"I... don't know," I admit. "We slept together, and then I left while he was still sleeping, and we haven't talked since."

"Well, do you want to be with him? Do you like him?" Maple asks me, and I swallow hard.

"Yeah, I do," I whisper.

"Then talk to him! Tell him that you want to really be his girlfriend," Olive tells me.

"I..." I trail off, and they all share a knowing look.

"It can be scary," Maple says gently, and I nod.

"What if he doesn't want to be with me? What if it was just a one-night stand for him or a mistake? Then I'll have to keep living next door to him and seeing him all of the time, and he's still fixing up my house, so that's going to make it even more awkward, and then I'll have to sell the house, and move to avoid him and—"

"Whoa! Slow down, Saffron. It's going to be okay," Olive says, her eyes wide with concern.

"You don't know that," I groan miserably.

"You need to talk to him," Lilou says, and I nod.

"I know, I'm just scared."

An image of Nolan above me, moving inside of me, fills my head, and I swallow hard. Last night felt so real, and I can't help but wonder if it just felt that way for me or if he felt it, too. Was it just a fling for him? Or something more?

"Just be brave and ask him. The worst that he can say is that it was just a one-time thing, and then you can work on moving on," Maple says.

"Hey! You guys all hanging out without us?" Ginger and Mira ask as they come into the bookstore.

"Saffron is freaking out, and we're helping her," Olive tells them, and I groan.

"Why?" Ginger asks.

"She slept with Nolan last night," Maple tells them.

"Woohoo!" Mira cheers, and I shake my head.

"I'm worried that it's just a one-night stand for him," I explain.

"It's not. I've seen him look at you, and he's always mooning over you," Mira says.

"Yeah! I mean, I wish that someone would look at me like that," Lilou agrees.

"Babe, I keep telling you that I'll look at you any way that you want me to," Milo says as he joins us in the store, and Lilou jumps, whirling around.

"We need to get a bell for the doors," she grumbles.

"How do you want me to look at you?" he asks her as he leans on the counter across from her. "Maybe like this? Over dinner?"

"No."

He just smiles at her, and her face flames bright red as she looks at anyone except him.

"Should we talk about Christmas? Is it too early for you to meet my parents?"

"Oh my god!" she shouts and throws her hands into the air.

His phone starts to ring and he smiles at Lilou before he answers it and heads back outside to his car.

"When is that going to happen?" Mira asks Lilou, and she glares at all of us when we giggle.

"Never."

"He's not going to give up," I point out. "He's been after you since he got to town. I haven't even seen him look at another girl."

"Never," she growls and we all know to drop it. At least for now.

"Now, when are you going to talk to your man?" Lilou asks me, and I sigh.

"I'll talk to him tonight," I tell them.

I even manage to sound confident as I say it, but deep down, I'm terrified that I might be the only one feeling this way.

I spend the rest of the day dreading when I have to go home and talk to Nolan. By the time I'm closing up Shelf Indulgence, I'm on edge and feel nauseous.

Time to get this over with.

TEN

Nolan

I WAKE UP ALONE, and it takes me a few moments before I remember where I am and what happened yesterday. I smile as I remember everything that Saffron and I did to each other last night. I sit up in bed and frown as I look around. Saffron's side of the bed is cold, so I know that she must have gotten up a while ago.

I toss the covers back and pull on my boxers as I go in search of my girl. I can't help but wonder if it's a bad sign that she wasn't still in bed with me as I make my way through the house.

It takes me only a few minutes to realize that Saffron isn't here. She must have gone to the bookstore already.

I frown as I stand alone in her half-remodeled kitchen and wonder what to do now. I want to talk to Saffron about last night and our future together, but I know her well enough to know that she won't want to have that conversation at work.

So, I'll stay here. I'll work on the house and practice what I want to say to her when she comes home. Then we can have our talk and get on with our relationship. Our *real* relationship.

I've finished a lot of the bigger renovations around here already. The bathroom cabinets came in a few days ago so that room is done. The kitchen counters are on backorder so that will be a few more days, so instead, I get to work on a special project.

Saffron has a room off of the living room that she has no idea what to do with, but I know. It's going to be her home library. I've already sketched out the layout for the custom built-in bookshelves and a cozy reading nook.

I head into the room and start bringing in all of the supplies and cutting the boards to size. I'm going to leave the wood raw and let Saffron pick out all of the colors that she wants.

The repetitive task and the hum of the saw helps me clear my head and figure out what I want to say to Saffron when she gets home. I want to tell her that this was never fake for me and ask her to officially make this relationship real.

When my phone rings a few hours later, my heart lodges in my throat, and I hurry to answer it, hoping that it's Saffron calling to tell me that she's coming home early. Instead, it's my mom. I debate ignoring the call, but I know that she'll just call me again.

"Hey, mom."

"Nolan! I was just calling to make sure that you and Saffron made it home safely."

"Oh, yeah, sorry, I should have let you know."

"No worries. I know that you two were probably busy. We loved meeting her by the way! She sure is a keeper."

"She sure is," I agree.

"Are you going to bring her back for Christmas?"

"Um, I'm not sure. I think that she might be celebrating it with her sisters."

"Oh, well, you two could come down before or after too! We'd love to see you both again. Oh! Or maybe for New Year's!"

"Maybe," I tell her noncommittally. "I'll have to ask Saffron."

Right after I ask her to be my girlfriend for real.

"Okay, well let me know. I'll let you go and talk to you later."

"Sounds good. Talk to you soon, mom."

"Love you."

"Love you too."

I hang up, and a minute later, I hear Saffron's car pull into the driveway. My heart takes off like a shot, and I head out of the library to greet her at the door.

I take a deep breath as she walks up the front porch steps, and as soon as she walks inside, I open my mouth and blurt out, "We need to talk."

ELEVEN

Saffron

THINGS AREN'T OFF to a great start.

I planned on out everything when I left work. I would walk into my house and find Nolan, then try to figure out how he was feeling about last night and how awkward things were before I asked him if we could talk.

Instead, he beat me to the punch.

"Uhh," I start, my hand still on the doorknob.

"About last night," he says, trying to comfort me.

Really, it has the opposite effect.

We stare at each other for a beat and then I close the door and peel off my coat and hang it up.

"Okay."

He swallows, and we head into the kitchen, each of us standing on either side of the counter as we stare at each other.

"How was work?" he asks, and I blink.

"Good. How about you?"

"Good. I have a surprise for you."

"Really?"

"Yeah, but first, I wanted to talk to you about last night and about...us."

"Okay," I whisper.

"I..." he closes his mouth, and I watch him swallow hard once more. "I love you."

"What!" I gasp, my mouth dropping open.

"I love you, Saffron. I have for months, well before I asked you to be my fake girlfriend for Thanksgiving. God, I never should have done that. I never want anything between us to be fake."

My knees feel weak, and for a second, it feels like I'm in the middle of one of my romance books.

"You regret it?" I ask him and he frowns.

"No, not really. I can't ever regret any time that I spent with you."

I grin, and he seems to relax.

"You love me?" I ask him softly, and he nods.

"So much, Saffron. So damn much. I should have just talked to you. I should have asked you out weeks ago, I should have told you about how I felt from the beginning, definitely before we slept together."

"I kind of panicked this morning. I should have stayed and talked to you and told you how I was feeling," I tell him, stepping closer to the kitchen island.

He nods, a hopeful look in his dark blue eyes.

"I love you too, Nolan. I've had a crush on you since I moved to town and first saw you, but I never thought that you would be interested in me. I didn't think that you noticed me at all," I admit.

"You were all that I noticed," he tells me, and I smile as a blush spreads across my cheeks.

"So, last night..."

"Was everything that I dreamed it would be and more," he finishes.

"Yeah, it was."

We share a smile, and he takes a step towards me.

"So, we're doing this? We're together? Officially?" I ask, and he nods.

"Fuck yes. You're my girl, Saffron. For real."

"For real," I agree.

We close the distance between us, and he wraps his arms around my waist, pulling me flush against him. My hands cup his face and he smiles down at me as his lips slowly lower to claim mine.

His lips move against mine slowly, like he's cherishing me, like he has all of the time in the world to kiss me. I moan as I lean against him, loving the feel of his strong body against mine.

"Mine," he whispers, and I nod.

Nolan's lips mold to mine and I get swept away by his kiss, by the feel of his hands on my back, pulling me closer and closer still.

When he finally pulls back, I feel like I'm floating, drugged by his kisses. His hands rub up and down my back, like he can't stop touching me, and I smile up at him.

"Do I get my surprise now?" I ask him, and he grins.

"Yeah, come on."

He takes my hand and to my surprise, leads me down the hallway to the bedroom off of the living room. I'm not sure what I was expecting, but it wasn't a wall of bookcases. If I wasn't in love with him before, seeing this would have had me falling head over heels for him.

"Oh my gosh! It's perfect!" I gush as I rush over to run my fingers over the wooden shelves.

"I didn't paint or stain them yet. I thought that you might want to pick out the colors and stuff."

"I love it! Thank you so much!"

"Of course," he says, smiling as I run over to him and wrap him up in a tight hug.

It doesn't take long for both of our bodies to react. It's like we can't be in the same room with each other now without needing to rip each other's clothes off.

"I need you," I whisper, and he nods.

His hands grab my hips, and he pulls me into him. I can feel his dick starting to swell against my thigh, and I can't help but rub against it. I feel wanton and desired as his cock hardens even more. I shift so that the thick ridge is between my legs, right where I need him most, and I can't help but moan. It feels so good, so hard.

"Fuck, Saffron," he groans, and I smile shyly up at him.

Nolan's head dips, his warm breath hitting my face, and my eyelids flutter shut as his lips land on mine. My heart is racing, and as my hands rub up his chest, I can feel that his heart is beating out of control, too.

My fingers climb higher, and I run my hands over his collarbone, memorizing every line of his body as I go. Nolan backs me up a step, and I go willingly. My fingers trace along his jawline, and he pulls away, staring down at me. I trace around his ear, my fingers tangling in his dark locks, toying with the long strands. I want to run my hands over all of him, to trace his body, and map it in my brain.

"I really love you," he murmurs, and I grin.

"I really love you too."

His lips capture mine as his hands move up my ribcage until he's cupping my breasts in his big, capable hands. His hands knead the soft globes, and I break the kiss, pulling away as I moan, my head falling back.

Nolan kisses down my neck, his lips finding the pulse point at the base of my throat. I push into him, wanting his hands on my skin, on every inch of me.

I raise my hands over my head, letting him drag the thin cotton of my shirt over my head. He wastes no time and drags the cup of my bra down next, exposing my nipples to the cold air. They pucker instantly, tightening into stiff peaks.

"Fuck, you're so perfect, Saffron," Nolan whispers against my heated skin, and I gasp as his warm mouth sucks the tight bud into his mouth.

His tongue swirls around it, and I arch into him. My eyes flutter open, and I watch as the fan spins round and round on the ceiling above us. Nolan's hands go around my back, and he pulls me into him, his hands tangling in my purple hair as he devours my breasts.

I swear that I'm about to explode. My whole body feels like it's on fire. I'm hot and needy, aching for him to make me come.

Everything about Nolan turns me on. The toned abs, the full lips, and dark blue eyes, the chiseled lines of him, all of the dips and planes. All of it is a work of art that I want to admire for hours. He's so strong, so smart and capable. He's sexy and funny, but right now, it's his body that is doing it for me.

Nolan pulls back, and I bite back a needy whine, missing having his mouth on me.

"Bed. Now," he orders, and I nod.

We take off up the stairs and into my bedroom. I giggle as we seem to race for my room, and as soon as I'm there, I'm pushing down my pants as I back up toward the mattress.

Nolan's eyes are burning, glinting in the sun as he takes

me in and I straighten my shoulders, wanting him to look his fill. It's obvious that my body turns him on just as much as he turns me on.

Nolan pushes me down onto the bed, and I start to wiggle out of my panties, letting Nolan pull them the rest of the way off.

"Fuck. Every inch of you is a dream, Saffron."

My body warms at the compliment, and I hold my hand out to him, wanting to feel his weight on top of me. He pulls his shirt off first, kicking his shoes off as he pushes his pants down his toned legs.

He comes down over me, and I spread my legs. He's still wearing his boxers, so we're not skin-on-skin, but I can still feel how hard and hot he is.

His head dips again, and his mouth latches onto one of my nipples, sucking the whole thing into his mouth. His mouth is so hot and wet, the suction so perfect that I'm close to coming in seconds.

My toes curl into the sheets as my hips rock restlessly against his, and he switches to my other breast.

That spot between my legs is getting wet, tiny sparks going off with every bite, suck, and caress that he gives my breasts. It's not quite enough, though. The nagging emptiness between my legs just won't go away, and the dull ache is starting to drive me crazy with need. I need to do something. I need him. I push on his chest, and he lets my nipple go with a pop, leaning up to look at me questioningly.

"I want to take care of you," I say, my fingers running down his chest, following his happy trail down to the band of his boxers.

Nolan pushes off of the bed, reaching for his boxers, and I drop to my knees, helping him pull them down his legs.

They pool at his feet, and he steps out of them as I reach up, fisting his thick length.

I open my mouth wide, sucking in the tip of his cock as Nolan's hand tangles in my hair. He doesn't push on my head, he just rests his hands there, his fingers tugging on the strands as my head starts to bob.

The feeling lights up my scalp, and I moan as I take more of him into my mouth. I work my hand in time with my mouth, and my body only burns hotter as I feel him swell against my tongue, hear the moans and the way that he says my name like it's a prayer.

"Fuck," Nolan says, pulling me off of him, and he reaches down, dragging me up to my feet and then pushing me onto the bed.

I pull him down, and our lips meet; we cling together as we take our time exploring each other. The earlier rush is gone, and I moan, rolling him onto his back and straddling his hips.

"Let me lick your pussy," Nolan says, but I shake my head.

I'm already wet enough, and I know that if I let him do that, he'll take control again, and I want to set the pace this time.

I reach behind me, grabbing his dick and lining it up with my opening as I slowly sink down, taking him into my body inch by delicious inch.

"Fuck," he hisses out as I slowly sink down until he's fully seated inside of me. "You're so wet. So fucking hot."

I grin at him, resting my hands on his chest as I slowly roll my hips. We both moan with every rock of my hips, every in and out, every push and pull of his cock inside of my snug channel.

His hands go to my ass, groping the globes, using them

to pull me down harder onto him. I pant as I grind against him, and he leans up, sucking one of my tits into his mouth.

He takes over, thrusting up from beneath me as our mouths fuse together, and I can feel myself starting to splinter apart around him as the pressure inside of me builds.

He hits a certain spot deep inside of me, and that's all it takes to send me flying over the edge of the cliff into oblivion.

Nolan's brow furrows in concentration as he grips my hips and drives into me in perfect precision.

Seeing him like that is intoxicating, and I can't look away as he finds his own release inside of me.

He rolls us to our sides, and we both suck in a deep breath as he pulls me against his chest.

"Love you, Saffy," he says, making me laugh.

"Love you too," I tell him as I drape my arms around his shoulders.

I feel his lips brush against my forehead, and I smile as I cuddle into his side.

"I'm going to need to do that again," he tells me, and I grin.

"Uh huh," I agree.

"But first, I should probably feed you."

"Just when I thought that you couldn't get any more perfect," I joke, and he grins. "My own knight in shining armor."

"I'll be anything that you need, Saffron," he whispers against my lips, and I smile.

"The food can wait," I whisper back, and he grins as I press my hips against him in invitation.

"Whatever you want, Saffy."

And he proceeds to give me everything that I want.
All. Night. Long.

TWELVE

Nolan

FIVE YEARS LATER...

I CARRY OUR THREE-YEAR-OLD SON, Finn, on one hip as I balance a casserole dish with my other hand. Finn is busy babbling about the dinosaurs he saw in his picture book this morning, completely oblivious to the fact that I'm breaking a sweat trying not to drop him or the sweet potato casserole I promised Saffron's sisters I'd bring.

"Daddy, I'm a T-Rex!" Finn announces proudly, lifting his arms and giving a tiny, ferocious roar.

"Yeah, buddy. You're the scariest one," I reply, grinning despite the precarious juggling act I'm managing.

Behind me, Saffron is closing the car door, holding our six-month-old daughter, Ellie, against her chest. Ellie's in that perfect stage where she's still soft and sleepy most of the time, and her big green eyes—the same ones Saffron has —blink up at me with curiosity.

"Need help?" Saffron asks, arching a brow as I readjust Finn for the third time.

"I've got it," I lie.

Saffron laughs softly, knowing better. She steps closer, brushing her shoulder against mine as she smiles. Even after all these years, she still manages to steal my breath every time she looks at me like that, like I'm the only person in the room.

"Ready for the chaos?" she teases, giving me a knowing grin.

"Is anyone ever really ready for Baker-family chaos?" I shoot back, pressing a quick kiss to her temple.

She snickers, and together, we head up the walkway to Olive's house. The front door is already cracked open, and we can hear the laughter and noise pouring out from inside.

The moment we step through the door, the usual Thanksgiving madness unfolds. Olive is directing traffic, shouting instructions about platters and pies from the kitchen. Ginger and Ryder are already in the thick of a lively debate with Townes and Mira about something to do with the parade floats on TV, and Kip is chasing his twin daughters around the living room, narrowly avoiding disaster as they shriek with laughter.

"Uncle Nolan!" one of them yells the second she spots me.

Before I know it, Finn's squirming out of my grip, eager to join the chaos. He takes off toward the twins without a second glance back, roaring like a dinosaur the whole way.

"Bye, buddy," I call after him, though he's already gone, wrapped up in the whirlwind of his cousins.

Olive swoops in before we can catch a breath. "Finally!

The dream team is here." She beams at Saffron and me, then takes the casserole dish from my hand. "You two are late, by the way."

"Blame the kids," I say, nodding toward Finn, who's now wrestling on the floor with Kip's girls.

"Excuses, excuses." Olive grins and winks at Saffron. "Glad you survived the morning, though. I know what it's like."

Saffron snorts, adjusting Ellie in her arms. "Barely. But hey, we're here."

We settle in quickly, the flow of conversation and noise wrapping around us like a familiar, chaotic blanket. Xavier waves me over to where he's stationed with Fisher and Huxley, beers in hand, already immersed in the sacred Thanksgiving tradition of sports talk. I grab a drink and join them, feeling more relaxed than I did years ago at my first Baker Thanksgiving.

It's not just familiarity—it's the comfort that comes with knowing you belong. This group, with all their quirks and teasing, is my family now. And Saffron? She's everything good in my life wrapped up in one perfect, chaotic package.

At some point, I catch sight of her across the room, Ellie now asleep against her shoulder. Saffron's laughing at something Olive said, her face lighting up in that way I can never get enough of.

We've had our fair share of hard days, raising two kids isn't exactly a walk in the park, but moments like this remind me how lucky I am. Watching her, surrounded by the people who love her, I feel like the luckiest man alive.

We moved into the house after I had finished fixing it up and I sold my old one. We got married there at the house, in a small ceremony in the backyard with just our friends and families there in attendance.

I started my own remodeling business a few years ago, and it's really taken off. I've hired a few guys to work for me and that gives me ample time to spend with my family or helping Saffron out at the bookstore. I even volunteer as the classroom monitor at the kid's preschool every Monday.

Since our wedding, we've taken turns switching between who's family we spend holidays with. It doesn't make the holidays any less chaotic, but Saffron says that it's the only fair way to split things up.

She catches me staring and gives me a soft, knowing smile. I smile back, my heart feeling so full I can hardly stand it.

"Time to eat!" Olive calls, and I tear my gaze away from my wife to find my Finn.

Dinner is, predictably, a mess in the best way. Kip's twins start an impromptu food fight over the mashed potatoes, which Finn is all too eager to join. Saffron scolds him, but I can see the smile she's trying to hide.

"Boys," she mutters, shaking her head. "They get it from you, you know."

"Not sure what you mean." I grin, wiping mashed potatoes off Finn's nose and earning a giggle from him.

Once the food is demolished and everyone's too stuffed to move, Olive pulls out a stack of games. It's tradition now. Thanksgiving isn't complete without a little friendly competition.

"Alright," Olive announces, holding up the cards for couples' trivia. "Let's see if the reigning champions can defend their title."

I groan dramatically. "You mean the reigning cheaters?"

Ginger gasps in mock offense. "Excuse me, we *never* cheat."

Saffron laughs beside me, nudging my arm. "We're

winning this year," she says, her eyes sparkling with mischief.

"You think so?" I ask, wrapping an arm around her shoulders and pulling her close.

"I know so."

The game goes about as well as expected, with plenty of trash-talking and not-so-subtle hints that certain couples are "totally peeking" at the answers. Saffron and I do better than I thought we would—five years together has given us an edge, even if we do bicker over which of us snores more (it's totally her, but I let it slide).

When the final question rolls around: "What's one thing your partner does that drives you crazy?"—I don't even have to think.

"She talks to her plants," I say with a grin, earning an uproar of laughter from the room.

Saffron just rolls her eyes, clearly used to this one by now. "They need encouragement," she says matter-of-factly, earning even more laughter.

"And I wouldn't change it for anything," I add quietly, just for her.

She looks up at me, her eyes soft, and smiles in that way that makes my heart feel like it's going to burst right out of my chest.

Later, when the kids are asleep in the guest room, and the house has finally quieted down, Saffron and I step out onto the porch to catch a moment of peace. The stars are bright above us, the air crisp and cold. I pull her close, wrapping an arm around her shoulders, and she leans into me, her head resting against my chest.

"You good?" I ask, pressing a kiss to her hair.

"Mmm. Better than good," she murmurs, her voice soft and content.

I hold her a little tighter, letting the quiet settle around us.

"Thanks for everything," she says after a while, her voice barely above a whisper.

I smile, brushing a strand of hair from her face. "You don't have to thank me, Saffron."

She tilts her head back to look up at me, her eyes shining in the moonlight. "I know. But I want to."

And just like that, I know I'd do it all over again—every chaotic holiday, every sleepless night, every crazy, beautiful moment we've built together.

Because with her?

This life is exactly where I want to be.

**WANT MORE OF SAFFRON AND NOLAN?
CHECK OUT THIS BONUS SCENE OF THEIR
FIRST CHRISTMAS TOGETHER!**

A VERY GRUMPY CHRISTMAS

I have a secret admirer…

Ginger:

When I got the first letter from my secret admirer, I was flattered.

With the second, I grew intrigued.

By the third, I'm starting to fall in love with him.

I wish that I could meet him in person, but I don't know how to arrange that.

Kip:

I've wanted Ginger Baker since the moment that I saw her.

She's so beautiful, so full of light.

I need that in my life, but I know that she would never be interested in me.

So, I do the only thing that I can to be close to her and start writing her letters.

When she writes back, demanding to meet, I know that I have a choice to make.

I can do as she asks and meet her under the mistletoe at the town party, or I can stay in the shadows, loving Ginger from a distance.

ONE

Kip

I LINGER in the shadows of the parking lot, waiting for her to come out and feeling like a creepy stalker.

Well, I mean, I guess I kind of am a stalker.

Shit.

Only hers, though. I've never done anything like this before, never wanted to. Not until I saw her.

Ginger Baker.

She moved to town with her sisters about a year ago, and I've been watching her ever since, trying to learn everything that I can about her. It's become an obsession, a compulsion. My feelings for her are out of control.

I'd like to say that it started as a mild interest, but the truth is that I've been obsessed with my curvy girl since the moment that she stepped foot in this town. It's why I've been doing crazy things, things that I never would have done in the past. Things like following her around and leaving notes for the last few months.

The sun is dipping below the horizon, painting the sky in swirls of orange and pink, but I'm not paying attention to the view. My focus is on Ginger. It's always on her.

I just need to get my daily dose of her, just one glimpse. That's why I'm out here, freezing my ass off.

Over the last year, I've learned a lot. I've learned that she's everything I'm not. She's bright, open, and full of life. Every time I see her, it feels like my chest tightens just a little bit more. She has my heart in a vise grip and doesn't even know it.

I've wanted to talk to her, *really* talk to her, for months now, to say something—anything—but every time I get close to her, the words get stuck in my throat, and I end up nodding or grunting at her like an asshole. And that scar on my face feels like it burns, reminding me of why someone like her would never want someone like me.

But I couldn't stay away from her, not for long. I had to get close, to bask in her light, to hear her infectious laugh. So, I did what any lovesick fool would do, and I started writing her secret love notes.

The first note was simple. I wrote that I loved seeing her smile, that her laugh was my favorite sound, and that I couldn't stop thinking about her. Then I left it on the windshield of her car, hoping it would make her smile.

And it had.

Now, it's been three months of me leaving letters, of pouring out my heart without ever signing my name. She's kept every note. I've seen them tucked into the pocket of her bag and coat, seen her rereading them sometimes when she's at work and it's slow. It's a small miracle, watching her read the words I'm too much of a coward to say out loud.

Tonight, there's another note, the same stationery as all of the others, carefully folded and placed under her windshield wiper. I stand far enough away that she won't notice me, my heart racing like a teenager waiting for his crush to notice him. It's pathetic, really. *I'm* pathetic. But when she walks out of Shelf Indulgence, her sister's bookstore, her dark red hair catching the last bit of daylight, all I can do is watch and hope she likes what I've written this time.

My eyes drink her in greedily, and I can't look away from her as she heads over to her old beat-up car.

I hate that damn thing. I've lost track of the number of hours that I've spent leaning over the hood, fixing the radiator and then the alternator, and then the spark plugs. The damn thing has been on its last leg for way too long, and she needs to replace it. For whatever reason, she refuses to, though, so I spend half of my nights making sure that it runs and my girl doesn't get stranded somewhere.

She reaches her car and spots the note almost instantly. She smiles, and it's like the whole world comes grinding to a halt. Her smile is the kind that makes you forget everything else. The kind that feels like warmth on a cold winter day. I watch as she takes the letter, her fingers brushing the edge of the paper as she opens it carefully, like she's afraid to damage it, like my note is something precious to her.

My breath hitches as she starts reading. I don't know why it still surprises me that she reads them so quickly, so eagerly. Or why I get so nervous as I watch her.

By the time she's finished, her smile has softened into something sweeter, something I wish was meant just for me.

"Are you stalking her again, Kip?"

I jump, startled, and glance to my right to find my best friend, Huxley, standing next to me, his arms crossed and a knowing smirk tugging at his lips.

"Not stalking," I lie, keeping my eyes on Ginger as she climbs into her car. She's still holding the letter as she starts the engine, and I can't help but feel a flicker of pride, or maybe it's hope.

"Sure," Huxley says with a shrug. "That's why you've been standing out here in the freezing cold for the last half an hour. Who doesn't love being outside when it's negative ten?"

"Exactly. I love it. It's... bracing."

He laughs, and I sigh. He's right, it's cold as fuck out here, and I'm pretty miserable. Seeing Ginger, though, makes it worth it.

"You could always try to watch her from indoors, ya know," he says.

I shoot him a glare, but he just chuckles. Huxley's been my best friend since birth, pretty much. We grew up together, graduated, and both joined the Marines. When I was shot and blown up last year and got out, he did too and joined me here in Wolf Valley. Now we own and run our own tourist helicopter business here in town called Semper Fly.

Huxley is the only one who knows how I feel about Ginger and about my letters to her. He's also the only one who doesn't think it's completely insane. At least, not most of the time.

"You know, you could just talk to her like a normal person," he suggests, his tone light but laced with a hint of seriousness. "Instead of... this."

"She wouldn't be interested," I say automatically, the words bitter on my tongue.

Huxley raises an eyebrow. "How would you know? You haven't even tried."

I don't answer. Instead, I watch as Ginger's taillights disappear down the road, a heavy sigh escaping my lips and coming out in a puff of white air. It's not that I don't want to talk to her. It's just... complicated. When I first moved to Wolf Valley after getting out of the military, I didn't expect much. I figured that I would move to a small town and try to blend in. I would do my best to enjoy a slow, quiet, lonely life.

Then I saw her and the way she lights up a room without even trying, the way she treats everyone like they matter. She was everything I needed but didn't think I deserved. Still don't.

"Man, you've got to do something," Huxley says, nudging me. "I can't keep watching you pine after her. It's getting nauseating."

I flip him off as I turn to head to my own truck, and he falls into step beside me.

"It's Christmas soon and then a new year. You gonna be that creepy guy leaving notes forever? Or are you actually going to tell her how you feel?"

"She's happy," I say, ignoring the sting in my chest. "She's fine without me. Besides, it's better this way."

"Better for who? You, hiding in the shadows, freezing to death? Or her, thinking she's falling for some fantasy dude who doesn't even exist?"

His words hit harder than I expect, and I clench my jaw. "I'm not some fantasy," I snap, but even as I say it, I don't fully believe it. Huxley's right. The person she's falling for isn't the real me. It's the version of myself I wish I could be. The guy who isn't broken or scarred, who isn't weighed down by his past.

But that's not who I am. Not anymore.

"Look, all I'm saying is, you've got to stop playing this game," Huxley says, his voice softening. "If you like her, really like her, then tell her. Don't let this secret admirer thing blow up in your face."

I stay silent, staring at the empty spot where Ginger's car was just moments ago. Huxley's right, but that doesn't make it any easier. If I tell her the truth, if I show her who I really am... what then? What if she looks at me the way I've always feared she would? With pity, or worse, disgust?

I've been hiding behind these letters because they're safe. It's easy to be confident on paper, to say all the things I could never say to her face. But sooner or later, I'm going to have to face the reality that I can't stay invisible forever. Not if I want a chance with her.

"She's going to the Christmas party," Huxley adds, almost as if reading my mind. "You know, the one she's been volunteering for and setting up?" He says, twirling his finger around us at all of the decorations.

I groan. Of course, he would bring that up. Every year, the town throws a huge holiday festival, complete with an insane amount of decorations and an obnoxious amount of mistletoe. It's supposed to be festive and light-hearted or whatever, but all I can think about is how impossible it would be to blend into the background at a place like that.

"So?" I ask, even though I already know where this conversation is headed.

"So, what happens if she stands under the mistletoe with someone else? What happens if she kisses someone else? Are you going to be okay with that?"

"Fuck no. She won't do that," I argue, and he gives me a skeptical look.

"You sure about that? She seems like she loves Christmas. I bet she would, even if it was just for the whole festive tradition."

"So, I'll stop her."

"How?"

"I don't know," I snap. "I'll figure it out.

"You going to shoot any guy who comes near her?" He asks, referencing the fact that we were snipers in the Marines. I don't bother to respond to that, mainly because the thought has crossed my mind before, and I know that if I answer, Huxley will be able to tell.

"Or," Huxley says with a grin, "this could be your chance. Show up. Talk to her. Maybe even be the one to kiss her under the mistletoe."

I shake my head. "You make it sound so simple."

"Because it is," he insists. "Look, I know you're scared, but you can't keep hiding. If you want something to happen, you've got to put yourself out there. Otherwise, you're just going to spend the rest of your life wondering what could've been."

I roll my eyes, but his words sink in deeper than I'd like to admit. Huxley's always been the fearless one, the guy who dives headfirst into everything without thinking twice. I used to be like that, too, once upon a time. But that was before the attack, before everything fell apart.

Now, I'm just a guy who writes letters to a girl who doesn't even know I exist.

But maybe... maybe I could change that.

"I'll think about it," I finally say, my voice barely above a whisper.

Huxley claps me on the back, his grin widening. "That's all I'm asking, man. Just think about it. You never know— Christmas miracles and all that."

I huff out a laugh, but the knot in my chest tightens all the same. The idea of actually talking to Ginger, of seeing the look on her face when she realizes who's been writing to her all this time—it's terrifying. But it's also tempting.

What if, just once, I let myself believe that she might want me too?

As Huxley rambles on about some plan to get me to the party, I glance down the road, imagining Ginger's face as she reads my next letter. It's a fantasy, I know that. But maybe it's time to stop hiding behind words and start living in the real world.

I'll talk to her, I decide, straightening my shoulders as we walk over to my truck.

Eventually...

TWO

Ginger

I WASN'T SUPPOSED to be the one getting the letter. That's what I told myself when I found the first one.

It was a cold, rainy day in early September and I'd had one of those mornings where everything seemed to go wrong, the kind of day that makes you question why you even bothered getting out of bed that morning.

I was late opening the bookstore, spilled coffee on my favorite sweater, and locked my keys inside the car. I had to walk back to my apartment to grab the spare and when I got back, that was when I found it.

I almost didn't see the letter tucked under my windshield wiper at first. I was rushing, trying to get back inside before the rain drenched me any more than it already had, but there it was—a folded piece of paper neatly placed under the wiper, its edges curling slightly from the damp air and drizzle.

I remember frowning, wondering if I had gotten a ticket

or something, but then I opened it and saw that it was on stationery. Stark white with a heart with an arrow on it in the bottom left corner.

My first thought when I realized that it was a love note, was that it had been meant for someone else. Wolf Valley was small, but we weren't immune to mistakes, and I figured someone had left it for the wrong person, that my car was common, and they had put it on the wrong windshield.

The words in the note were simple and kind. There was no name, no signature, just an anonymous message that made my heart race and my palms sweat for reasons I couldn't quite explain.

But instead of feeling flattered, I felt confused. I almost left a note of my own, telling whoever it was that they had the wrong person. I didn't get anonymous love letters. That sort of thing happened in romance novels, not real life. And certainly not to me.

Yet, for reasons I still don't fully understand, I didn't leave a note. I tucked the letter into my bag, and that was that. A fluke, I told myself. Just some strange, one-off occurrence.

Then came the second letter.

I decided to leave that letter on my car and write my own note, explaining that it was my car and they must have the wrong person.

Then I got the third note, that one addressed to me, and I realized that it wasn't a mistake. The letters were meant for me. There was no denying it anymore—I had a secret admirer.

It showed up a week later, tucked into the door of the bookstore this time. The stationery and handwriting were the same—careful, deliberate—but the words were different. This one was more personal, like whoever was writing to me knew me a little better now. They complimented me and told me that they used to love the color blue, but after seeing my eyes, it had changed to green.

By the time I read the fourth letter, I was hooked and starting to fall for him. Hard.

It's funny how quickly your perspective can shift. One moment, I was convinced the letters weren't meant for me, and the next, I was eagerly waiting for the next one, wondering what my mystery man would say. Every time I got a new one, it felt like a piece of a puzzle falling into place. I was dying to solve it and figure out who my secret admirer was. To tell him that I was obsessed with him too.

But there was a problem.

There was no pattern to the letters. Sometimes they'd show up at the bookstore or the bakery, whichever one of my sister's businesses I was working at that day. Other times they were slipped under my welcome mat at home, or on my car, and once, even slipped into my mailbox. They came at different times, on different days, with no rhyme or reason. I never knew when the next one would appear, and it was driving me crazy.

I needed to know who he was. I needed to figure out who the man that I was in love with was.

"Maybe it's the new guy in town," Cora says, leaning across my little kitchen table, her eyes twinkling with amusement as I tell her about the latest letter. "You know, Huxley? He's always looking at you."

I snort, shaking my head. "Huxley isn't looking at me, Cora. He's looking at you."

She laughs, the sound bright and full of mischief. "No, he's not."

I don't bother to correct her. Cora is sure that no one wants her, and I know that if I point out that he can't take his eyes off her, she'll just argue with me. Huxley is for sure in love with her, but he'll have to be the one to convince her of that.

Cora and I have been friends ever since she moved to Wolf Valley a few months after my sisters and I did. We became fast friends and hang out at least once a week. She's one of the only people here, besides my sisters, who know about the letters.

"I just wish I knew who he was," I admit, leaning back against the kitchen counter. "It's been months, Cora. Months of these letters and still no clue."

"Well," Cora says thoughtfully, tapping her chin, "there's got to be some kind of pattern, right? Have you noticed anything? Does he say anything that might give him away?"

I shake my head, pulling the most recent letter from my pocket and handing it to her. She unfolds it carefully, her eyes scanning the familiar handwriting as I watch her face for any sign of recognition.

"'Your smile is like sunshine on a rainy day,'" she reads aloud, her voice softening as she reaches the end. "'I hope one day I'll be brave enough to tell you this in person, but until then, I'll keep admiring you from afar.'"

Cora looks up at me, her eyes wide with excitement. "Ginger, this is so romantic! It's like you're living in a freaking romance novel!"

I chuckle, but my heart clenches in my chest. "Yeah, except in romance novels, the guy usually reveals himself by now."

"Well, maybe he's shy," Cora suggests, folding the letter and handing it back to me. "Or maybe he's waiting for the perfect moment."

I tuck the letter back into my pocket, biting my lip. "I

don't know, Cora. You don't think that if he wanted to, he would have said something by now? What if he never reveals himself? What if I'm just stuck here, reading these letters and wondering who he is for the rest of my life?"

Cora taps her fingers against the counter, her expression thoughtful. "Well, who do you think it could be? I mean, someone's got to be writing these letters. Let's make a list."

I laugh, shaking my head. "A list?"

"Yeah! A list of possible suspects," she says, her eyes gleaming with excitement. "Come on, it'll be fun."

I groan, but I can't help but smile at her enthusiasm. "Fine, but you're not going to find anything. I don't have a clue who it could be."

Cora pulls out a notepad from her purse and grabs a pen, poised to start writing. "Okay, first up: Huxley."

I roll my eyes again. "We already covered this. He's not interested in me."

"Okay, fine. What about his friend? Kip?"

My heart skips a beat at the mention of his name, and I quickly look away, pretending to rearrange the books on the counter.

Kip. The one person I'd been trying not to think about in connection to these letters.

"Why would you say Kip?" I ask, keeping my voice as casual as possible.

Cora gives me a knowing look. "Oh, I don't know. Maybe because you blush every time you hear his name?"

I feel the heat rise to my cheeks, and I curse my fair complexion. "I do not."

"Sure, you don't," she says, smirking. "But come on, Ginger. He's quiet, he keeps to himself, and he's always hanging around, but never too close. Sounds like secret admirer material to me."

I bite my lip, trying to ignore the way my heart flutters at the thought of Kip being the one behind the letters. The truth is, I've had a crush on Kip for as long as I can remember. Ever since I first saw him, there's been something about him that's drawn me in—something quiet, almost mysterious. But I never thought he'd be interested in me. Not really.

"Even if it is Kip," I say, trying to keep my voice steady, "why would he write me letters instead of just talking to me? He knows where I work. He could come in anytime."

"Shy, remember?" Cora asks and I sigh. "Or maybe he's scared. Or... I don't know. I mean, I barely know the guy. He keeps to himself."

I nod, my heart aching a little at the thought. I don't know much about Kip's past, but I've heard enough to know that he's been hurt. The scar on his face is a constant reminder of whatever happened to him, and I can only imagine the toll it's taken.

But could he really be the one writing me letters? Could Kip, the quiet, reserved guy who barely says more than a few words at a time, really be my secret admirer?

The thought sends a thrill through me, and I can't help the small smile that tugs at my lips.

"Okay, maybe it's Kip," I admit, glancing at Cora. "Or maybe I just want it to be him. But, how do I find out for sure?"

Cora grins, leaning forward with a gleam in her eye. "Leave him a note. Ask him to meet you. If it's him, he'll show up."

I bite my lip, considering the idea. It's risky. What if it's not him? What if I'm wrong, and I end up embarrassing myself? But at the same time, the idea of finally knowing the truth, of finally meeting my secret admirer face-to-face, is too tempting to resist.

"I'll think about it," I say.

"You'd better," Cora says with a wink. I laugh, shaking my head as I grab a few more books from the counter, trying to distract myself from the swirling thoughts in my head. Holiday magic, sure. But real life isn't a romance novel. Magic doesn't just happen, not without some effort. And writing a note? Asking Kip—or whoever this mystery man was—to meet me? That felt like a lot more effort than I was ready for.

Still, the idea buzzes in the back of my mind, refusing to let go.

"Are you helping out with the festival?" She asks me and I sigh.

"No, my car was making a weird sound last night and wouldn't start. I was going to try to take a look before I bring it over to the mechanics."

"You know how to fix cars?" She asks and I shake my head.

"Nope, no clue, but I want to at least try before I pay for someone else to do it. What if it's an easy fix?"

"Alright, let's go. I'll try to help."

She pulls her phone out as we head outside to where my old car is sitting.

"Uh, try to start it now?" She asks, already googling car starter issues.

I climb behind the wheel and send up a silent prayer as I stick the key in the ignition and turn.

"What the—" I mumble as my car starts right up.

"Sounds fine to me," Cora says, poking her head into the driver's side door.

"Yeah, that's so weird. It wouldn't start yesterday, and I

tried a bunch. This car is so old that before I moved here, I was bringing it in for work like at least once a month. Ever since, though, it's been running great."

"Maybe you should sell it or trade it in before it breaks for good," she suggests.

"It was my mom's," I whisper, and she nods, her eyes softening.

I turn the car off and climb out, locking the door behind me.

"I need to check in with Saffron," I tell her, and she nods, following me over to the bookstore and inside.

We both try to warm up a bit as I look around for my sister.

"We should talk about the holiday festival," Cora says, straightening up from the counter.

"Yeah, did you come up with any new ideas?" I ask her.

"Not really," she admits with a sigh.

"What are you two scheming about now?" My sister, Saffron, asks as she sweeps into the bookstore, her arms full of decorations.

Saffron owns the bookstore and I cover for her when-ever she needs it. I do the same for my other sisters, Olive and Maple at their businesses. I'm the youngest of us and the only one who has no idea what she wants to do with her life.

As soon as we moved here, Olive, the oldest, opened her own bakery. She's always loved to cook so it made sense. Maple opened up her own adult toy store here in town and Saffron quickly followed with the bookstore. I was last, and so far, I've just been happy to help them out and hang out in town.

"Just trying to figure out who Ginger's secret admirer is," Cora says with a mischievous grin.

"Oh, please." Saffron rolls her eyes as she sets down a box of garlands. "That's easy. It's Kip."

I nearly drop the stack of books I'm holding, my heart thudding painfully in my chest. "Why does everyone think it's Kip?"

"Because it's obvious," Saffron says with a shrug, as if it's the most natural conclusion in the world. "He's been into you since the day he moved here, but he's too shy to make a move. The letters? Classic move from someone who's too nervous to talk to you in person."

I gape at her, feeling a blush creep up my neck. "That's ridiculous. If Kip liked me, he would've said something by now."

Saffron arches an eyebrow, giving me a look that's somewhere between amusement and disbelief. "Ginger, he's practically in here every day. Don't you think it's a little suspicious that he always finds a reason to hang around?"

I open my mouth to argue, but the words die on my lips. I can't deny that Kip is always around, always hovering in the background but never quite stepping into the spotlight. He's quiet, yes, but there's something else, something deeper. Maybe I've been too wrapped up in the mystery of the letters to see what's been right in front of me all along.

"Maybe he just likes reading," I argue, and Saffron snorts.

"*I* love reading, and even I'm not reading a book a day like he is. He's always buying books. Since you started helping out here more, he's become my best customer, and when I talked to Olive, she said the same thing. He's even asked what pastries you worked on, and he only buys those whenever you help out at the bakery."

Cora snickers, clearly enjoying my discomfort. "See? Even Saffron agrees. It's Kip."

I huff, crossing my arms. "I still think it could be someone else."

"Like who?" Saffron asks, tilting her head. "Name one other person who's shown even a fraction of the interest in you that Kip has."

I frown, feeling cornered. "I don't know. Maybe it is Kip. But what if it's not?"

"Then you'll never know unless you ask," Cora chimes in. "Come on, Ginger. What have you got to lose?"

I sigh, glancing between my sister and my best friend. They both look at me with such confidence, as if it's already decided—Kip is the one, and all I have to do is ask him to meet me. But the truth is, I'm scared. Scared of being wrong, scared of getting my hopes up, scared of getting hurt. Scared of what it means if Kip really is the one behind the letters.

"I'll think about it," I mutter, though I can tell by the way they're grinning that they don't believe me for a second.

"Don't think too long," Saffron says, grabbing the decorations again. "I'm going to start decorating for Christmas. Unless... you want to do it."

She gives me a teasing smirk. It's well-known in my family that I love Christmas. There's just something about that time of year that makes me happy. I've had my apartment decorated for weeks, and my tree has been up since the middle of November.

"You know I want to," I grumble, snatching the box of decorations out of her hands.

I hear her and Cora laugh as I head over to the front windows and get to work. I smile as I go, and my mind drifts back to Kip.

I wonder if he'll be at the holiday festival next week. He

hasn't really gone to any of the other town events, but maybe this time will be different.

Cora and I have volunteered to help set up, and I need to finish up here quickly so that we can head over to town hall to get to work.

Cora joins me at the front windows and we have the display set up in no time. I step back to admire our work and she bumps her shoulder against mine.

"We should go, or we'll be late," she points out, and I nod.

We both bundle up and wave goodbye to Saffron as we head out. It's a quiet, cold evening as we head down to the town square. The smell of pine and cinnamon hangs in the air, and a few snowflakes are starting to fall, lightly dusting the streets of Wolf Valley. It's the kind of picturesque setting that you'd find on the cover of a Christmas card, and under normal circumstances, I'd be soaking it all in.

But tonight, my mind is elsewhere.

"Where do you want us?" Cora calls to the organizer.

"Start on the lights, please!" She calls back, and we nod and get to work.

As we start stringing up lights and hanging garlands, I catch myself glancing around, half-expecting to see Kip lurking nearby. He's always been good at blending in, disappearing into the background, but now I wonder if I've been blind to his presence this whole time.

"It's really coming along, huh?" Cora asks, and I blink, looking around at the town square and all of our hard work.

"Yeah, it's nice."

"Hey," Cora says, nudging me with her elbow. "You okay? You've been quiet since we left the bookstore."

I shrug, trying to play it off. "Just thinking."

"About Kip?" she asks, her tone teasing but not unkind.

I sigh, shaking my head. "About the letters. About everything. What if... what if I'm wrong, Cora? What if it's not him? I don't want to make a fool of myself."

Cora's expression softens, and she tugs me over to the side, away from the others. "Ginger, you're not going to make a fool of yourself. Whoever this guy is, he clearly cares about you. He's been writing you letters for months. And if it is Kip... well, you'd be lucky to have him. He seems like a good guy."

I bite my lip, feeling the weight of her words. "I know he is. I just... I don't know if I'm ready."

Cora gives me a small, understanding smile. "You don't have to be ready right this second. But don't close yourself off, okay? You deserve to be happy, Ginger."

I nod, though my heart is still heavy with uncertainty. Cora's right, of course. Whoever this mystery man is, he's taken the time to get to know me, to write to me, to admire me from a distance. Maybe it's time I let myself open up to the possibility that someone—whether it's Kip or not—actually wants me.

By the time we finish decorating the square, I'm exhausted. I touch the most recent letter in my coat pocket, the paper crinkling against the fabric as I head toward my car. My sisters are meeting me later tonight for dinner, but for now, I just need a moment to clear my head.

The streets are quiet as I drive through town, my thoughts swirling like the snowflakes outside. When I finally pull into the driveway of Olive's house, I take a deep breath, steeling myself for the evening ahead.

I'm not sure what tomorrow will bring, or if I'll ever find out who's been writing me these letters. But there's one thing I do know.

I'm falling for him.

And if it's Kip... well, maybe that wouldn't be so bad after all.

THREE

Kip

I STAND IN THE SHADOWS, clutching the letter in my hand as if it's the only thing tethering me to reality. It's late, and the streets are empty, but my heart is pounding like I'm in the middle of a crowd, all eyes on me.

I shouldn't be here. I shouldn't be doing this. It's too risky. I know that she'll be out here any minute.

And yet, I have to.

I glance around, checking to make sure no one is watching, before I walk over to Ginger's car and slip the letter under her windshield wiper. My hands shake as I pull away, and for a second, I think about leaving. Not just this spot, but the whole thing—the letters, the secrets, the cowardice. But then Ginger's face flashes in my mind, the way her smile lights up everything around her. The way her eyes spark when she reads one of my notes, and I know I can't stop. Not now. It's a stupid, childish thing, leaving these letters for her, but it's all I have. It's the only way I can be close to her without actually having to face her.

I'm about to slip away when a sound startles me—a door slamming at the coffeehouse down the block. My heart jumps into my throat as I duck behind a nearby building, peeking around the corner just in time to see Ginger walking toward her car.

Shit. That was too close.

I press my back against the cold brick wall, holding my breath as she approaches her car. My pulse races as I watch her reach for the note I left behind. She pauses, her eyes scanning the parking lot for a second before she pulls the paper from under the wiper.

Something's wrong.

She's off today.

I watch her read the note, and my body starts to grow cold as I catalog her reaction.

She doesn't smile this time.

I frown, watching as she reads the letter, her brow furrowing. There's frustration in the way her shoulders tense, and I can feel the anxiety bubbling up inside me. She's been reading my letters for months now, but I've never seen her look like this.

She's upset.

I hate that I can't do anything about it. I hate that I'm too much of a coward to walk up to her, to tell her that it's me, that I'm the guy who's been pining for her from afar. Instead, I stand here, frozen in place, watching her.

I watch as she reads my note and takes a deep breath. She's not smiling like she usually is after I leave her and note, and a pit starts to form in my stomach, growing by the second as I watch her. She looks like she's debating something, and my mind races as I try to figure out what she's thinking.

Suddenly, Ginger pulls something out of her bag—a pen and a scrap of paper. My heart lurches as I watch her scribble something down, her movements quick and sharp, as if she's trying to get the words out before she changes her mind. Then, with a determined look, she tucks the note under her own windshield wiper and walks away.

I don't move. I don't breathe. I wait until she's disappeared down the street, my mind racing with what she could've written. Did she figure it out? Does she know it's me?

Or worse—does she want it to stop?

When she's long gone, I force myself to move, my legs stiff and heavy as I approach her car. My fingers tremble as I reach for the note she left behind, my pulse pounding in my ears. The moment I open it, my breath catches in my throat.

MEET ME.

THE WORDS ARE bold and underlined, like she's daring me to step out of the shadows. Like she's tired of waiting, tired of the mystery. She wants to know who I am, and now I'm faced with a choice I've been both dreading and looking forward to from the moment that I wrote that first letter.

I should be happy, right? I mean, if she wants to meet, then she must have liked my letters. She must be interested in me.

Right?

I've spent months dreaming about this moment, imagining what it would be like for her to finally know. But now that it's here, all I can feel is panic. My scars feel like they're burning under my skin, a constant reminder.

She thinks she's falling for someone who doesn't exist. The man in those letters isn't real. He's a fantasy, a version of myself that I'll never be. And if she finds out the truth... she'll hate me. She'll look at me like everyone else in town does—with pity, or worse, disgust.

I crumple the note in my hand, my chest tight with fear. Then I hurry to straighten it back out. I can't bear to destroy anything that Ginger gives to me.

What the hell am I supposed to do now? Do I meet her and risk everything? Or do I keep hiding, keep pretending that this is enough?

I know the answer. I've known it for a while now.

I can't keep hiding.

But the fear is paralyzing, and I'm not ready. Not yet.

With a heavy sigh, I shove the note into my pocket and head to my truck. I need to head to work and wrap up a few things, but even as I drive toward the helicopter hangar, my mind keeps drifting back to that note and the decision I'll have to make.

By the time I get to work, Huxley is already there, prepping one of the choppers for the morning flight. He glances up as I approach, wiping grease off his hands with a rag.

"Hey, wasn't expecting to see you here," he says with a grin. "Miss me?"

I grunt in response, trying to shake the tension from my shoulders as I grab my gear. I can feel his eyes on me, but I'm not in the mood to explain. Not yet.

"Everything okay?" Huxley asks, his voice softening. He knows me well enough to pick up on my mood, even when I try to hide it.

"Yeah," I mutter. "Just... stuff on my mind."

Huxley arches an eyebrow, but he doesn't push. Instead, he changes the subject, knowing that I'll talk when I'm ready.

"So, have you made a decision? Are you going to the town's holiday festival?" he asks, his tone casual. "The one with all the mistletoe and terrible music?" He asks as if I need a reminder.

I shrug, trying to play it off. "Maybe. I haven't decided yet. What about you?"

He snorts. "Hell no."

I glance over at him, narrowing my eyes. "Why not? No holiday spirit?"

"Not interested."

"Cora will be there," I point out, and he tenses.

We haven't talked about it much, but I've seen the way that he looks at her, and I know that he likes her just as much as I like Ginger.

"Did you get Ginger's car fixed last night?" He asks, and I nod. "How long did it take you?"

"Four hours, and you're changing the subject."

He sighs, tossing the rag onto a nearby table. "Fine, I'll go, and we both know that you're going. You'll show up, even if you keep your distance. Just like always."

I huff out a laugh, but it's forced. Huxley knows me too well. He knows I can't stay away from Ginger, even if it means lingering in the background, just out of sight. The idea of watching her laugh and smile with other people, of seeing her with someone else under the mistletoe—it makes my stomach twist.

But showing up? Actually talking to her, revealing that I'm the one behind the letters? I don't know if I have it in me.

"Yeah, maybe," I say, turning away from him and

focusing on the helicopter in front of me. "I'll think about it."

Huxley doesn't say anything, but I can feel his eyes on me, like he's waiting for me to make a decision. And maybe I am too.

As the night drags on, my mind keeps wandering back to that damn note in my pocket. The weight of it feels heavier with every passing hour. Ginger wants to meet, and if I don't show up, if I keep hiding, I'll lose her before I ever really had her.

But if I do show up... what then? What if she sees me and regrets everything? What if she realizes that the guy in the letters isn't the guy standing in front of her? Can I handle that rejection?

The doubt gnaws at me, refusing to let go.

By the time I finish up and head home, I'm no closer to an answer. I drive home in silence, the streets dark and empty, and all I can think about is the holiday party. I know Ginger will be there. I know she'll be waiting for me.

And I know I'm running out of time to decide what to do.

As I pull into my driveway, I lean my head back against the seat, closing my eyes for a moment. The house is quiet, empty, and for the first time in a long time, I feel the weight of my loneliness. I've spent so long pushing people away, hiding behind these letters, that I've forgotten what it's like to really be close to someone.

Ginger could change that. She could be the one to pull me out of this darkness.

If I'm brave enough to let her.

I glance at the note in my pocket one last time before heading inside. I'll have to make a choice soon.

But not tonight.

FOUR

Ginger

IT'S BEEN three days since I left my secret admirer the note, and still nothing.

I keep checking my car, mailbox, under my welcome mat and everywhere else that I can think about. I know that I'm driving my sisters crazy by looking all over their businesses every morning, every afternoon, even late at night after work, hoping—no, *praying*—that there will be something waiting for me. Another letter. A sign. *Anything*. But there's been nothing.

The note I left is gone, so I know he got it. He must've read it. He had to have seen that I asked to meet, and still nothing.

The silence has been deafening.

I don't know what I expected. Maybe I thought he'd be excited, that he'd jump at the chance to finally come out of the shadows and show me who he is, but that doesn't really make sense with the whole anonymous letter thing that he's been doing. I guess I had just hoped that he would want to meet face-to-face, to talk about all of this.

Instead, all I'm left with is doubt and frustration, wondering if I crossed some invisible line. Did I scare him off? Was it too much too soon? Or maybe he's not the person I imagined him to be. Maybe he doesn't want to meet at all.

That thought makes my chest tighten, and I hate it. I hate how much I've let myself get attached to a man I've never even met, how much I've invested in the words of a stranger. But I can't help it. Every letter he's written feels like a piece of him, and I've been falling in love with those pieces for months now.

I can't just let it go. Not yet.

With a determined breath, I grab a pen and a sheet of paper from behind the counter of Wet and Wild, my sister Maple's adult toy store. I was here covering for her while she went out to lunch with her boyfriend, Ryder. She just got back, though, so I know that I'll be headed out soon. Maple is in the back, working on some inventory, and I'm thankful for the moment of privacy. I scribble down the words quickly, not letting myself overthink it.

MEET ME. **I'm not waiting any longer. I need to know who you are.**

I STARE at the note for a long moment, my fingers tightening around the edges of the paper. This is it—my last attempt, my last push. If he doesn't reply after this, I'll have to let it go. I'll have to accept that maybe I'm just chasing a fantasy, a ghost.

But I need to try.

I fold the note carefully, slipping it into my bag. I'll leave it on my car after work, just like I did the last time, and hope that this time, he'll be brave enough to answer.

When I head into the back room, Maple looks up from her computer, raising an eyebrow as I approach.

"You okay? You've been kind of... off today."

I force a smile, though it feels weak, like I can't quite muster the energy to fake it. "Yeah, I'm fine. Just... thinking about stuff."

She narrows her eyes, clearly not buying it. "Is this about your secret admirer again?"

I sigh, leaning against the counter as I cross my arms. "Yeah. I left him a note a few days ago, asking him to meet me, but I haven't heard anything. I'm starting to think I messed up."

Maple frowns, setting aside the stack of lingerie she was organizing. "Why would you think that? Maybe he's just nervous."

"Or maybe he doesn't want to meet me," I say, the bitterness creeping into my voice. "Maybe he's been having fun with the mystery and doesn't actually want anything more."

My sister gives me a sympathetic look, but before she can say anything, the bell over the door jingles, and Cora walks in, her face lighting up when she spots me.

"Ginger! I've been looking for you all afternoon," she says, bounding over to the counter with a grin. "Got time for a coffee break?"

I glance over at Maple, who waves me off with a smile. "Go ahead. I've got it covered from here. Thanks for helping out today."

"Anytime."

With a sigh of relief, I grab my coat and bag, following Cora out of the sex shop. The crisp winter air bites at my cheeks, and for a moment, the cold wakes me up, shaking off some of the frustration I've been carrying around all day.

Cora nudges me as we walk. "So, what's the latest with your mystery man?"

I groan, pulling the folded note from my bag and waving it in front of her. "Still nothing. I'm leaving him another note today, basically demanding that he meet me in person. I'm tired of waiting."

Cora's eyes widen in surprise, and then she grins. "Good for you! It's about time you took charge."

"Yeah, well, if this doesn't work, I don't know what will. I've been falling for this guy, Cora, and I don't even know who he is. It's ridiculous."

She gives me a sympathetic look as we walk into the coffee shop, the smell of roasted beans and cinnamon immediately wrapping around us. We order our usual drinks and settle into a booth by the window, the snow lightly falling outside as people bustle around the square, decorating for the holiday festival.

"Have you thought about, you know, putting yourself out there?" Cora asks, her tone gentle but probing.

"What do you mean?" I ask, sipping my coffee.

"I mean, maybe it's time to meet someone, Ginger. In person. Secret admirers are fun and romantic, but they're not exactly... real. You don't even know if this guy is who you think he is."

I frown, swirling my coffee in its cup. "You think I should just... move on? Start dating other people?"

Cora shrugs. "Maybe. Look, you've been waiting for months, and you're still waiting. What if he never shows up? You deserve to be happy, and you deserve someone who's willing to put themselves out there for you."

I know she's right. As much as I want to believe that my mystery man will come forward, there's no guarantee. And I can't keep putting my life on hold for someone who might never appear.

"I don't know," I say, leaning back in my seat. "It feels weird, starting over, dating someone new when I'm still hung up on this."

Cora grins, her eyes twinkling with mischief. "You know what you need? A little liquid courage."

I laugh, shaking my head. "Oh no. I know where this is going."

But Cora is already up, pulling me out of the booth. "Come on. We're going to your place, and we're going to have some fun. You need to loosen up a bit, Ginger. Trust me."

I groan, but I don't resist. Maybe she's right. Maybe a night of letting loose is exactly what I need to get out of my own head.

Two hours and a bottle of wine later, Cora and I are sprawled out on my couch, giggling like schoolgirls as we scroll through dating profiles on my laptop.

"I can't believe we're doing this," I say, covering my face with my hands as Cora types furiously on the keyboard.

"You need to put yourself out there," she says, laughing as she adds another detail to my profile. That's been her mantra tonight. I swear that she's told me the same thing a dozen times in the last two hours, and she just keeps repeating it as she gets even more drunk.

I groan, but I can't help but laugh along with her. I'm definitely tipsy, my head buzzing pleasantly from the wine, and for the first time in days, I'm not thinking about my mystery man. I'm not obsessing over the letters or the lack of a response. Instead, I'm just... here, in the moment, laughing with my best friend.

"Okay, let's see," Cora says, reading off the screen. "Loves Christmas, works at a bookstore, a bakery, and an adult toy store, terrible at dating—check, check, and check."

I snort, rolling my eyes. "Thanks for that glowing endorsement. I'll have guys hitting me up left and right with that bio!"

Cora grins, setting the laptop down on the coffee table. "It will work and you'll thank me later. Besides, if this doesn't work out, we'll just delete it. No harm, no foul."

I sigh, leaning back against the cushions, feeling a little lighter than I have in days. "I guess you're right. Maybe this is what I need."

"Exactly," Cora says, her voice slurring slightly as she grabs her glass. "Now, let's just relax and let the magic happen."

I smile, closing my eyes as the warmth of the wine settles over me, making my limbs heavy and my mind foggy. Cora leans her head on my shoulder, and before I know it, the sounds of the world start to fade away, and I'm drifting off to sleep.

When I wake up the next morning, my head throbs, and the first thing I see is Cora sprawled out on the floor, snoring softly. The empty bottle of wine sits on the coffee table, and my laptop is still open to my brand-new dating profile.

I groan, rubbing my temples as I sit up, the events of last night slowly coming back to me. I glance at the clock and realize I'm late to help Olive out at the bakery—really late.

Shit.

I scramble off the couch, nudging Cora with my foot as I try to gather my bearings. "Cora, wake up. We overslept."

She groans, burying her face in the couch cushions. "Five more minutes..."

I laugh despite the pounding in my head, and as I rush to get ready for the day, I can't help but feel nervous. I'm not ready to try online dating, not when I'm still so hung up on my secret admirer.

What other choice do I have, though? If he won't meet me, then I need to try something else. Who knows, maybe putting myself out there won't be such a bad idea after all.

FIVE

Kip

I THOUGHT I had more time. I thought I could delay meeting her a little longer, could maybe come up with the perfect way to reveal myself.

But then I found out about the dating profile.

When Huxley told me, I almost didn't believe him. He'd mentioned it in passing, as if it were no big deal, but my heart had dropped like a stone. Ginger Baker, my Ginger, had made an online dating profile. And now, the thought of her meeting some random guy, letting him get close to her—*my* girl—it was driving me insane.

I shouldn't be this angry. I know that. But I can't help it. After all these months of writing to her, pouring out everything I'm too afraid to say in person, the thought of someone else stepping in where I haven't had the courage to go... it's too much.

I grab my phone, my hands shaking with frustration as I open the dating app Huxley mentioned. It takes me a few minutes to find her, but when I do, my stomach twists. There she is, smiling at the camera, her profile casual and sweet, just like her.

I stare at the screen, my heart pounding as I hover over the message button. This is a terrible idea. I shouldn't be doing this. But I can't stop myself. My thumb taps the button, and before I know it, I'm typing out the first thing that comes to mind.

TAKE YOUR DATING PROFILE DOWN.

I HIT SEND BEFORE I can think better of it, my pulse racing as I wait for her to respond. What the hell am I doing? This isn't the way to handle this, but I can't shake the fear gnawing at me—the fear of losing her before I've even had a chance to show her who I really am.

The phone buzzes in my hand, and I look down at her reply.

EXCUSE ME? *Why? Who is this?*

I SWALLOW HARD, my mind racing as I try to figure out what to say next. I can't exactly tell her the truth, not yet. But I also can't stand the idea of her going out with someone else. I clench my jaw and type out my next message.

THE GUY *who's been writing to you. Take the profile down.*

. . .

THERE'S A LONG PAUSE, and I wonder if I've crossed a line. My palms are sweating, and I almost want to take it all back, but then her reply comes through, and I can practically feel the heat in her words.

YOU'RE *the one who's been leaving me notes, and now you think you can just tell me what to do? Who do you think you are?*

I GROAN, running a hand through my hair. This is going terribly. I take a deep breath and type out my reply, trying to explain myself without sounding like a complete asshole.

I DON'T WANT *you to meet anyone else. I'll explain everything, just... take the profile down.*

THERE'S ANOTHER LONG PAUSE, and I can almost hear the frustration in her silence. When her next message comes through, it's clear she's had enough.

EITHER YOU MEET *me under the mistletoe at the town holiday party at 9 PM, or I'm done taking orders from you. If you don't show, I'm putting this profile to good use.*

. . .

MY HEART LURCHES in my chest as I read her words, the ultimatum hanging in the air like a threat. She's not playing around anymore. I've pushed her too far, and now I'm backed into a corner. I either meet her at the party, face-to-face, or I lose her.

I close my eyes, my chest tight with anxiety. This is it. I've run out of time.

I stare at the screen, my fingers hovering over the keyboard. There's so much I want to say, but none of it feels right. In the end, I don't reply. I can't. I have to figure this out, and the clock is ticking.

I'm so worked up, and I know that I need to find something to keep busy, so I head to work. I find Huxley in the garage, tinkering with one of the helicopters. He glances up as I approach, wiping grease off his hands with a rag.

"Hey, you look like you've seen a ghost. What's up?"

I pace back and forth, the anxiety gnawing at me. "I messed up, man. She's going to be at the holiday party. She told me I either meet her there at 9 PM, or she's done."

Huxley raises an eyebrow, leaning against the workbench. "And you're freaking out because...?"

I glare at him. "Because I'm not ready, Hux. I can't just show up and... what if she takes one look at me and regrets everything? What if I ruin this? I mean, she's expecting some handsome, charming guy and I'm--," I throw my hands out, my words cutting off.

He lets out a sigh, crossing his arms over his chest. "Kip, you've been writing to her for months. She's falling for you, not some other guy. If she's into you in those letters, she's going to be into you in person. You're over-thinking this."

I shake my head, the doubts swirling in my mind. "You don't know that. The guy she's falling for isn't the real me.

It's the version of me that I wish I could be, the guy who isn't broken."

Huxley rolls his eyes. "You're not broken, Kip. And she'll see that. You just have to show up."

I stop pacing, staring down at the floor. "What if I don't go?"

Huxley's expression hardens. "Then you lose her. And you'll spend the rest of your life wondering what could've happened if you'd just had the guts to show up."

I swallow hard, the weight of his words sinking in. He's right. If I don't go, if I let my fear win, I'll lose Ginger forever. And I can't let that happen.

"I have to go, don't I?" I say, my voice barely above a whisper.

Huxley grins. "Yep. And it's going to be fine. Hell, this could be the best Christmas of your life."

"Or the worst," I mutter, rubbing the back of my neck. The thought of standing under the mistletoe, waiting for Ginger to show up, only for her to take one look at me and walk away—it's terrifying.

Huxley slaps me on the back. "Come on, man. You've got this. And hey, maybe we can make it easier on you. You know, blend in a little."

I frown, not understanding what he's getting at. "What do you mean?"

Huxley's grin widens. "We'll volunteer to help out with the party. That way, you can be there without all the pressure of just waiting around. You'll have something to do, and you'll look like a hero for helping out. Win-win."

I blink at him, considering the idea. It's not a terrible plan. Volunteering would give me an excuse to be there, to keep myself busy, and maybe it would help with the nerves. And if it means I get to be closer to Ginger, even better.

"Yeah, okay," I say slowly, nodding. "I'll do it. But... I'm not sure this is going to end well."

Huxley laughs, slinging an arm around my shoulders as we head out of the garage. "Hey, worst case, you get rejected, and we go to your place and get drunk. Best case, you get the girl. Either way, you'll finally know, and you can stop living in limbo."

I shake my head, but I can't help the small smile tugging at my lips. He's right. This is it—the moment I've been avoiding for months. It's either going to be the best Christmas I've ever had, or the worst.

I just have to show up.

SIX

Ginger

I STRETCH ON MY TOES, trying to hang the last string of lights along the rafters, but of course, the bulbs decide to burn out right as I'm almost done. I groan in frustration, letting the string drop from my hands and dangle uselessly. There's always something, isn't there?

It's just a few days before the big holiday party, and the town square is buzzing with last-minute preparations. I've been volunteering for hours, trying to make sure everything is perfect for the event. The twinkling lights, the pine-scented garlands, the mistletoe—it's supposed to feel magical, but right now, all I feel is exhausted.

I grab the burned-out string of lights and start untangling them, but my thoughts are far from the task at hand. The note I left for my secret admirer is still on my mind. It's been days since I demanded that he meet me under the mistletoe at the party, and I haven't heard a word back. I know he took my last note, but the silence since then has been eating away at me.

What if he doesn't show up? What if he just... disappears?

"Uh...need a hand with that?"

The deep voice jolts me out of my thoughts, and I look up, startled. Standing just a few feet away are Kip and Huxley, both of them dressed casually but looking like they belong in a magazine spread for rugged, outdoorsy men. I wasn't expecting them, and the sight of Kip—his broad shoulders, his quiet confidence—sends a shiver down my spine.

"Oh, uh, yeah," I stammer, holding up the string of lights. "These decided to burn out on me."

Kip steps forward, his expression calm but focused as he takes the lights from my hands. He angles his head to the right, and I know that he's trying to hide the scars that mar that side of his face and neck. It's obvious that he's self-conscious about them, but I don't know why. It makes him look edgy and sexy.

His fingers brush mine for a split second, and I feel a spark of warmth shoot through me. "I'll take care of it," he says, his voice low and rough.

I glance at Cora, who's been helping me decorate, and she gives me a wide-eyed look before quickly turning her attention back to a garland she's hanging on the light post outside of the Nosh Diner. I can tell she's trying not to smirk.

Kip carefully inspects the lights, his brow furrowed in concentration as he works on replacing the burned-out bulbs. Huxley, meanwhile, is chatting with some of the other volunteers, making jokes and keeping things light as usual. But my attention is locked on Kip.

"Should be good now," he says, pulling me out of my thoughts. He plugs in the lights, and they flicker to life, casting a soft, warm glow over the room.

"Thanks," I say, smiling up at him. "You're a lifesaver."

He shrugs, offering me a small smile in return. "No problem."

For a moment, we just stand there, the twinkling lights between us, and I can't help but feel a strange sense of connection. It's quiet, but it's there—a warmth, an under-standing. I wonder if he feels it too, or if it's just my imagi-nation running wild.

"So, are you helping out with the festival?" I ask, trying to keep the conversation going.

Kip nods, glancing around at the decorations. "Yeah. Huxley and I thought we'd lend a hand."

"Well, it's good to have more volunteers," I say, hoping I don't sound as nervous as I feel. "This place is going to look amazing once we're done."

He nods again, his eyes scanning the block, but there's something thoughtful in his gaze, like he's thinking about something else entirely. I want to ask him what's on his mind, but I don't. Instead, I focus on the task at hand, hanging more lights and garlands while we work side by side in comfortable silence.

At one point, our hands brush again as we both reach for the same string of lights, and I feel my heart skip a beat. I glance up at him, and for a split second, I think I see some-thing flicker in his eyes—something more than just casual friendliness.

Could he feel the same way about me? Could he...?

No, stop it, Ginger. Don't let your mind go there. He's probably just being nice.

But the thought lingers, and as we finish hanging the

last of the decorations, I find myself wishing—*hoping*—that Kip could be the one behind the letters. It would make sense, wouldn't it? He's always around, always so quiet and careful. And the way he looks at me sometimes...

"Ready to head out?" Kip's voice breaks through my thoughts, and I blink, realizing that we've finished. The town square looks magical now, the lights twinkling and the decorations perfectly in place.

I glance at Cora, who's already putting on her coat. "Yeah, I'm ready."

Kip walks with me as we step out into the cold night, our breaths visible in the frosty air. The snow has started falling again, soft and gentle, blanketing the streets in white. It's beautiful, the kind of night that makes you want to hold someone close and never let go.

We walk in silence for a while, our footsteps crunching in the snow. I sneak glances at Kip, wondering if he's going to say something, if he feels the same pull I do. There's a tension between us—something unspoken but undeniable.

When we reach my front door, I stop, turning to face him. My heart is pounding, and I'm not sure why I'm so nervous. He looks down at me, his eyes unreadable in the dim light, and for a moment, I think he might kiss me.

I *want* him to kiss me.

But he doesn't. He hesitates, then gives me a small, almost shy smile. "Goodnight, Ginger."

Disappointment floods me, but I force a smile. "Goodnight, Kip."

He lingers for a second longer, as if he's debating something, but then he turns and walks away, his figure disappearing into the falling snow.

I watch him go, my heart aching in my chest. Part of me wonders if I should have said something, done something to close the distance between us. But instead, I turn the key in my door and step inside, the warmth of the house doing nothing to ease the chill in my chest.

I lean against the door, closing my eyes as I replay the night in my mind. I don't know if Kip will ever see me the way I see him, or if my secret admirer will ever reveal himself.

But for now, I'll keep hoping. Maybe, just maybe, this Christmas will bring me the love I've been waiting for.

And if Kip *is* my secret admirer... well, that would be the best gift of all.

SEVEN

Kip

I ALMOST KISSED her last night.

It was so close, I could feel the electricity in the air between us. Her eyes were soft, full of hope and warmth, and I swear my heart stopped when she looked up at me like that. But I chickened out. My feet moved before my brain could catch up, and I walked away like an idiot.

Now, it's two days until the holiday party, and I can't stop thinking about it. About her. About kissing her and doing a hell of a lot more than that to her.

I'm back at the town hall, helping Huxley and the girls finish up the last of the decorations. The square is coming together beautifully, with garlands, lights, and other decorations strung along the lamp posts and buildings, and the smell of pine and cinnamon filling the air. But I can't focus on any of it. All I can think about is how close I was to kissing Ginger, how her lips would have felt against mine, how she might have—

"Yo, Kip, you spacing out?" Huxley's voice cuts through my thoughts, and I shake my head, trying to snap back to the present.

"Nah, just... focusing," I mutter, grabbing another string of lights and draping them over a nearby archway.

"Thinking about Ginger?" Huxley asks with a knowing smirk.

I grunt in response, which only makes him chuckle.

As we work, I catch glimpses of Ginger across the square. She's helping with the mistletoe, her auburn hair catching the light as she laughs with Cora. Every time she smiles, it feels like a punch to my chest. She's beautiful, in that effortless way that makes it hard to look at her without wanting more.

And then, just as I'm starting to focus again, I see them —two guys, strangers, walking up to her. They're laughing, chatting her up, their eyes lingering on her in a way that makes my blood boil.

I set down the lights, my jaw clenching as I watch them. One of the guys steps closer to Ginger, and I can see the way her smile falters, her discomfort clear.

That's it.

Before I even realize what I'm doing, I'm moving toward them, my fists clenched at my sides. When I reach them, I step right between Ginger and the guys, my eyes cold as I look at them.

"You need something?" I ask, my voice low and dangerous.

The guys glance at each other, clearly not expecting to be interrupted. "Uh, we were just—"

"You were just leaving," I growl, cutting them off.

They stare at me for a moment, but one look at my face is enough to make them reconsider. With mumbled excuses, they back off and shuffle away, leaving me standing there, fuming.

"Wow," Ginger says from behind me, her voice soft with surprise. "That was... intense."

I turn to face her, my anger fading the moment I see her face. She's not upset—if anything, she looks amused. "Sorry," I mutter, running a hand through my hair. "They were bothering you."

She smiles, a real one this time, and it sends a wave of warmth through me. "Thanks, Kip. But I could've handled it."

"I know," I say, trying not to sound too defensive. "But I didn't like the way they were looking at you."

Her smile softens, and for a moment, we just stand there, the noise of the town fading into the background. There's something between us, something I can't quite put into words, but it's there. It's always been there.

"Hey, I need to head back to the bookstore for a bit," Ginger says, breaking the silence. "Want to walk with me?"

I nod, eager for any excuse to spend more time with her. "Sure."

We leave the town hall together, the cold winter air biting at our faces as we walk down the snow-covered streets. It's quiet, the town peaceful in the early evening, and for once, I feel calm. Just being near her makes everything feel right.

As we reach the bookstore, something catches my eye— mistletoe, hanging just above the door. My heart skips a beat, and I glance at Ginger, wondering if she's noticed it too.

She does. Her eyes flick up to the mistletoe, then back to me, a nervous smile playing on her lips.

This is it. No backing out this time.

I take a step closer to her, my heart pounding in my chest as I reach for her hand. She doesn't pull away. If anything, she steps closer too, her breath visible in the cold air between us.

And then, without overthinking it, I lean in and press my lips to hers.

It's soft at first, tentative, like we're both testing the waters. But then she kisses me back, and everything else disappears. The cold, the snow, the world—it's all gone, replaced by the warmth of her lips, the way she fits perfectly against me.

It feels right. More right than anything has in a long time.

When we finally pull apart, my heart is racing, and I can see the same surprise in her eyes that I feel. For a moment, I wonder if she knows—if she realizes that I'm the one who's been writing to her all these months.

But before I can say anything, she smiles, and it's like the whole world lights up. "I guess that's what happens under mistletoe, huh?"

I chuckle, though my mind is still racing. "Yeah, I guess so."

We stand there for a moment longer, the weight of the kiss lingering between us, but then she steps back, her smile soft and shy. "I should get back to work."

"Right," I say, nodding. "I'll, uh... see you later?"

She nods, her cheeks flushed as she heads into the bookstore. I stand there for a second, watching her disappear behind the door, and I can't help but wonder—did she kiss me because she wanted to? Or was it just because of the mistletoe?

The question gnaws at me as I turn and walk away, my mind spinning with uncertainty. Does she like me? Or is she just caught up in the tradition, the magic of the season?

I head towards work, the snow crunching beneath my boots as I try to make sense of it all. By the time I reach the garage, Huxley is there, working on one of the helicopters.

"How'd it go with Ginger?" he asks, not looking up from the engine.

I hesitate, the memory of the kiss still fresh in my mind. "We kissed."

Huxley looks up, eyebrows raised. "Seriously? That's great, man!"

I shrug, though my heart is still pounding. "Yeah, but... I don't know. It was under mistletoe. What if it was just because of that? What if she doesn't actually..."

Huxley shakes his head, grinning. "Come on, Kip. If she kissed you, it's not just because of mistletoe. Trust me."

I don't respond, the doubts still lingering in the back of my mind. But then Huxley changes the subject, his grin widening.

"Speaking of girls, I need your help with something."

I raise an eyebrow. "With what?"

He rubs the back of his neck, looking unusually sheepish. "Cora."

I laugh, shaking my head. "You're finally admitting it, huh?"

"Yeah, yeah," Huxley mutters, though there's a smile on his face. "But I have no idea what to do. She's... difficult."

I snort. "Difficult? She's perfect for you, and you know it."

"Maybe, but she's also impossible to figure out. Every time I try to get close, she pushes me away. What am I supposed to do?"

I think for a moment, then grin. "Stop pissing her off, for one."

Huxley laughs, shaking his head. "Yeah, well, easier said than done."

We spend the next hour brainstorming ideas, throwing out everything from grand romantic gestures to simple conversations. But in the back of my mind, all I can think about is Ginger. That kiss. And whether or not she feels the same way I do.

Because in two days, I'll know for sure.

The holiday party is coming up, and everything will be decided under that mistletoe.

Best or worst Christmas ever—I guess I'm about to find out.

EIGHT

Ginger

IT'S the day of the holiday party, and I can't stop thinking about the kiss.

For two days, that moment has been playing on a loop in my mind. The warmth of his lips, the way he stepped close to me under the mistletoe, how my heart raced like it was about to burst out of my chest. I've been floating on this strange, giddy feeling ever since, and no matter how much I try to focus on anything else, all I can think about is *Kip*.

And his kiss.

And the fact that he's my secret admirer. He's the man who wrote me such sweet words, who made me feel special and seen and beautiful. I know it.

I've been helping set up for the party all day, but my mind keeps drifting. Every time I pass the mistletoe, my stomach flips, because tonight... tonight is the night.

Will he show? Will he admit that he's the one who has been sending me letters?

It's almost 9 PM, and the party is in full swing, with people milling about, grabbing hot chocolate and other treats, and looking at the little vendor tables. But I'm standing here, waiting. Waiting for Kip to show up, waiting for him to kiss me again.

I already know it's him. I knew the moment I saw how he reacted to those guys flirting with me. The jealousy in his eyes, the way he stepped in without hesitation—that's when it clicked. The guy I'd been hoping for, the guy I'd been falling in love with through words, was Kip all along.

Now, I just need him to show up.

I glance around the town square, feeling that familiar twinge of nerves. The twinkling lights, the smell of cinnamon and pine, the sound of laughter and Christmas carols—it's all perfect. But my heart is pounding, and I can't focus on any of it. All I care about is *him*.

I check the clock again. Two minutes to nine. My hands are sweaty, and my heart is racing. I've never been this nervous in my life.

And then, I see him.

Kip walks through the crowd, looking as nervous as I feel. His dark hair is a little messy from the cold wind, and his strong jaw is clenched like he's trying to steel himself for something. He's scanning the space, and when his eyes land on me, his whole body seems to relax, even if it's just for a moment.

He starts walking toward me, but before he can get too far, I do the only thing I can think of—I run.

I don't wait for him to reach the mistletoe. I don't care about anything else in this moment. All I care about is *him*. I run across the square, my boots slipping slightly on the icy sidewalk, and when I reach him, I leap into his arms.

He catches me, his eyes wide with surprise, but I don't

give him time to react. I press my lips to his, and everything else falls away. The music, the people, the noise—it's all gone, replaced by the warmth of his kiss.

His arms tighten around me, holding me close, and I can feel his heart pounding in his chest. When we finally pull apart, I'm breathless, and I can see the shock in his eyes.

"I love your letters," I whisper, my hands still resting on his shoulders.

He blinks, looking like I've just knocked the wind out of him. "You... you knew?"

I smile, my heart swelling with affection for him. "I figured it out the other day when you got all jealous about those guys talking to me. Plus, when I showed Saffron the stationery, she told me that you were the only one to buy it in the last few months."

His brow furrows. "They were hitting on you."

I roll my eyes, laughing softly. "They were just talking to me. You didn't need to scare them off."

He shakes his head, a small grin tugging at his lips. "Trust me, they weren't just talking."

I tighten my hold on him, and uncertainty flashes across his face.

"Are you disappointed?" He whispers, and I bite my lip, feeling the butterflies in my stomach fluttering wildly.

"Well... I was kind of hoping it was you."

His eyes widen.

"Really?"

"Yeah, why are you so surprised?"

His finger absently runs across the scars on his face, and my heart hurts.

"I don't mind your scars. I like them. They make you look like a badass. Plus, it means that you can scare off any guys who try to flirt with me."

"Damn right," he growls, and I giggle.

He smiles at me softly, his whole face softening, and I can see it then. He loves me. He would do anything for me.

"I'll always protect you, Ginger."

"I know," I whisper, and for a moment, we just stand there, staring at each other.

The space feels small, like it's just the two of us, and I can't help but feel like everything has been leading to this moment.

"I can't believe you figured it out," Kip says, his voice low and a little shy. "I thought I was doing a pretty good job of hiding it."

I laugh, shaking my head. "You were... until you weren't."

"Yeah, I was starting to crack. It was hard being close to you, but not close enough," he says with a chuckle, but then his expression shifts, turning more serious. "I wanted to tell you. I just... I didn't know if you'd want me."

I feel my heart ache at the vulnerability in his voice. How could he ever think I wouldn't want him? Kip has always been the one I wanted, even when I didn't know it was him behind the letters.

"I've always wanted you," I whisper, my voice trembling with emotion. "You don't have to hide from me, Kip. I like you... and your letters."

His eyes widen at my words, and before I can say anything else, he kisses me again, pulling me closer, his lips soft and warm against mine. It's perfect. It's everything I've been dreaming of.

But then a shiver runs down my spine, the cold seeping into my bones from standing still in the cold, away from the heaters and crowd. Kip pulls back, concern flickering in his eyes.

"You're cold," he says, his voice soft as he starts to shrug off his coat.

I laugh, shaking my head. "I have a better idea for how you could warm me up," I say suggestively.

His eyebrows lift in surprise, but then a slow, hopeful, smile spreads across his face. "Oh yeah?"

"Uh-huh," I nod, biting my lip as I take his hand and start leading him toward the parking lot. "Let me tell you about it on the way to your place."

The cold winter air hits us as we step away from the buildings, but it doesn't matter. I've never felt warmer in my life, because tonight, I'm with Kip.

We can't stop smiling at each other as we make the short drive to Kip's house. He lives on the outskirts of town, next to his business, Semper Fly.

"I should have taken my car so you don't have to drive me back to town," I say as we pull into his driveway.

"That old thing might have never made it all of the way out here," he grunts, and I laugh.

"It's actually been running pretty smoothly lately!" I tell him, and he shakes his head.

"No, it hasn't," he grumbles quietly and it clicks then.

"Oh. My. God," I gasp as I turn to face him. "You've been sneaking around and fixing my car!"

He blushes, actually blushes, and clears his throat.

"Yeah, I didn't want you driving around in an unreliable car."

"How many times?" I ask him, my mind racing as I try to remember all of the times when my car wouldn't start or when it seemed like it was starting to act up and then magically was fine.

"I don't know. A few."

"It had to be more than just a few! I mean..." I trail off as I count in my head. "Jeez, Kip, it had to have been like once a month for the last six months at least."

"It's not a big deal," he grumbles, and I shake my head.

"Yes. It is. That was so... amazing of you. You're so sweet, Kip. Thank you."

He nods, and we stare at each other in the dark cab of his truck. I'm not sure who moves first, but soon we're both leaning over the center console, our lips a breath apart.

"Ginger..." His voice is low and rough like he's holding back.

I don't wait. I can't.

Without thinking, I reach for him, my hand sliding up his neck as I lean over the console. I feel the warmth of his skin beneath my fingers, the roughness of his jawline, and before I know it, my lips are on his.

The moment our mouths meet, it's like everything else falls away. The world outside the truck disappears, leaving only the heat of his kiss, the way his lips move against mine with such intensity it makes my head spin. He kisses me back, his hand tangling in my hair as he pulls me closer, and it's like we're both caught in this moment—wild, breathless, unstoppable.

I don't think I've ever wanted someone like this, felt this kind of urgency. My heart is racing, my whole body trembling as I press against him, deepening the kiss. His lips are soft, warm, and when I feel his tongue brush against mine, a shiver runs down my spine. I can't get enough of him. I never want this to stop.

Kip groans softly against my mouth, and the sound sends a jolt of electricity through me. His other hand slides to my waist, gripping me firmly as he pulls me even closer, like he's afraid I'll slip away. But I'm not going anywhere. I want to be right here, in this moment, with him.

I shift in my seat, turning toward him, my hands roaming over his chest, feeling the solid muscle beneath his shirt. He's strong, every inch of him, and it drives me wild knowing he's holding back for me, controlling that strength even as the tension between us builds.

"Kip..." I whisper against his lips, my breath ragged, my heart pounding. His name comes out like a plea, and he responds by kissing me harder, deeper, his fingers tightening in my hair.

I don't know how long we kiss—seconds, minutes, it could be hours for all I know. Time doesn't seem to matter when I'm with him like this, lost in the feel of him, the taste of him. The windows of the truck fog up, the world outside blurring into nothingness as we lose ourselves in each other.

When we finally break apart, we're both breathless, our foreheads resting against each other as we struggle to catch our breath. My lips feel swollen, tingling from the heat of the kiss, and my heart is still racing in my chest.

Kip looks at me, his eyes dark with desire, his breath warm against my skin. "I've been wanting to do that all night," he murmurs, his voice rough with need.

I smile, my fingers still tracing the line of his jaw, my own desire mirrored in his gaze. "Me too."

For a moment, we just stay like that, our bodies pressed close, the heat between us still simmering. I can feel his heart pounding against mine, and there's a part of me that wants more. I decide to listen to that part of me.

"Let's go inside," I whisper, and he nods.

We climb out of the truck, and he rushes over to my side, helping me down and taking my hand as we head up to the front porch.

He unlocks the door and ushers me in ahead of him. I scan his place, as I take off my jacket, hat, and mittens, taking in the mostly bare living room and kitchen.

"Nice place."

"Thanks."

He turns on some lights, and I wander further into the house.

"Want the tour?" He asks, and I nod. "Well, you've already seen the living room and kitchen."

I nod. "Very nice."

He takes my hand, and we head down the long hallway.

"This is the guest bathroom," he says, nudging the first door open. "And this is the first guest bedroom...and the second," he says, pushing open the next two doors. "And this... is my room."

I step into his room, and the tension between us grows as I wander closer to the king-size bed. The bed is neatly made, the corners of the dark blue comforter perfectly folded down, and I wonder if that was a habit that he always had or if he picked it up in the military.

"I like it."

"You can change anything that you don't like about the house," he says instantly.

I laugh, thinking that he's joking, but I turn to see him watching me with a serious look on his face.

"Wait, what?"

"Ginger," he starts, his voice low and rough. "I need to tell you something."

I nod, starting to get nervous as he shifts. He looks so anxious and I wonder what it is that he has to tell me.

"I... I've been falling in love with you," he tells me, the words coming out in a rush, like they've been trapped inside him for too long. "For a long time now."

My eyes widen, but not in shock.

"I love you," he says, his voice barely above a whisper. "I just needed you to know."

"I do know," I tell him. "I know, and I love you too. So much."

"So much?" He asks quietly, and I nod.

"So much."

For a moment, there's silence. Then, without warning, he leans forward, his lips crashing against mine in a kiss that's filled with everything—every unspoken word, every emotion we've both been holding back all these months.

It's soft at first, tentative, like we're testing the waters, but then something shifts. His hands tangle in my hair, pulling me closer, and I feel the heat between us ignite like a spark catching flame. I kiss him back with everything I have, pouring months of longing into every movement, every touch.

My body presses against his, and I feel him groan against my lips, the sound sending a rush of heat through me. His hands slide down to my waist as we deepen the kiss, my heart pounding in my chest. He feels so good, so *right*.

We break apart for air, our breaths coming in ragged gasps, and when I look into his dark blue eyes, I see everything—desire, love, tenderness, all mixed together in a way that makes my heart swell.

"I love you, Kip," I whisper as his forehead rests against mine. "I think I've loved you from your first letter."

We kiss again, slower this time, more deliberate, like we're savoring the moment. My hands roam over his chest, and I feel his pulse quicken, the heat between us growing with every passing second. I wonder if he can feel me trembling slightly as my fingers tighten in his shirt.

The kiss deepens, passion flaring hot and fast between us, and I lose myself in him—his touch, his scent, the sounds he makes as he holds me close. Nothing else matters. It's just us here in this moment, and I never want it to end.

Kip's hands slide down to my hips and toy with the hem of my sweater. I hum against his lips in agreement and a moment later, he's slipping the soft wool sweater over my head and tossing it aside. We stare at each other, both of us breathing hard. The lust is palpable in the air around us, and I feel like I'm burning up alive as he stares at me.

"I want you so fucking bad, Ginger," he whispers, and I swallow hard and nod.

"I'm yours. Take me."

That's all it takes and it's like a flip switches in Kip. He takes charge. There are no more soft kisses; it's all passion. I can taste his desperate need for me on his lips, and it drives me wild.

"Naked," he grunts at me, and I nod, scrambling to push my plaid leggings down my legs and kick them off. My thick wool socks follow, and then my panties.

"Bra," he orders as he drops to his knees at the edge of the bed.

I arch, reaching to unhook my bra, and his big hands grip my thighs, yanking me to the edge of the mattress. I blink, my brain trying to keep up with everything that he's doing.

"Kip," I breathe a second before he leans forward and buries his face in my pussy. "Fuck!" I shout, my bra long forgotten.

He's so enthusiastic as he licks me, practically devours me, and all I can do is lay there and let him have his way with me. So many emotions and feelings are building inside of me as his tongue licks over my clit, sucking the little pearl into his mouth.

"Kip! Oh, God," I gasp, moaning his name as his fingers spread me wider.

"So damn sweet," he moans against my core, and I grip the bedspread beneath me tighter as his tongue licks down to my opening, licking up more of my juices as he goes.

"Oh!" I gasp as his tongue wiggles into my snug hole just a little bit.

"So tight. Gonna have to loosen you up," he murmurs, and I nod desperately.

"I need you," I beg, and he runs a finger between my folds, the digit swirling over my clit and driving me wild. "Please, Kip," I pant. "Don't tease me."

I love seeing this confident side of him: how he's taking control, how needy he seems to be to have me, and how he looks and touches me like I'm something precious.

We lock eyes and stare at each other as he slowly works one thick finger into me. I wince at the sharp string of pressure as he stretches me and he swallows hard.

"Are you a virgin, baby?" He asks, his voice low and guttural.

I nod silently, and he closes his eyes for a moment.

"Were you saving yourself for me?" He croaks, and I nod again. "Thank fuck. I was waiting for you too, baby."

I want to ask if that means that he's a virgin, too, but before I can, his mouth is back on me, and I forget about everything else.

His mouth loves my clit while he adds another finger, stretching my pussy wider. He works them in and out of me slowly, and a pressure starts to build low in my stomach, coiling tighter and tighter until it snaps.

"Kip!" I cry out as I fall over the edge, riding his fingers as my orgasm flows through me.

"Fuck, that was so fucking hot," he groans, and I look down to see him licking his fingers clean.

I sit up, intending to return the favor, but before I can, Kip grabs me and moves me to the center of the bed. He strips quickly, and I can only stare at his perfect body as he joins me in the middle of the bed.

"Sorry. It's not pretty to look at," he whispers, and I blink, looking up at him with confusion.

"What?" I ask, and he looks away from me.

"The scars," he says, and I blink, taking him in again.

"These?" I whisper, my fingers stroking over the raised red lines on his face, down his neck, and down his chest to his shoulder.

"Yeah," he chokes out.

My fingers trail lower to the other scars and bumps on his hip, and I look up at him.

"Bullets and an IED," he tells me without me having to ask.

"I'm sorry that you went through that," I whisper, leaning forward and pressing a kiss to one scar and then the next, and then the next.

"Ginger," he says, and I can hear the doubt in his voice.

I'm no stranger to being self-conscious. I've always been a bigger girl, and I've had to work to be confident in my own skin.

"I love your body. You look like a warrior. You *are* a warrior," I tell him as I continue to trail kisses across the scars. "Look at how strong you are. How brave."

I kiss lower, pushing him onto his back as I settle between his thighs. His cock is hard and resting against his flat stomach, and I place a kiss next to his belly button.

He sucks in a sharp breath, and I smile up at him as I wrap my hands around his dick.

"I might not be good at this," I warn him.

"You're doing amazing already," he says hoarsely, and I smile.

"I'm not really doing anything," I point out and he swallows hard.

"You're sitting next to me, naked, with your hand on my cock. I'm about two seconds from coming," he says, and it's the biggest ego boost that I've ever gotten.

"Have you thought about me, about us, doing this before?" I ask him as I lean down and swipe my tongue over the tip of his cock, licking up the drop of precum there.

"Only every single day for the past year."

"And what do I do in these fantasies?" I ask him as I trail my tongue down the underside of his cock.

"Fuck, Ginger," he groans, and I grin.

"Uh huh, but *how* do we fuck?" I ask him, and he stares down at me with fierce eyes.

"Every way. There's not a single thing that we haven't done in my head," he tells me, and I nod.

"You'll have to make a list so that we can get to all of it."

"A... list?" He asks, his eyes going hazy as I wrap my lips around him and start to suck his cock.

"Hmm," I hum around him, and his thighs tense.

"Fuck," he grits out, his hand coming up to tangle in my dark red hair.

I take more of him, all of the way until he bumps against the back of my throat. His length is starting to swell on my tongue already, and I swallow around him, wanting to taste his release.

"Ginger...baby...," he pants, and I wrap my hand around the length that I can't get in my mouth, working him in time with my mouth. "Ginger. Ginger!" He shouts, his hand tightening in my hair.

A moment later, his salty release coats my tongue, and I hurry to swallow it all down. I sit back on my heels and watch him as he catches his breath. Finally, he opens his eyes and looks right at me.

"I love you."

He says it so fiercely, and I nod. This man loves me with every fiber of his being. And I love him.

"I know. I love you too. Now make me yours."

He moves, rolling me under him, and I spread my legs wider for him, offering him all of me.

"You've been mine since you stepped foot in this town. You'll always be mine," he tells me as he starts to push into me.

"Yours," I agree, my body already starting to race for my release as he slowly bottoms out inside of me.

I don't even feel when he takes my virginity. All I can feel is his love for me. All I can focus on is him.

He kisses me, his hands on my breast, in my hair. It's like he can't stop touching me, even as he makes love to me. I wrap my legs around his waist, clinging to him as my orgasm brews inside of me. He kisses me, whispers that he loves me and I come undone.

"Kip!" I scream as I come, and he groans my name as he follows me over the edge.

I'm not sure when he moves, but a moment later, we're lying on our sides facing each other, both of us still panting and flushed.

"So that's one fantasy," I tell him and he huffs out a laugh.

"One down. A million more to go," he whispers, and I smile as I cuddle into his side.

I just need to close my eyes for a moment. That's what I tell myself as I nestle against him and slowly let sleep claim me.

I feel Kip kiss my forehead right before I drift off.

"Merry Christmas, Ginger," he whispers, and I smile as I fall asleep.

NINE

Kip

"SO IT GOES OLIVE, then Maple, then Saffron, and you're the baby," I clarify, and she nods against my chest. "Did you like being the baby?"

"Yeah, I just wish that... I had more time with them," she finishes softly, and I know that she's talking about her parents.

"I know, baby. I'm sorry."

"What about you? Ever wish that you had siblings?"

"Sometimes. It was lonely growing up with two doctors for parents. They were always too busy off saving other people to remember me, and then I would feel guilty for wishing that they were with me when I knew that their patients needed them."

"You needed them, too," she reminds me, and I nod.

"Yeah."

"Do you ever talk to them?"

"Sometimes, but not a lot. They're disappointed in me. They wanted me to be a doctor too, but I couldn't. It's not what I wanted."

"I couldn't do it either. All of the blood and stuff," she says with a shudder, and I smile.

"What do you want to do?" I ask her as I rub her back lazily with my fingers.

"I don't know. I just... I always wanted to be a mom. I want a family. I want a home."

"I'll give you that," I promise her, and she smiles up at me.

"I know you will."

She kisses my chest, and I smile. I could stay like this with her forever.

"We should get up," Ginger whispers, and I tighten my arms around her.

We've been lying in bed and cuddling, talking about anything and everything for the last few hours, and I don't want it to stop. I love being with her like this. It feels so right, so natural, and effortless.

"Five more minutes," I argue, and she laughs.

"We're going to be late if we stay in bed any longer."

I groan as she pulls away from me and watch as she stands and heads towards the bathroom.

"Come on. I'll let you wash my back," she says with a wink, and I grin.

"Anything else you want me to wash?" I ask, and she giggles as she heads into my bathroom.

She invited me and Huxley to spend Christmas with her family and friends, and we're due to be at her eldest sister, Olive's, house in an hour. I'm nervous to be around so many people, but Ginger is so excited, and I know that I'll have to get used to it. These people are going to be my in-laws, my family, soon. Very soon, if I get my way.

I step into the bathroom after Ginger, watching as she turns on the shower, and she smiles at me in the mirror, giving me an idea.

"Eyes on me, baby," I tell her, my voice low and filled with promise.

Her breathing shallows, and she watches me excitedly as I step up behind her. I keep my eyes locked on hers until her ass squirms against me. Then I grin wickedly and let my eyes drop, taking in all of her sexy curves.

She's so perfect. Every inch of her is like a work of art.

Normally, I would be self-conscious to have my scars on full display, but with Ginger, I forget all about them. She makes me feel handsome, like I'm the sexiest man alive. She makes me see my scars in a new light.

"Spread your legs," I order, and she hurries to widen her stance. "Wider," I growl, and a crimson blush spreads from her face down to her full tits.

I can see how turned on she is before I even look between her legs.

"You're soaked for me, baby. Does someone need their man to give them a nice good fuck?" I ask her, and she nods eagerly.

"Kip," she gasps as my cock brushes against her drenched folds.

"Hmm?" I hum as I reach up, my hands cupping her breasts, feeling the weight of them in my palms.

"Please!" She begs, and I grin.

"Since you asked so nicely," I whisper against the shell of her ear, and she shivers against me, her eyes locked on me.

I grip her hips, jerking them back until I'm lined up with her tight opening. We lock eyes once again as I slowly start to sink into her, my hands gripping her hips tightly as inch after inch slowly stretches her pussy.

"Fucking dripping for me," I groan, and she nods, her breaths coming in short pants as I fill her completely.

She's so tight, and I let go of her hip, reaching around and finding her clit. As soon as my thumb starts to stroke that little button, Ginger gasps, her eyes darkening as her pussy clamps down on my length.

We stare at each other in the mirror, the glass starting to get foggy from the steam from the shower. I start to move in and out of her, when her phone rings.

"The party," she gasps, and I grunt in acknowledgment, my pace picking up.

My hips slam into her ass over and over again, driving both of us higher with each thrust. She's so damn tight, so wet and hot, and everything that I will ever need.

Ginger grips the bathroom counter tight as I pound into her. I can tell that she's close, and I am too, but I need her to come first.

"Give it to me, baby," I order, my thumb working her clit in tight circles.

She cries out my name, and I can't take it.

I pull out, spinning her around and lifting her onto the counter. Then I'm slamming into her in the next breath.

"Kip!" She screams, and I grip her legs, holding them open as I rut into her.

Her tits are bouncing with each thrust, and I grit my teeth, my eyes locking with hers as she starts to come. Her juices coat my cock, her walls tightening around me, forcing my own orgasm out of me.

"Fuck," I grit out, and she moans my name.

Steam fills the room as we catch our breath and she smiles at me.

"It keeps getting better and better," she tells me, and I nod.

"Always. Now, wrap your legs around my waist. I'm not done with you," I tell her as my hands cup her ass, and I lift her, carrying her under the hot spray of the shower.

"We're going to be late," she whispers against my mouth and I shake my head.

"I can multitask," I tell her, grabbing her shampoo and massaging it into her hair with one hand while the other keeps her on my cock.

She squirms against me, bouncing up and down slightly, and I plant my feet, giving her more leverage. It doesn't take long before we've both forgotten about the shampoo and shower.

Her back rests against the shower tile, and we make out like teenagers as I slide lazily in and out of her. My cock brushes over her clit, and she moans against me. I kiss down her neck, my lips wrapping around one stiff nipple and sucking it into my mouth. She pants above me, and the sound echoes off the walls of the shower. It's music to my ears.

"I love you, Ginger. More than anything," I whisper against her wet skin.

"I love you too."

Our lips find each other again, and our movements pick up. We move together perfectly and it doesn't take long before we're both reaching our peaks once again.

She sighs as I set her down on her feet, and I smile as I grab her body wash and start to rub it over her body until soap bubbles cover every inch of her.

"My turn," she says, doing the same to me, and I smile as her hands move over my body.

"Love you," I say as we step out, and I wrap her in a towel.

"Love you too."

We race to get dry and then to get dressed. We make a quick stop at Ginger's apartment to grab the gifts that she got for everyone and then make the short drive to Olive and Xavier's place.

"Ready?" She asks me, and I nod.

"Yeah, I'm ready."

We gather up the presents, and I pause, passing her the one that I got for her.

"For me?" She asks, delighted, and I smile.

"Yeah. Open it."

She tears at the wrapping paper, and I watch her face as she lifts the lid and looks inside.

"It's...paperwork?" She asks as she pulls out the papers.

"No...well, yeah, for right now. I got you a puppy."

She looks up at me in surprise and I smile.

"I've seen you with all of the dogs in town. You love them. I just... I thought... I—"

"Thank you!" She shouts, wrapping her arms around me so tightly that I almost can't breathe. "Thank you, thank you."

"Of course. I'd do anything to make you happy, Ginger."

"I can't have a dog in my apartment," she tells me and I grin.

"Guess you'll have to move in with me then."

"Oh yeah?" She asks with a wide smile.

"Yeah."

"We'll see," she says, but I can tell that she's in.

"Merry Christmas, Ginger."

"Merry Christmas, Kip. I love you."

"I love you too."

"Best Christmas ever," she says, and I can't help but agree.

It's our first Christmas together, and I intend to make every other one perfect.

TEN

Ginger

FIVE YEARS LATER...

FIVE YEARS. It's hard to believe that it's been five years since that Christmas when everything changed. Since I found out that my secret admirer—the man I'd been falling for in those letters—was Kip. Five years since that fateful kiss under the mistletoe that sealed my heart to his.

Now, here we are, five years later, and Christmas has become even more magical than it used to be.

I stand in the doorway of our cozy little house, watching the snow fall softly outside. The world is quiet, blanketed in white, and the Christmas lights twinkle in the trees lining our street. It's perfect—just like the life we've built together.

Kip is in the living room, decorating the tree with the same focus and intensity he puts into everything. He's carefully hanging ornaments, stepping back every now and then to make sure everything is in its right place. I can't help but smile as I watch him, remembering how far we've come from that first Christmas.

"Kip," I call softly, stepping into the room. "You're going to run out of branches if you keep hanging ornaments that close together."

He looks over his shoulder at me, a grin spreading across his face. "I'm just making sure it's perfect."

"It's already perfect," I say, crossing the room to stand beside him. I wrap my arms around his waist, resting my chin on his shoulder as we both look at the tree.

Five years ago, I never would have imagined we'd be here. But now, with the tree glowing warmly in front of us, the house filled with the smell of fresh pine and the faint sound of Christmas music playing in the background, I can't imagine my life any other way.

"It's beautiful," I murmur, my arms tightening around him.

He leans down, pressing a kiss to the top of my head. "Not as beautiful as you."

I laugh softly, rolling my eyes. "You've been saying that for years, you know."

"Because it's true," he says, turning in my arms so that we're face to face.

I look up at him, my heart swelling with love. There's still a part of me that's amazed by how far we've come, how lucky I am to have found someone like Kip. He's everything I've ever wanted, and more than I ever thought I deserved. Five years, and I'm still falling in love with him every single day.

Goldfish comes into the room, and I bend down to

scratch him behind the ears before he heads over to his dog bed in the corner.

Kip and I got married six months after we got together, in a small ceremony here in Wolf Valley. Then we spent two weeks in Hawaii, enjoying the sun and water and each other. Two weeks after we got back home, we found out that I was pregnant.

To say that it was a whirlwind would be an understatement, but Kip was so strong and supportive throughout it all. It made me fall in love with him even more.

Since then, we've had our son, moved into a bigger house, and grown the business. I started working with Kip and Huxley at their company, and I've been handling the admin work ever since.

"You know," Kip says, his voice soft, "I was thinking about that first Christmas, when I finally got the nerve to kiss you under the mistletoe."

I smile, remembering it as if it were yesterday. "You mean when I ran across the room and practically jumped into your arms?"

He chuckles, his eyes crinkling at the corners. "Yeah, that part. I still think about how scared I was that night, wondering if you'd actually want me after you found out I was the one writing those letters."

My smile widens, and I press a kiss to his jaw. "I wanted you more than anything."

"And now?" he asks, his voice playful but with a hint of seriousness beneath it.

"Now," I say, leaning up on my tiptoes to kiss him softly, "I still want you. Always."

His arms wrap around me, pulling me closer, and for a moment, we're lost in each other, the rest of the world fading away like it always does when we're together.

But then a sound breaks the silence—a tiny voice from the other side of the room.

"Mama! Dada!"

Kip and I both turn at the sound, and my heart swells as I see our little boy, Sawyer, standing by the fireplace, his wide green eyes sparkling with excitement. He's holding one of the Christmas ornaments in his small hands, his dark hair a messy mop on his head.

"Look!" Sawyer says, holding up the ornament proudly.

I walk over, kneeling down in front of him as he shows me the ornament—a small wooden heart with the word *Love* carved into it. It's one of the first ornaments Kip and I ever bought together, back when we were just starting out, before our lives got filled with all the little moments and memories that now decorate our tree.

"Do you want to put it on the tree?" I ask, smiling at him.

Sawyer nods enthusiastically, his face lighting up with excitement. I stand up and help him reach one of the branches near the bottom of the tree, and he carefully hangs the ornament in place, his little face serious with concentration.

"Tada!" he says proudly.

"It's perfect!" I compliment him.

Kip walks over, ruffling Sawyer's hair with a grin. "You're right, buddy. It's perfect."

I step back, watching the two of them, and my heart feels like it might burst. This is our life now—our little family, our home filled with warmth and love, and it's more than I ever could have dreamed of.

The doorbell rings, and Sawyer's eyes widen with excitement. "Is it Santa?" he asks, bouncing on his toes.

I laugh, shaking my head. "No, sweetheart, it's probably Aunt Cora and Uncle Huxley."

Sawyer's face lights up even more at the mention of his favorite aunt and uncle, and he races toward the door, his little feet barely touching the ground as he runs.

I glance at Kip, who's grinning as he watches Sawyer disappear down the hallway. "You know, five years ago, I wouldn't have imagined us here," I say softly.

Kip turns to me, his expression softening. "Yeah. It's crazy to think about how much has changed."

I nod, my gaze drifting back to the tree, the soft glow of the lights casting a warm, golden hue over the room. "I didn't think I'd ever find this—find *you*—and now I can't imagine life without it."

Kip steps closer, wrapping his arms around me from behind. "I couldn't imagine it either."

I smile, leaning back against him as we stand there, soaking in the quiet of the moment.

The door opens, and I hear the familiar sound of laughter as Cora and Huxley step inside, Sawyer's excited voice echoing through the house as he tells them all about the tree and the ornaments he helped hang.

"Merry Christmas!" Cora calls out as she walks into the living room, her arms full of gifts, her face glowing with happiness.

"Merry Christmas," I reply, stepping forward to give her a hug. "You're just in time."

Huxley grins, clapping Kip on the back. "This place looks amazing. You guys went all out this year."

Kip chuckles. "Well, you know Ginger. She doesn't do anything halfway when it comes to Christmas."

I smile, shaking my head at him as I help Cora with the

gifts. It's true—I've always loved Christmas, and ever since Kip and I started this tradition of decorating together, it's become even more special. Especially now that we get to share it with Sawyer and our friends.

The evening passes in a blur of laughter and warmth, the house filled with the sound of music and the smell of gingerbread cookies baking in the oven. Sawyer is bouncing around, showing off the decorations to Cora and Huxley, while Kip and I steal quiet glances at each other, little moments of connection that remind me how lucky I am.

As the night winds down, and the house falls into a comfortable silence, I find myself standing by the window, watching the snow fall gently outside. The world is peaceful, and my heart feels full.

Kip walks up behind me, his arms wrapping around my waist as he rests his chin on my shoulder. "You okay?"

I nod, leaning back into him. "Yeah. I'm more than okay."

We stand there for a while, watching the snow, and I think about how far we've come, how much has changed. Five years ago, I was standing under the mistletoe, waiting for Kip to show up, nervous and unsure of what the future would bring.

Now, as I stand here with him, with our son asleep upstairs and our friends gathered in the warmth of our home, I know that I've found everything I've ever wanted.

"I love you," Kip whispers, his breath warm against my neck.

I smile, turning in his arms to face him. "I love you too."

And as we kiss, the snow falling softly outside, the lights twinkling around us, I know one thing for sure—this is the Christmas I'll remember for the rest of my life.

Because this is *our* Christmas. Our family. Our love. And it's perfect.

Want more of Kip and Ginger? Then be sure to check out this bonus scene of the night that their son, Sawyer, is born!

WANT A FREE BOOK?

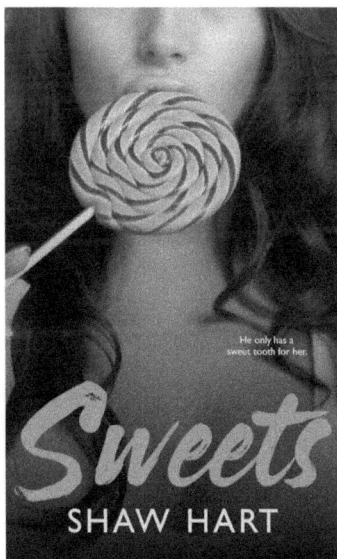

You can grab Sweets Here.
Check out my website, www.shawhart.com for more free books!

ABOUT THE AUTHOR

CONNECT WITH ME!

If you enjoyed this story, please consider leaving a review on Amazon or any other reader site or blog that you like. Don't forget to recommend it to your other reader friends.

If you want to chat with me, please consider joining my VIP list or connecting with me on one of my Social Media platforms. I love talking with each of my readers. Links below!

Website
Newsletter

SERIES BY SHAW HART

<u>Cherry Falls</u>

<u>803 Wishing Lane</u>

<u>1012 Curvy Way</u>

<u>Eye Candy Ink</u>

<u>Atlas</u>

<u>Mischa</u>

<u>Sam</u>

<u>Zeke</u>

<u>Nico</u>

<u>Eye Candy Ink: Second Generation</u>

Ames

Harvey

Rooney

Gray

Ender

Banks

<u>Fallen Peak</u>

A Very Mountain Man Valentine's Day

A Very Mountain Man Halloween

A Very Mountain Man Thanksgiving

A Very Mountain Man Christmas

A Very Mountain Man New Year

Folklore

Kidnapping His Forever

Claiming His Forever

Finding His Forever

Rescuing His Forever

Chasing His Forever

Folklore: The Complete Series

Holiday Hearts

Be Mine

Falling in Love

Holly Jolly Holidays

Love Notes

Signing Off With Love

Care Package Love

Wrong Number, Right Love

Kings Gym

Fighting Fire With Fire

Fighting Tooth and Nail

Fighting Back From Hell

Mine To

Mine to Love

Mine to Protect

Mine to Cherish

ALSO BY SHAW HART

Still in the mood for Christmas books?

Stuffing Her Stocking, Mistletoe Kisses, Snowed in For Christmas, Coming Down Her Chimney

Love holiday books? Check out these!

For Better or Worse, Riding His Broomstick, Thankful for His FAKE Girlfriend, His New Year Resolution, Hop Stuff, Taming Her Beast, Hungry For Dash, His Firework

Looking for some OTT love stories?

Her Scottish Savior, Baby Mama, Tempted By My Roommate, Blame It On The Rum, Wild Ride, Always

Looking for a celebrity love story?

Bedroom Eyes, Seducing Archer, Finding Their Rhythm

In the mood for some young love books?

Study Dates, His Forever, My Girl

Some other books by Shaw:

The Billionaire's Bet, Her Guardian Angel, Falling Again, Stealing Her, Dreamboat, Making Her His, Trouble

A VERY GRUMPY NEW YEAR

*

Moving in with him is starting to feel like a mistake...

Cora

When my rental house gets condemned, I'm not exactly surprised.

I mean, the place was always a dump, but it was all that I could afford.

Now I have a problem.

I need to find a new place to live, which is easier said than done in a small town like Wolf Valley.

Then I learn that the new guy in town is looking for a roommate.

He may just be the answer to my problem... and the man of my dreams.

Huxley

I've wanted Cora since the moment that I saw her.

When I find out where she's living, I know that it's not safe for my girl.

So, I may have pulled a few strings to get her out of there and moved in with me.

Now that we're living together, I have her right where I want her.

I just need to figure out how to make it a permanent thing.

ONE

Cora

I'M NOT SURPRISED.

I mean, I knew that this place was a dump when I first moved in. It was all that I could afford, though, so I did my best to make do. There's no making do with this, though.

I stare at the gaping hole in the ground, the one that my foot went straight through a week ago, and sigh. I had thought that the floorboards in this rental house were alright, but I guess not. My face flushes with embarrassment as I remember walking across the living room and then just crashing straight through it. I would think it was because of my weight, if not for the fact that the whole house is pretty much falling apart.

Still, I would have bet money that the roof or porch would have collapsed before the living room floor. Maybe I should go on a diet...

"What are you thinking about?" A deep voice asks me, and I spin around to face him.

Huxley Jacobs.

My new roommate.

"That I should go on a diet," I tell him, and he frowns.

"No."

With that, he picks up another box and heads out to his truck. I roll my eyes and watch him go.

Huxley was the one who found me struggling to get my leg out of the hole. He had picked me up like I weighed nothing, taken one look at the hole, and announced that I was moving in with him.

A part of me is grateful that he did. I mean, I am grateful that he saved me, though I wish that he had caught me in a sexier position than covered in sweat and dirt and crawling out of the floorboards.

It was a relief to not have to stress and worry about where I would be staying. It's hard to find roommates or rentals in this small town, and I don't know what I would have done if he hadn't declared us roommates.

I could always have asked my friends; I just would have felt guilty. All of them just got into new relationships, and I don't want to be the one to get in the way of any happy couple. My single friends are all living in cramped apartments, and I know that they wouldn't be able to let me crash with them. At least not comfortably.

Speaking of friends, my phone rings with Noelle's name on the screen.

"Hey," I answer with a smile.

"Hey, I was just calling to see if you needed any help with the move," she says.

"Oh, that was nice of you, but we've got it. We're actually just finishing up now."

"That was fast!"

"Yeah, I don't have much," I say with a laugh.

"Okay, well, let me know if you need anything."

"I will," I promise her.

Noelle was one of the first friends that I made when I moved to Wolf Valley. I wish that we could hang out more, but her family keeps her under their thumb quite a bit. It seems like she's always busy with something or helping them out somehow. I hope that she'll put some distance between them soon, but I know that it can be hard to distance yourself from family.

"I'll talk to you later," I tell her as Huxley comes back into the room.

"Talk to you soon."

I hang up and look around the house one last time.

"Is that it?" Huxley asks me, and I turn to face him.

For such a big guy, I don't know how he's always able to get around so quietly, especially in this old house that creaks if you look at it funny.

"Did they teach you how to sneak up on someone in the Marines?" I ask him and he blinks.

"Yes."

I roll my eyes. The guy never gives me much. I've seen him laughing and smiling with his friend, Kip, so I know that he's capable of it. With me, though, he seems to only be able to manage one or two-word sentences. It's started to become a challenge for me to get him to say more than a handful of words at the same time. So far, I'm not winning.

"You're really good at it."

He grunts at me, and I frown at his back as he takes one last look around the place.

"I was never very good at sneaking around. I was always the first one caught in hide and seek," I tell him.

Another grunt.

"For the love of God, *use your words!*" I snap at him, and he blinks at me in surprise.

"Okay."

"Oh my God," I groan as I stomp past him.

I head out to my car and climb behind the wheel. Huxley is right behind me and he heads my way, leaning down to see me through the window. I stubbornly refuse to roll it down.

Alright, and maybe the window also doesn't work in my car so I couldn't roll it down even if I wanted to. Which I don't.

He sighs, shaking his head, and then stands and opens my door.

"You need a new car," he tells me, and I glare at him.

"Really? Why?" I ask sarcastically, but he answers me anyway.

"This thing can barely run. Half of the features don't even work," he says, reaching down and hitting the window button. My car screeches, and I swat his hand away.

"Yeah, well, in case it wasn't obvious based on my old living arrangements, I can't afford a new car or to fix this one."

"It's a good thing that this place is being condemned," he tells me and I want to punch him right in his handsome face.

"Good for you maybe," I grumble and he looks away.

I stare at my new roommate, trying to convince myself that moving in with him isn't going to be my biggest regret in life, but it's hard to believe that.

The man drives me crazy. Normally, I'm pretty laid back and easy going, but when I'm around Huxley, I'm on edge. I can't quite name the feeling and maybe that's what throws me off around him.

I mean, sure, I'm attracted to him. Who wouldn't be? The man is gorgeous. He's close to six and a half feet tall, tan from being outside so much, with deep green eyes and dark brown hair, and he has this whole rugged vibe thing going on that would make any girl swoon.

Including me.

Huxley doesn't seem to be interested in dating or girls, though. At least, not as far as I can tell. I've never seen him with anyone in town other than Kip. I've never seen him so much as look at any of the women in town, either.

Ginger, my best friend, is convinced that Huxley has a crush on me, but I think that she's just saying that because she's dating Huxley's best friend, Kip, and she thinks it would be fun if we were also dating best friends.

"You can follow me home. Hopefully, your car makes it," he mumbles, and I want to yell at him, but he slams my door shut and ambles over to his truck.

I glare at him the whole way.

Why did I think that moving in with him was going to be a good idea? I mean, my body can't decide if I hate him or want to jump him.

Why can't it be both? My subconscious asks, but I ignore her.

Huxley pulls out of my drive and I follow after him slowly.

This is a mistake, but I don't know what else to do. There's nowhere else in town that's renting, and I can't afford to buy anything.

I just need to make it through a few months with Huxley. I can save up and move out. Then I can avoid him for the rest of my life.

I just need to not kill the guy or buy into Ginger's whole fantasy that he wants me too. As long as I can keep my heart safe around the guy, then I can make it a few months as his roommate.

Right?

TWO

Huxley

"SHE KNOWS," I blurt as soon as Kip answers my call.

"Hello to you too," he says sarcastically, and I grit my teeth.

"She knows," I repeat.

"Who knows what?"

"Cora! She knows that I sabotaged her house and called the city to have it condemned."

"You did what?" He asks, alarmed.

"Her house was terrible. It wasn't safe."

"So... you made it even more unsafe?"

"I did what I had to do to keep her safe."

"That's why you were by her house the other day."

"Yeah, I needed to be close by in case she needed me."

"Needed you because you cut a floorboard in her living room and made her fall through."

"You've seen her house," I argue. "If it hadn't been that, it would have been the roof falling in on her. I made sure that the dirt was piled up so that she wouldn't fall far or get hurt. She was never in any real danger," I argue, and he sighs.

"You're crazy," he groans.

"Like you wouldn't have done the same for Ginger. You were sneaking around fixing her car for her for months," I remind him.

"Speaking of cars," he starts, and I cut him off.

"I know. Her car is going next."

My eyes cut back to my rearview mirror to check on my girl and make sure that her dumpster fire of a car is still behind me.

"How are you going to manage that? Cut her brake lines?" he asks me sarcastically, and I roll my eyes.

"No. I haven't figured that part out yet. Maybe I'll tell her that she won a prize or something."

Kip sighs, but doesn't say anything. It's not like he could. He would do the same thing for his girl, and we both know it.

"So, what's the plan then?" He asks me.

"Well, she's moving in so I'm already one step closer to making her mine."

"I don't think so," he mumbles, and I frown.

"Why? What have you heard?"

"Ginger told me that Cora's plan is to save up money and move out fast. She said since you're not charging her rent, she thinks she can be out in two or three months. Maybe less if she picks up more shifts or holiday hours."

"Dammit," I curse under my breath.

"Should have charged her rent," he says unhelpfully.

"I don't need or want her money. I thought by not charging her rent, I would be showing her that I could be a good provider."

Kip hums on the other end of the line, and I groan.

"What the hell do I do?" I ask him, and he's silent. "Kip!"

"Dude, I don't know! I'm still not a hundred percent sure how I managed to get Ginger so I'm not going to be any help with your lady problems."

"I need to figure it out."

"Maybe just start by asking her out?" He suggests, and I mull over his idea as I turn down my street.

I've been obsessed with Cora since she moved to town, and who wouldn't be? I mean, she's gorgeous—the most beautiful woman that I've ever seen. It was her pale blonde hair that had first caught my attention, but then she had smiled at me, and her pretty hazel eyes had sparkled with so much joy. Her optimism and happiness were addicting.

I couldn't stay away from her, but I've never managed to have much of a conversation with her. I get so nervous and end up mumbling some nonsense or clamming up every single time that I've tried. Maybe being around her so much now that we're living together will fix that, though, and I can ask her out.

"Or I can make her dinner at home and secretly date her that way," I say.

"Yeah, I think that you might be secretly dating her while she has no idea then," he points out. "Just ask her out. You were always encouraging me to go for it with Ginger. Now you need to take your own advice."

"And if she says no and then is uncomfortable around me, and we have to live together?" I ask him.

"Then she moves in with me, I guess."

I growl, and he laughs.

"I wouldn't be that happy about it either, but we both know that Ginger would ask, and I can't tell my girl no."

I can't let Cora go. Not now when I finally have her close to me. This is my chance to finally show her how good we could be together. I just need to not mess it up.

"Are you going into work today?" He asks me as I turn into my driveway.

"Yeah, I'll be there in a bit. I need to get Cora settled here first."

Kip and I got out of the Marines last year after he almost died. I think that it shook both of us up, and since we've been best friends since like birth, I decided to get out too and follow him here to Wolf Valley. We opened up our own helicopter tourism business here called Semper Fly, and we run it together. We've even hired a fellow Marine, Ansel, to help us out starting in January.

"Alright, I'll see you in a bit then. We can show Ansel around the place, finish up his paperwork, and then we can brainstorm ideas while we finish up work."

"Thanks, man. I'll see you soon."

I end the call as I park in my driveway and climb out. Cora is looking around and I watch her. I hope that she likes the place.

Would it be too much to tell her that I'm obsessed with her, and that I would do anything for her, including remodeling this entire house or buying her a different place here in town?

Probably, I decide as I start to unload boxes from my truck.

We head up to the front door and I unlock it, motioning for her to go in ahead of me.

"Welcome home," I tell her

I send up a silent prayer that it really is her home, her permanent one, as I start to bring in boxes.

THREE

Cora

IT'S BEEN A FEW DAYS, and I finally feel like I've settled in. The house is beautiful, and I love my room with a view of the mountains and forest. Plus, it's just nice not to have to worry about something breaking or the floorboards giving out under me.

It also helps that Huxley has been away so much. He had a big tour come into town and has been working like crazy. Something that he curiously didn't seem happy about. You'd think that he would be thrilled since that meant that business was going well, but he just grumbled before he left each morning.

Then, there was a storm that hit a little further north of Wolf Valley, and he and Kip volunteered to help search the nearby ski resort for anyone who was injured or in need of help. So, for having lived with him for three days, I haven't actually seen that much of him.

That looks like it's about to change, I think as I hear his truck pull into the driveway.

"You're home early," I say from the couch as he walks in.

His dark green eyes find me, and I fight not to squirm under his gaze.

"Weather is getting bad, so all flights have been canceled for the rest of that day."

I nod and watch as he toes off his boots. I'm not sure if I'm hoping that he will come and join me in the living room or leave me alone.

He turns and heads over to the couch, and I swallow as I watch him drop down onto the cushioned seat next to me.

"What are you doing?" He asks me, his voice rough and deep.

"Nothing. I'm bored."

"No work today?"

"No, we're all off until after the holidays."

He nods and I roll my eyes at his lack of conversation skills.

"I love Christmas and New Years," I tell him, "But sometimes this time of year can be so boring. It feels like time seems to rush all of the way up until Christmas, and then it just grinds to a standstill for a few days."

"You don't like the break?"

"I do, I just wish that I had more to do sometimes."

He nods, and I sigh, sitting up more.

"What about you?"

"What about me?"

"What's your favorite holiday?"

"Um, Christmas, I guess."

"What did you do for Christmas when you were

younger?" I ask him, settling back against the pillows as I turn to face him.

He does the same, getting comfortable on the other end of the couch and watching me right back.

"We went to visit family most years. We would spend Christmas Eve and Christmas with my mom's side of the family and then make the drive to my dad's side and spend New Years with them."

"Where are you from again?" I ask him.

"Destiny Falls. It's this tiny town in Michigan."

"You didn't want to go back there when you left the Marines?"

"No, there's not a lot left there for me. My parents split up a few years ago, but they both still live in town. I've gone back to visit and I can't handle the constant arguing. The holidays are the worst because they both want me to spend them with each of them, and it gets tough having to choose and upset one or the other."

"I bet," I say softly.

He clears his throat, and I know that he's about to shift the conversation to me.

"What about you?"

"What about me?" I ask with a smile, and the corners of his lips tilt up.

"Where are you from?"

"Raleigh, North Carolina."

"You're a long way from home."

"Yep."

"You don't like North Carolina?" He pries, and I shake my head.

"No, my parents divorced when I was really young, but they had started a business together, so they never really got any space from each other."

"They didn't sell the business? Or split it?"

"Nope, neither one of them wanted to give it up. Both too stubborn, I guess."

"And you were in the middle," he guesses, and I nod.

"Always. I hated it. I always had to try to lighten the mood and diffuse any of the tension. When I got older, I just started leaving. I would say I was going to help with accounting just to escape them and I ended up kind of disappearing into the math. Stuff made sense there."

He nods, and I swallow hard. I hate talking about my family and childhood, but Huxley doesn't make me feel judged. If anything, he seems to understand how hard it is to be stuck in the middle.

"I'm sorry that you had to go through that."

"You too," I whisper.

"So, that's how you decided to go into accounting?" He asks, and I nod.

"Yeah, I loved it. I think that my parents thought that I would come back and work for them again after graduation, but I just couldn't. I mean, you should have seen them at my graduation ceremony. They got into a screaming match at dinner, and I decided for sure right then and there that I was going to go far away from them."

"Why Wolf Valley?" He asks, and I shrug.

"There was just something about this town. Some kind of magic," I say with a smile, hoping that I don't sound crazy.

"Yeah," he agrees, and my smile widens.

"Are you hungry?" I ask, and he nods.

"Almost always."

I giggle as I push to my feet.

"Want to make dinner with me and then watch a movie

or something? Looks like the weather is going to be too bad to go out tonight."

"Sure."

He follows me into the kitchen, and I ask him about helicopters and how they decided to start Semper Fly as we make spaghetti and carry it into the living room. He lets me pick the movie as he adds some more wood to the fireplace, and soon I'm snuggled under a blanket, watching Bridesmaids.

He's not that bad of a roommate, I think as my eyes start to drift shut.

I'm not sure when I fall asleep exactly, but I start to stir as I'm lifted into a pair of strong, muscular arms.

"Shh, I've got you," Huxley whispers, and I smile.

He actually might just be the best roommate that I've ever had.

FOUR

Huxley

"STORM HAS PASSED," I say as soon as Cora walks into the kitchen.

"Huh?" She asks sleepily, and all I can think is *fuck, she's so adorable.*

"The storm passed, and I was thinking... you said that you were bored and didn't have anything to do. Well, what if you came to Semper Fly with me today? I can take you up for a tour."

"You don't have any tours already booked?" She asks me, and I shake my head.

"Not until the New Year."

She bites on her bottom lip, and I can see her debating it in her head.

"Alright," she agrees, and it feels like I just won the biggest prize.

She trusts me.

"Great. I'm ready whenever you are."

"I'll just go get dressed," she says, turning and back-tracking to her room.

She doesn't know it, but I put her in the master bedroom. I just couldn't stand the thought of her living in our house and not being in our bedroom. I'll tell her soon enough.

She's back downstairs a few minutes later, and I pass her a bowl as I head for the door.

"Thanks! This stuff is my favorite," she says as she takes a big bite of the yogurt parfait.

"I know," I tell her without thinking, and she frowns for a second.

Understanding dawns in her hazel eyes, and I'm sure that she's figured out just how crazy in love with her I am. Part of me is eager for her to know the truth, for it to be out in the open so that we can both deal with it. I just need one of us to say it out loud, but when she opens her mouth, that's not what comes out.

"Because the fridge is full of yogurt and fruit, huh? Sorry about that, I won't buy this stuff in bulk next time."

"What? No... no, it's fine," I say as I lead her over to my truck.

Disappointment hits me, but I push it aside as I help her into the passenger seat and climb behind the wheel. I'm alone with my girl, and we're going to spend the whole day together. I'll just have to show her how much she means to me.

It's a short drive over to Semper Fly, and I park out front. We're the only ones here, probably because Kip is at home with his girl. It's quiet as we head inside, and I lead her past our offices and over to the hangar.

"You're sure that this is safe, right?" Cora asks me as I lead her over to my helicopter.

"Yeah, visibility is good this morning, and the chance of icing is low. We'll be safe."

She nods, and I help her into the seat, passing her a pair of headphones so that we'll be able to hear each other.

"I'm going to do a check, and then we'll be good to go," I tell her, and she nods, looking around at all of the buttons while I go to check out the helicopter.

I finish my check and climb inside next to my girl. I slide my own headphones on and look over at Cora.

"Ready?" I ask her, and she nods.

She looks nervous, but also excited as the roof parts, revealing the bright blue sky above us.

"Whoa," she whispers, and I grin as I start the helicopter, the blades whirring loudly above us.

I clear our flight with the nearest tower, and off we go. I still get the same almost giddy feeling as we take flight. When I first decided to join the military with Kip, I was kind of hoping that we would pick the Air Force. I always liked flying, and I think that if I hadn't joined the military, I would have become a pilot.

We went into the Marines, though, and I wound up being Kip's partner. He was a sniper, and I was his scout. I watched his back, just like I did when we were growing up. I can't say that I regret my choice now. We were trained in so many different things, and I love my life now.

"Whoa!" Cora exclaims as we start to fly over the forest and towards the mountains. "It's beautiful."

Her voice sounds tinny in my ears, and I smile over at her as we fly through the crisp winter sky. I point out a few landmarks, giving her the same tour that I do for all of my clients, and by the time we land and climb out of the helicopter, we're both grinning, high off the thrill of flying.

"That was so much fun! Thanks for taking me."

"Anytime," I tell her as I shut down the helicopter, closing the roof and wiping down the windshield of the helicopter.

Cora's stomach growls and I bite back a smile.

"Hungry? Want to go out to lunch with me?" I ask her, and she nods.

"Sure. What are you hungry for?" She asks.

"I'm good with whatever. What are you in the mood for?"

"How about tacos?"

"Sounds good. Felix's?"

She nods, and we head out of Semper Fly and over to my truck. I open the passenger door for her and soon enough, we're on the way toward town to Felix's taco stand.

We're here early enough, so we walk right up to the counter to place our order and then take a seat at a booth in the back of the restaurant.

"My New Year's resolution is going to be to stop coming here so much," Cora says as she pops a chip and some salsa into her mouth.

"Why?"

"Cause I eat here at least once a week."

"It's good," I agree, and she snorts.

"Too good."

Our food is dropped off, and we both dig in.

"What about you?" She asks. "What are your New Year's resolutions?"

"I don't know if I have any of them. Not yet, anyway."

"You still have a few days to figure it out."

"Not many," I say when I realize that New Year's Day is in two days.

"Do you usually do resolutions?" She asks me, and I shake my head.

"I think the last time I did it was when I was in middle school. What about you?"

"That's becoming our catchphrase," Cora says with a giggle, and I smile. She's right, we do say that a lot.

"I'm curious about you," I tell her, and she blushes slightly.

"You shouldn't be, I'm boring."

"You could never be boring."

Her blush darkens, and she clears her throat.

"I try to do resolutions every year. This year, my word was growth, and I just tried to learn a new skill and grow as a person and in my career. I think I did that."

I nod and watch as she polishes off the last of her taco.

"Want another?" I ask, nodding at the two tacos on my plate.

"No, I'm good. I'm going to eat all of these chips and salsa, though. Fair warning to take more now if you want any."

I laugh and grab my next taco.

"What other resolutions do you have for next year?" I ask her.

"I'm going to try to lose some weight, make more—"

"Why?" I interrupt her.

"Why do I want to lose weight?" She asks with a frown.

"Yeah."

"Well, to...lose weight... I mean, look at me."

"I am. You look hot."

Cora's face flames red hot, and she stares at me in surprise.

"I..." she trails off and never finishes her sentence.

We finish lunch and head back out to my truck to make the drive home.

"Want to watch another movie?" I ask as we head inside.

"I need to do laundry and clean my room. Maybe later?"

"Sure. I'll be around."

She smiles and heads back to her room, and I watch her go. Maybe her cleaning up is a good thing. It gives me time to figure out how to show her that we would be perfect together.

Now I just need to figure out how exactly to do that.

FIVE

Cora

"ARE you going to Olive and Xavier's New Year's Eve party?" I ask Noelle as I fold my clothes and put them away in the dresser.

"No, I'm going to hang out with Ansel and just have a quiet night in," she says and I can hear the smile in her voice.

"That sounds fun!"

"Yeah, it's been nice having him back in town. I missed him."

"I bet. Well, have fun. I'll see you in the New Year!"

"Have fun at the party! Tell them all that I said hi and Happy New Year."

"I will," I promise. "Talk to you soon."

"See you."

We hang up, and I finish putting the rest of my clothes away.

"Are you going to the party?" Huxley asks, and I smile at him over my shoulder.

"Yep. You?"

"Yeah."

I nod, and he hovers in the open doorway.

"Are you hungry?" He asks finally, and I nod.

"I could eat. Are we cooking here tonight?"

"Yeah, unless you wanted to go out."

"No, that's fine."

"Omelets?" He asks me, and I nod.

"Sounds perfect."

We head out to the kitchen, and as we get to work on dinner, I can't help but think back to when I first moved in with him and how I was so sure that it was going to be awkward or a mistake. That's not the case, though. I feel so at ease around Huxley, so at home in this house. I know that it's only been a few days, but this place already feels like home.

"What are you thinking?" He asks me, and I blink, getting back to cutting up the vegetables.

"Just thinking about dinner," I lie. "What about you?"

I smile as I look over at him and see him smiling down at the frying pan on the stove.

"New Year's resolutions," he says, and I blink again.

"Really? Are you making one this year?"

"Yeah, thinking about it."

We add the vegetables to the eggs, and Huxley gets started on our omelets while I move to make us some toast.

"What have you come up with so far?" I ask him as he flips the omelet in the pan.

"Well, I think growing the business," he says as he plates our food.

"Sounds good. Like hiring more people?" I ask him as I set the table, and we sit down.

"We actually just hired another Marine. You might know him; he grew up here in town."

"What's his name?"

"Ansel James."

"Noelle's Ansel?" I blurt, and he frowns.

"Uh, yeah, I think that he does have a girl named Noelle. He was always talking about her on our deployments and writing to her."

"Oh my gosh! What a small world," I say with a grin as we both dive into our food.

"What about you?" He asks me.

"I'd like to maybe find a new job or another one. Make some more money, grow my savings," I list.

"What else?" He asks as he finishes his food.

"I'd like to pick up a new hobby. Lose some weight and start working out more, even if it's just going for a walk."

"Hm," he says, and I quirk a brow.

"Got something to say?"

"You don't need to lose weight," he grumbles.

"I'd *like* to," I stress.

He grumbles some more as I pop the last bite of omelet into my mouth.

"I'll do the dishes," I say as I push to my feet and carry my plate over to the sink.

"I can get them."

"You did most of the cooking. I'll clean."

Huxley joins me at the sink as I load the dishwasher. He washes off his plate and passes it to me to put in the dishwasher.

"Did you come up with any other resolutions?" I ask him as I close the dishwasher.

"Yeah," he says softly as he washes and rinses the pan, leaving it in the rack to dry.

"What is it?"

He takes a deep breath and looks down at me. He looks so thoughtful, and the energy between us shifts, growing more serious.

"I want to be braver," he whispers, and I lick my lips.

"Braver? You were in the military. You were a Marine. I thought that there was no one braver."

"There's not."

"Then what do you need to be braver about?"

"There's just something that I haven't been able to say... until now."

I stare at him, and he takes a step closer to me until our toes are touching.

"Cora, I... I want you. Badly. I have for a while."

My heart is racing like a runaway train, and I take a shaky breath. I'm not sure what to say, and my mind races as I try to process this new information.

Huxley likes me, really likes me, and as way more than just a roommate. He wants me, but what do I do with that information? Do I act on my feelings? Or try to forget about them?

Maybe it's time that I start to be brave, too, and admit something to Huxley and myself.

"I want you too," I whisper, and he lets out a rough exhale.

"Say it again," he commands, and I swallow hard.

"I want you, Huxley. I like you too."

Huxley's eyes are dark and stormy, and I can feel the tension radiating off him as he steps closer, closing the space between us until we're pressed up against each other. My heart races, my pulse pounding in my ears as I look up at him, the intensity in his gaze making my breath hitch. I can feel the heat simmering between us, something raw and undeniable that neither of us can ignore any longer.

As I watch, it's like the beast that he's kept caged inside of him is let loose. His hands cup my face, and he tugs me against him as his lips claim mine.

"Cora," he says, his voice low and rough, his hands reaching out to grip my waist. His fingers dig in, pulling me against him with a possessiveness that makes me shiver. He's so close I can feel the warmth of his breath, his hand moving up to cup the back of my neck, tilting my head up to meet his gaze.

I barely have time to react before his mouth crashes down on mine, rough and demanding. It's not gentle, not soft—this kiss is fierce, all-consuming, and I lose myself in it completely. I press into him, my hands clutching his shoulders, and he growls low in his throat, his grip on me tightening as his lips move against mine, urgent and hungry.

He kisses me like he's claiming me, his mouth hard and unrelenting, and I respond with just as much intensity, my hands sliding up into his hair, pulling him closer. I can feel the tension in his body, the way he's barely holding himself back, and it ignites something wild in me. I tug on his hair, and he lets out a low, feral sound that sends a thrill down my spine.

"Cora," he groans against my mouth, his voice thick with desire, and the sound of my name on his lips makes me ache with need.

I pull him even closer, desperate, needing more. His hands roam over my body, rough and possessive, leaving a trail of heat wherever he touches. His mouth moves down to my neck, his teeth grazing my skin, and I gasp, clutching him tighter. He nips at my collarbone, then soothes the spot with his tongue, making me shiver as I tilt my head back, giving him all the access he wants.

"God, Huxley," I breathe, my fingers digging into his shoulders, and he pulls back just enough to look down at me, his eyes blazing.

He doesn't say a word, just crushes his mouth to mine again, his kiss rough and desperate, like he can't get close enough. I can feel the heat between us building, the fire and intensity that neither of us can contain. It's raw, wild, and I lose myself in it, in him, in the way he kisses me like he's wanted this for as long as I have.

There's nothing soft about it—just heat, need, and the feeling that neither of us is holding back anymore. And as his hands tangle in my hair and his mouth claims mine over and over, I know I'm his, and he's mine.

This is raw passion.

Pure need.

"Cora," he murmurs, his voice low and rough, sending a shiver down my spine. He brushes a strand of hair from my face, his fingertips grazing my cheek with a touch that's achingly gentle. My pulse quickens, and I can feel my cheeks flush under his gaze, heat pooling low in my belly as his fingers slide down to trace the line of my jaw.

I melt against him, my hands tangling in his hair as he pulls me even closer. His lips move slowly, exploring, tasting, igniting a fire inside me that I can't ignore. I press into him, needing more, and he responds with a low, rumbling sound that vibrates through me, pulling me deeper into the kiss.

His hands are everywhere, one on my waist, the other sliding up my back, his fingertips pressing into me as if he can't get close enough. His lips part against mine, and I let out a soft sigh as his tongue brushes against mine, sending sparks through every nerve. I sink into him, into the warmth and strength of his body, feeling the world around us fall away as his kiss deepens, becoming urgent, desperate.

"Huxley," I breathe, his name a whisper against his lips, and he pulls back just enough to meet my gaze, his eyes dark and hungry. The look he gives me sends another wave of heat through me, and I can barely catch my breath as he leans down, his lips grazing my ear.

"You have no idea how long I've wanted this," he murmurs, his voice thick with desire, and I feel a shiver run through me.

"Then don't stop," I whisper, my hands tightening in his hair as he captures my mouth again, harder this time, more insistent, his hands roaming over my body, igniting every inch of skin he touches. I press against him, feeling the heat and strength of him, wanting more, needing more.

The kiss grows deeper, hotter, his mouth trailing down my jaw to my neck, leaving a trail of fire in its wake. I tilt my head back, giving him better access, and he doesn't hesitate, his lips brushing over the sensitive skin just below my ear, making me gasp.

I'm lost in him, in the feel of his hands and his mouth and the way he holds me like he never wants to let go.

"Bed," he mumbles against my lips, too wrapped up in me to pull away enough to talk.

"Uh-huh," I mumble back, and then he's lifting me and carrying me to my room like I weigh nothing. My body heats even more at his show of strength, and I moan, writhing against him.

"Fuck, Cora. You're going to make me come before I've even got you naked."

I gasp as he lays me down on the bed and grinds against me, thrusting between my legs and driving me wild.

"Been dreaming about you naked and beneath me for so long," he whispers as we rock together.

"Then do it. I don't want to wait any longer," I beg him.

He nods, standing between my legs and pulling his shirt over his head as he stares down at me with so much heat and longing in his deep green eyes. His dark brown hair is slightly mussed, and I know that it's from my fingers being in it.

"You turn," he says, and I sit up, pulling my shirt off and dropping it on the floor.

I have a moment of panic and self-doubt as I stare at Huxley's ripped body, but when I look up at him, his eyes are locked on my curves, and as I watch him, he licks his lips. He wants me. He's staring at me like he's never seen anything sexier, and that helps my confidence level grow.

"Bra," he rasps out.

I reach behind me and unhook the clasp, letting the straps slowly slide down my arms until they're off. Then I let the cups drop, and the bra falls to the floor next to my shirt.

"Fuckkk," he groans, and I blush.

"Take off the rest of it," I tell him.

We both reach for our pants at the same time, and it's like we're racing to get naked. I win, but Huxley is right behind me, and then he's on me.

His lips land on mine as he lifts me and drags me to the very center of the bed. His knees nudge my legs wider, and he lets some of his weight press onto me. It feels delicious to have him on me like this, his hot skin branding mine everywhere it touches.

His tongue tangles with mine, and his fingers tangle in my hair, tugging at the strands until he has my head angled just right. The kiss deepens, and his cock rubs against my drenched core, the tip rubbing back and forth over my clit, until I'm right on the edge and begging him to put it in.

"Please!" I scream, and he hums against my lips.

"Need to taste you," he says, and I push on his chest until he lifts off of me a bit, then reach down and swipe two of my fingers up my pussy and hold it out to him.

"Here. Taste. Then you fuck me before I scream."

"Oh, Cora, baby, I'm going to make you scream," he promises me wickedly.

His lips wrap around my fingers, and when his tongue swirls around the digits, I almost combust.

"Put it in," I pant, and he moans as he licks my fingers clean.

"In a minute. I need another taste."

He grabs my hand and runs my fingers through my juices again. Then brings those fingers back to his mouth.

"Oh my god," I pant.

"Say my name," he orders.

"Please, Huxley."

He kisses the tips of my fingers and then starts to kiss his way down my body. He cups my breasts, and I arch into his hold as his lips wrap around one nipple, his tongue rolling over the stiff peak.

My hips are restless against his. His cock keeps rubbing against me, so close to where I need him, but I can't get him to where I want him.

"Huxley," I cry out, and he grins against my breast before he switches to my other nipple.

I let out a frustrated groan, and he chuckles as his teeth nip at my skin.

"Be patient. I've been dreaming about this for so long. I want to take my time."

"I'm so close to just taking care of myself and saying screw you," I warn him.

He growls but starts to kiss down my body. His hands grip my thighs, and he holds them open as he licks a path up my center, and then he buries his face in my core.

I scream as he sucks my clit into his mouth and come so hard that I see stars. My thighs clamp down around his head, but that doesn't faze him. He keeps licking me, his tongue circling my little button until I come again.

He licks up all of his juices, and I reach down, tugging at his hair to get him to stop.

"Fuck me," I order, and he licks my clit once more and then prowls up my body.

He kisses me, and I taste myself on his tongue. His cock nudges at my opening, and I wrap my legs around his waist as he starts to push into me.

"Wait!" I gasp. "Shouldn't I...take care of you first?" I ask him.

"You can do that later," he promises me as he sinks in another inch, nudging up against my virginity.

"Thank fuck," he groans, and I frown.

"Wha—" I start, and then he thrusts into me, popping my cherry and bottoming out inside of me.

We both groan, and as he fills me, and my legs tighten around his waist. He kisses me and then looks into my eyes, studying my every reaction as he starts to slide out of me and then push back in.

He buries himself inside of me over and over again, lighting up all of my nerve endings and pushing me closer to the edge with each thrust.

I'm soaking wet, and Huxley starts to really pound into me. His pace is rough, and I love it. Normally, I feel big and heavy, but having Huxley take charge and move me wherever he wants me makes me feel dainty and sexy.

"Oh!" I cry out as he hits a spot inside of me that makes me feel like a firecracker about to go off.

"That's it, baby. Let me hear how much you love it. I want to hear you scream my name until you're hoarse."

"Fuck," I pant, and he shakes his head.

"Not good enough."

He kneels between my thighs, putting my ankles on his shoulders and dragging my ass into his lap. He's so deep this way and I suck in a sharp breath as he pounds against that spot inside of me.

"Huxley... HUXLEY!" I scream as I start to come on his cock.

"That's it," he says, his cock grinding against my clit as he pulses against me.

"Oh," I cry out as his fingers rub against my clit, making my orgasm go on and on.

He holds my thighs tight and practically bends me in half as he starts to fuck me harder. Stars burst behind my eyes as another orgasm starts to build in me. I can tell that Huxley is close too. His pace is starting to grow erratic, and I can feel him swell in me, and I can see him losing control in his eyes and the set of his mouth.

We lock eyes, and he stares at me with a look close to love as we both come.

"Cora," he whispers, and I've never heard anyone say my name like that. With so much longing, love, and need.

I love it.

I might even love him.

Wait. No, that must just be the post-orgasm high messing with my brain.

Huxley pulls out slowly, and I look away from him,

trying to hide my feelings before he can see them. He rolls onto his side, both of us breathing hard, and I try to look normal as I snuggle under the comforters next to him. He pulls me into his side, and I rest my head on his chest, listening to his racing heart as I try to sort through my feelings.

I can't be in love with Huxley... can I? I haven't really known him that long. Plus, I can't date my roommate. If we break up, it would be so awkward. Although, sleeping with my roommate may have already made things awkward...

I'm so warm, so comfortable, that soon enough, my eyes grow heavy, and I start to drift off. As I fall asleep, my last thought is that maybe falling for Huxley isn't the worst thing in the world.

SIX

Huxley

I WAKE up and instantly know that I'm alone. I can feel it. The house is cold, and that can only mean that Cora is gone. Normally, when she's home, I can sense it. The house feels cozier. It's more welcoming and warmer.

"Dammit," I groan as I roll over and sit up in bed.

My feet touch the cold floor, and I welcome the chill. It helps to wake me up. My phone rings, and I lunge for it, hoping that it's Cora, but Kip's name is on the screen.

"Hello?" I answer, my voice groggy and rough with sleep. I clear my throat, trying to sound more human. "What's going on?"

"Are you going to the Baker's New Year's Eve party?" He asks me.

"Yeah. You?"

"Yeah, Ginger just headed over to Olive's house to help her set up for tonight. I'm going to go over there around nine. I need to head up to Semper Fly so that I can wrap up a few things before we start fresh on Monday."

"I'll join you."

"Sounds good. I'll see you soon, then."

"See you."

We end the call, and I climb out of bed and head out of Cora's room and into my own room next door. I hate to wash the scent of Cora off of me, but if I have my way, I'll smell like her again soon enough.

Images from last night play in my head as I rinse off, and by the time I step out to dry off, my cock is rock hard, and I'm ready to do all of those things with Cora all over again.

Maybe I should skip work and head over to Olive's house. I can help them set up and hang out with Cora more.

My phone buzzes, and I see a text from Kip.

KIP: **Want me to pick you up?**
Huxley: Sure. Be ready in five.

HE SENDS BACK A THUMBS UP, and I rush to get dressed and grab a protein bar for breakfast. I'm shoving the last bite into my mouth when he pulls up, and I head out to his truck.

"So?" He asks as soon as I shut the door.

"What?"

"How's Cora? Have you talked to her yet?"

"Kind of."

"Sounds promising," he teases me as we pull out of my driveway and head towards Semper Fly.

"We slept together," I blurt out.

He whips his head to look at me so fast that I slam my hand on the dashboard.

"ROAD!" I shout, and he jerks his eyes back to the snow-covered road.

"That's huge man! Congrats! So, you two are like officially together?"

"Not quite."

"What? What exactly happened?"

I give him a look and he laughs.

"Okay, not exactly. I mean, what did you tell her? Does she know that you're obsessed with her?"

"Don't think so."

He sighs, and I take a deep breath and sigh, too.

"I told her that I like her."

"You mean love."

"I do, but I didn't say that. I was afraid that I'd freak her out, and I mean, she lives with me, so I need her to feel comfortable."

"So, you're just going to take your time," he says, and I nod.

"Exactly."

"Okay, so maybe next New Year's Eve you'll tell her that you love her?"

I groan, scrubbing my hands down my face.

"Are you just going to keep sleeping with her for months before you tell her that you love her? What's the plan here, man?"

"I don't know. Don't really have one," I admit.

"Well, you need to come up with one pretty fast."

We park outside of the Semper Fly offices and climb out of his truck. It's starting to snow and I hope that Cora has made it to Olive's house safely.

"What's with the frown?" Kip asks me as he unlocks the doors.

"Cora's car," I bite out, and understanding dawns in his dark green eyes.

"Does it have snow tires?"

"I doubt it. It barely even works. The thing is falling apart."

"Why don't you text her and make sure that she made it to Olive's place safe and sound," he suggests.

"Good idea."

Kip heads into his office, and I head across the hall to mine, pulling out my phone as I go. I find Cora's name and start to type, hesitating before I hit send.

HUXLEY: **Morning. Did you make it to Olive's okay?**

CRAP. *Should I have said something about last night? Should I have asked how she was?*

Panic and doubt swirl inside of me, but it's too late to change the message now.

CORA: **Morning! Yep, we made it here and were busy decorating now! See you tonight! You're still coming right?**
Huxley: Yep

SHE HEARTS MY MESSAGE, and I relax. She seems

normal. Not like she's upset or anxious about last night. That has to be a good sign, right?

Unless she thinks that it was just a one-time thing and is trying to be normal now.

I groan and bury my face in my hands.

"Is this what I was like when I was chasing after Ginger?" Kip asks me, and I glare at him.

"You were so much worse," I tell him, and he grins.

"It will be alright. She likes you too, or she wouldn't have slept with you last night. It's basically a done deal, man. You just need to tell her exactly how you feel and make the whole thing official."

I nod, wanting to believe his words.

"You're right. I'll tell her tonight at the party."

"Good. Then we can both go into the New Year with our women."

I nod, and he switches topics and starts to talk about the schedule for January. We go over budgets, schedules, and maintenance lists. Soon enough, it's time to head home and get ready for the party.

"Want me to drive you over there?" Kip asks as he pulls up outside of my place.

"Yeah. That way I can drive Cora home and make sure that she gets here in one piece."

"Alright, I'll swing back here in half an hour."

"Thanks. See you soon."

I hurry inside and take another shower, trying to calm down and go over what I want to say to Cora. I pull on a dark green wool sweater and a fresh pair of jeans and then head back downstairs. I know that Kip will be here any minute, and I glance at my phone. No new messages from Cora.

As if my thoughts have conjured her, her name flashes on my screen.

CORA: **On your way?**
Huxley: About to be. Do you need anything from the house or in town?
Cora: Maybe a light sweater? My pink one. It should be hanging up in my closet.
Huxley: Got it. I'll see you soon.

I JOG upstairs and grab her sweater. My eyes stray to the messy bed, and I wonder if I should have made it or changed the sheets for her.

HUXLEY: **Do you want me to make your bed?**
Cora: ?
Huxley: Never mind.

A CAR HORN HONKS OUTSIDE, and I rush downstairs and out to Kip's truck.

"Ready to party?" He asks me, and I nod.

We make the short drive to Olive's house, and Kip parks on the dirt road behind all of the other cars and trucks.

"Did they invite the whole town?" I ask, and Kip laughs.

"Practically. I mean, between the whole Baker family and all of their friends," he says, and I nod.

We head inside, and I scan the crowded house for my

girl. My eyes spot her by the kitchen and I take a deep breath as I make my way over to her.

It's time to make this official.

I hope.

SEVEN

Cora

HUXLEY BEELINES FOR ME, and I bite back a smile as I watch him make his way through the crowd towards me. He stops right in front of me, and I crane my head back to maintain eye contact with him.

"Here," he says, handing me my sweater, and I smile up at him as I slip it on.

"Thanks."

"We should—"

"Are you hungry?" I ask at the same time.

I laugh, and some of the tension between us seems to fade.

"What were you going to say?" I ask him.

"We should... grab something to eat," he says, and I know that he's lying, but I decide not to push him.

"Yeah, there's a ton of food. Come on."

I turn and head into the kitchen with Huxley following right behind me. I can see Ginger looking at me, and when we make eye contact, she raises her eyebrows, silently asking me if I've talked to him yet. I shake my head at her, and she frowns.

I spent most of today helping set up, cooking for the party, and being grilled by my friends about what is going on between me and Huxley. I told them that we slept together last night and that I really liked him, but Ginger knows me better than that. She cornered me and asked if I was willing to admit that I had feelings for him, that I loved him.

It had been scary to admit that, even to my best friend, and she spent the rest of the day trying to talk me up and convince me to talk to him tonight and make things between us official. She wants me to tell him that I like him, a lot—maybe even tell him that I love him—but I'm not sure that I can do that tonight.

Maybe after some liquid courage, I think as I head over to the counter filled with liquor and start to make myself a rum and coke.

"Do you want one?" I ask Huxley, but he shakes his head.

"I'm good for now."

I take a big sip of my drink and grab a plate as we head over to the buffet of food.

"I'll hold your plate for you," Huxley says, and I smile.

"Thanks."

I add some dips and other appetizers to the plate and then pop a strawberry in my mouth as we take a seat at the long table that's been set up in the corner of the kitchen. Huxley heads back to make his own plate of food and I start to eat as I study him.

He looks so handsome in his forest green sweater and dark-wash jeans. He smiles and greets Kip as he joins him in line for food and they start to whisper to each other. Kip claps him on the back, and Huxley nods as he turns and makes his way back over to me.

We eat in silence for a while, and I try to think of something to say. *Do I ask him about his day? Do I mention last night and how amazing it was?*

"What did you do today?" I ask him as we eat.

"Kip and I ended up going in to work for a bit. We got a lot of stuff figured out and ready for January."

"That's good. It must be a relief, huh?"

"Yeah, it's nice to have it out of the way."

I nod, and we eat in silence for another minute.

"What about you?" He asks and I grin.

"I'm going to get that printed on a shirt for you," I tell him, and he laughs.

"Fine. What did you do today?" He asks me.

"I helped out here. I made the seven-layer dip," I tell him, pointing to it on his plate.

"It's delicious. The best thing here."

"And I made the chicken wings."

"Love them too."

I laugh and smile at him and he stares at me.

"We need to talk," Huxley says and I drop the tortilla chip in my hand as I stare at him.

"Okay. Right now?" I ask him, and he nods.

"Yeah."

He sounds so resigned, or maybe it's determination that I hear. Either way, I get an anxious ball in my stomach as I stand and follow him to the front door. We both pull on our coats, boots, and winter gear and then head outside.

"What's up?" I ask him as we head to the far end of the porch.

"I need to tell you something."

I nod, watching him anxiously and waiting for him to go on.

"About last night..." he starts, and I swallow hard.

"It was nice," I say and he nods animatedly.

"Yes, nice."

His mouth opens and closes a few times and I bite back a smile at how out of his depth he looks.

"It was amazing."

He nods again and I watch him swallow hard, his fingers stretching and then tightening into fists. He rolls his shoulders back and takes a deep breath, looking like he's trying to psych himself up for something.

"Cora, I like you," he says finally, and I blink.

"I like you too."

"I more than like you. That doesn't even begin to describe how I feel about you."

"Okay..."

"I'm obsessed with you. I have been for months. Since you moved to town."

"I—"

"I love you. So much. More than you know. More than is probably healthy."

"Huxley," I try again, but it seems like now he's on a roll, like now the floodgates are open and he has to get it all out.

"I had your house condemned so that you would have to move in with me."

"What!?"

"I moved out of the master bedroom so that you could have it because, fuck, I want you to be mine. I needed to see you in my bed, even if I wasn't in it with you."

"You had my house condemned?" I ask again, and he nods.

"It wasn't safe for you to live there. I don't regret it, and I would do it again in a heartbeat. I'm working on getting rid of that thing next," he tells me, nodding behind me to my car.

"My car isn't that bad!" I argue, and he glares at it.

"It's the worst. I can't stand it. Do you have any idea how many times I've followed you home or to town just to make sure that you got there safely? How many nights I've spent lying awake and wondering if you had made it home?"

"How were you going to get rid of it? Break something on that too?" I ask him, crossing my arms over my chest as I glare up at him.

"No, I wouldn't need to do that. A strong wind comes through, and that thing will break down."

"It's not that bad!" I scream, and he shakes his head.

"It is. I've been toying with the idea of setting up a fake contest to have you win one, or buying another car for myself and then insisting that you use it because it's safer in this weather."

"You're crazy," I whisper, and he nods.

"I know. Don't you think that I know that? You drive me crazy, Cora. I've never been like this with anyone before. I've never felt even a fraction of the things that I feel for you for anyone else. I don't know how to act around you or how to control my instincts when it comes to you."

"What were you going to do when I moved out?" I ask him.

"Not let you."

"How were you going to do that?"

"I was hoping that I'd be able to convince you to stay. I was hoping that I would have enough time to show you that we were perfect together. I was hoping that I would be able to get you to fall in love with me too."

We stare at each other in silence for a beat; the only sounds are the muted voices and music from the party.

"Well, you did," I say softly, and he blinks.

"Did what?" He asks carefully, like he's afraid to believe that I might be saying that I love him too, and I smile up at him.

"You made me fall for you too."

"What?" He asks, his eyes wide in shock.

"I love you too."

He closes the distance between us quickly, and his lips find mine. He kisses me passionately, his hands tangling in my hair as his tongue licks into my mouth.

The wind whips my hair around us, and I can hear the sounds of the party from inside, but all I can focus on is Huxley. His hand slips around my waist, pulling me close, and the rest of the noise and distractions fade away. His green eyes meet mine, intense and smoldering, and I feel my breath catch as I stare up at him.

The snow falls gently around us, blanketing the world in quiet as we stand on the porch, close enough that I can feel the warmth of him radiating against the cold. Huxley's eyes are intense, his gaze fixed on me, his breaths visible in the winter air. It's almost surreal, this moment, this silence that pulses with an unspoken electricity between us.

He reaches out, brushing a snowflake from my cheek with the back of his hand, his fingers lingering just long enough to make my skin tingle. My heart thuds in my chest as he tilts his head, his eyes searching mine, his face close enough that I can see the flecks of green in his dark eyes.

"Cora," he murmurs, his voice rough and low, filled with something that sends a thrill down my spine.

He leans in, and before I can think, before I can even take another breath, his lips find mine. The kiss is soft at first, just a whisper of warmth in the cold, his mouth gentle but possessive, as if he's savoring this moment. I let myself melt into it, my hands finding his shoulders, feeling the strength beneath his jacket, the solidness of him.

The kiss deepens, and a shiver runs through me, though it has nothing to do with the chill. His hands slide to my waist, pulling me closer, his body heat seeping through our clothes. I feel him press into me, every inch of him as he wraps me up in his arms, the world falling away until there's nothing but the two of us and this kiss. My hands slide up to his neck, fingers tangling in his hair as his lips move over mine, slow and deliberate, coaxing, exploring.

He pulls back just enough to look at me, his breath mingling with mine, his eyes dark and hungry. "You're driving me crazy, you know that?"

"Good," I whisper, breathless, and that's all it takes.

His mouth crashes against mine, harder this time, his kiss filled with a raw need that makes my knees go weak. He presses me back against the porch railing, his hands roaming over my back, pulling me even closer, as if he can't get enough. I feel his warmth everywhere, igniting something inside me that I've never felt before.

He breaks away just long enough to murmur my name against my lips, his voice rough with longing, his hands framing my face as he gazes at me, his eyes filled with an intensity that takes my breath away.

And then his mouth is on mine again, his kisses deep and insistent, making my head spin. I lose myself in him, in the warmth and strength of his embrace, in the way he holds me as if I'm the only thing that matters. The snow falls softly around us, silent witnesses to a moment I know I'll never forget.

He's really mine, I think with a smile.

"Are you two coming back inside?" Ginger calls, and we pull apart.

"Yeah, in a second!" I call back, and she gives me a knowing smile before she heads back inside.

"I love you, Cora," Huxley whispers as he presses his forehead against mine.

"I know, crazy," I say, and he glares at me until I laugh. "I love you too."

He smiles and presses another kiss to my lips. I shiver as the wind picks up and pull back.

"It's freezing. Let's go inside," I tell him, and he nods.

He takes my hand in his as we make our way back towards the door.

"You're my girl," he says as we stop outside the front door.

"Yeah."

"And we're going out. We're not just roommates now."

"Uh-huh."

"And I'm moving back into the master bedroom. I don't want to spend another night without you next to me."

"Okay," I say, leaning up and kissing his cheek. "Now, let's go inside and hang out with our friends. Then in a few hours, if you're lucky, I'll let you be my midnight kiss."

"Damn right, I'm going to be your kiss," he grumbles as we head inside, and I smile as we rejoin the party.

"So?" Ginger asks, pulling me aside, and I see Kip giving Huxley a questioning look.

"Meet my boyfriend," I tell the party, and everyone cheers.

Huxley tucks me into his side, and I grin up at him.

"It's about time!" Ryder says, and I laugh.

Our friends all congratulate us, and Huxley keeps me close to his side for the rest of the night. He's so attentive, always watching me and getting me something before I can even try to get it myself or ask for it. He seems more relaxed and at peace, too. It's like now that I know how crazy obsessed with me he is, he can relax and just be himself.

Midnight comes so fast, and as we all countdown and watch the ball drop, I smile up at Huxley.

"Happy New Year," I tell him and he smirks down at me.

"Happy New Year. I'm going to make sure that it's your best year yet," he promises me as he leans down and kisses me as the ball drops on the TV.

I close my eyes and smile as I kiss my man back.

EIGHT

Huxley

CORA KISSES me as soon as we're through the door, and I grin as I kiss her back. She might be a little tipsy from the champagne, and it's making her giggly and horny. Not that I'm complaining.

"Need you," she moans, and I nod.

"How do you want it?" I ask as she sits on the arm of the couch to pull her boots off.

She tips backward, laughing as she bounces on the cushions, and I grin as I move to help her take her boots off.

"Here," she says, wrapping her legs around my waist.

"I'd love to, but we both have about ten layers that we need to lose first," I tell her.

She nods and rolls off the couch to her feet. I watch as she starts to take off her coat, wiggling out of the sleeves. She raises an eyebrow at me and nods to my own coat, and I start to strip too.

Cora shivers as she takes off her clothes and I move to

the fireplace, building up a fire quickly and then standing to take off the rest of my clothes. She makes her way over to me as I kick off my boxers and grins as she trails a finger down my chest, all of the way to my hard cock. As I watch, she licks her lips, her hazel eyes lighting with excitement as she drops to her knees in front of me.

My cock jerks as she comes to eye level with it. Her hand wraps around my length, and she leans forward and licks the tip. It's obvious that she hasn't done this before, but her inexperience is a turn on for me. Hell, everything that Cora does is a turn on. She could be doing her taxes, and I would probably be rock hard.

Her full lips wrap around my dick, and I have to grit my teeth to stop from coming immediately. Her tongue swirls around my tip, and I tilt my head back and try to think about all of my deployments instead of focusing on my girl's perfect fuckin' mouth.

I fail.

"Fuck, you're good at that."

She moans, the sound vibrating down my length to my balls. I bump up against the back of her throat, and she swallows around me.

"Oh, fuck!" I shout and she hums around me.

Then she does it again.

I brace myself against the fireplace, my knuckles turning white as I hold on and try not to come down her throat so soon.

"Cora," I moan.

Her hand twists as she jerks my cock in time with her mouth. She opens her mouth, sticking her tongue out as she looks up at me.

"Fuck, Cora. I've never seen anything hotter in my life."

She smiles wickedly up at me and continues to jerk me

off. Her hand twists as she strokes up and down my cock. My balls tighten with each stroke, and I groan.

"Cora, I'm close," I warn her, and her lips wrap around my cock again.

She takes me all the way to the back of her throat, and my fingers thread into her hair, holding her in place as I come. She moans as she swallows down my release, licking the tip to get every drop.

She smiles up at me, and I reach down, picking her up and carrying her back over to the couch. I sit her down with her ass on the back of the couch and kiss her. She grabs my hips and tugs me closer to her.

We're close to the same height when she's sitting there, and when she tugs me closer, my cock nudges her snug opening.

I rest my forehead against hers and we both look down as I start to push into her. We exhale together as I sink balls deep inside of her.

"So damn perfect," I whisper, and she nods, her forehead rubbing against mine with the movement.

"Hold on," I order her as I pull out and then slam back in.

She gasps and grips the back of the couch as we start to move together. Her blonde hair falls in her eyes, and I reach up and push it out of the way as I continue to thrust in and out of her.

"I love you," she tells me, and I smile, loving that she said it first this time.

"I love you more."

She wraps her arms around my neck and kisses me as we move together. My hands move up and down her body, running over her curves and cupping her breasts. My fingers find her hard nipples, and I pinch the sensitive peaks. She gasps and I smile against her lips.

I can tell that she's close, her breathing always starts to get choppy when she's close to the edge. Her pussy is gripping my cock like a vice, and I grit my teeth so that I don't come before her.

"Give it to me, Cora. I need to feel you come all over my cock."

She cries out, and I pinch her nipples, sending her over the edge. She screams my name as she comes, and I follow her over the edge, coming with her and choking out her name as I fill her up.

We're breathing hard as we rest against each other, and she smiles at me, kissing my nose adorably.

"Ready for bed?" I ask her, and she grins.

"Ready for round two?"

I grin back at her and then wrap my arms around her and turn to carry her back to our room.

"Ready for anything," I tell her, kissing her as we fall down into bed together.

It's a long night of passion, and the perfect way to start the New Year. I hope that we make it a tradition and do it every year. And if I have my way, we will.

NINE

Cora

I WAKE up the next morning to Huxley moving stuff around in the closet.

"What are you doing?" I mumble as I rub the sleep from my eyes.

"Wanted to start this year off on the right foot," he says over his shoulder.

"By...robbing me?" I guess and he laughs.

"I'm not stealing anything. I was just moving your clothes over to make room for mine."

"Why?" I ask, still half asleep and feeling like I'm missing something.

"Cause I'm moving back in here with you. I don't want to sleep apart anymore."

I remember him telling me last night that he had moved out of the master bedroom so that I could have it because he didn't want me anywhere but his bed, and I smile as I climb out of bed.

"What if I want the whole closet?" I ask him as I move closer and lean against the doorway to watch him.

"Do you? Do you have more clothes that we didn't grab from the rental house?" He asks, looking around at the half-full closet.

"No, this is all of it. But what if I want to buy more? Then I'll need the room."

"I can move back to the other closet and –" he says, already grabbing his hangers to move back.

"I was joking!" I tell him before he can leave, and he blinks.

"It's too early for jokes," he grumbles, and I snort.

"You're the one who got up at the crack of dawn to move."

"It's almost eleven," he says, and my eyes widen as I turn to look at the clock.

"Whoa, I can't remember the last time that I slept in this late."

"Me either."

"What do you want to do today?" I ask him. "Besides, move. Today is my last day off. It's back to work tomorrow."

"I was thinking about that," he starts, and I narrow my eyes at him.

"I'm not quitting my job," I tell him, and he shakes his head.

"Not quit, but change jobs."

"To what?" I ask, crossing my arms over my chest.

"Come work for me. We need an accountant at Semper Fly. Plus, we could carpool, and you'd get to see Ginger more since Kip just hired her as his assistant."

"And what happens if we break up?"

"We're never breaking up. You're it for me. It will always only be you, Cora. And before you say it, I'm never letting you go, either. I would do anything to make you mine, and I'll do anything to keep you."

"Alright," I agree, and he raises an eyebrow at me.

"Alright, what?"

"Alright, I'll come to work for you guys at Semper Fly. I need to put in my two weeks' notice, though."

"Alright."

I giggle, and he smiles down at me.

"I love you, Cora."

"I know. I love you two, psycho."

"You're the only one who makes me crazy," he whispers, and I smirk as his lips land on mine.

His kiss is filled with so much promise for our future and I smile as I wrap my arms around his neck and kiss him back, trying to pour all of my love and hopes for the future with him into it.

"We're getting married," he announces against my lips and I laugh.

"Not today."

"Soon," he grumbles, and I nod.

"Soon."

He kisses me again, and I jump up, wrapping my legs around him.

"Now, I'll help you move back into this room in a little bit, but there's something that I wanted to do first," I tell him and he smirks.

"What's that?" He asks, already walking back towards the bed, his hard cock rubbing me through his boxers.

"Come back to bed, and I'll show you," I whisper, and he kisses me as we both fall down onto the mattress.

Then, the two of us get started making this year the best year yet.

TEN

Huxley

FIVE YEARS LATER...

SNOW BLANKETS the rolling hills of Wolf Valley, turning the town into a cozy postcard scene, and our house glows with warm light against the night. The party is in full swing, our house bustling with voices and laughter as we celebrate the coming New Year with our closest friends and family. Somewhere in the chaos, Kip is telling a story so dramatically I can hear the kids shrieking with laughter from here. Ginger shoots me a knowing smile, and I stifle a laugh as Kip continues his wild tale. It's good to see him and Ginger so happy and to know that all of us, the "found family" we built, are together to welcome another year.

"Alright, everyone!" Olive Baker's voice calls out as she swoops into the room, her hands full of drinks she's trying not to spill. "Who's ready for a toast?"

Everyone cheers, the excitement contagious as we start to gather in the main room. I feel Huxley's hand at the small of my back, pulling me close. He's wearing the sweater I bought him last Christmas—a dark, forest green that matches his eyes—and even after all this time, I still get butterflies just looking at him.

"Happy New Year," he murmurs into my ear, his voice warm as he squeezes me a little closer.

"Almost," I whisper back, smiling up at him. "But I'm not complaining about the early start."

I feel a rush of love and gratitude for this man who's been my partner through all of it—the laughter, the challenges, the quiet moments when it's just us, side by side, sharing a look or a touch that says everything we don't need words for.

As everyone gathers around, Huxley lifts his glass, and the room falls quiet. I glance up at him, surprised he's the one taking the lead, but he just smiles down at me, giving me a gentle wink.

"Alright, everyone," he begins, his voice deep and warm. "It's been another good year, and having all of you here with us means more than you know. Let's raise a glass to family, to friends, and to all the memories we've made and have yet to make." He pauses, and I can see the hint of emotion in his eyes. "Here's to many more years of laughter, love, and unforgettable moments."

Everyone cheers and clinks glasses, and I feel myself tearing up a little as Huxley pulls me in for a quick kiss. I glance around the room, taking in the faces of all the people who mean so much to us, feeling that familiar warmth of Wolf Valley.

As the festivities continue, people start to spread out.

Kip and Ginger join us, drinks in hand, and Kip grins at Huxley.

"Nice speech, man," Kip says, clapping Huxley on the shoulder. "Never thought I'd see the day you'd take the lead at a party."

"New year, new me," Huxley deadpans, and we all laugh. He may have loosened up over the years, but there's still that dry humor I love so much.

"Speaking of new," Ginger chimes in, looking a little too innocent, "have you two made any New Year's resolutions yet?"

I raise an eyebrow, glancing at Huxley, and he shrugs. "Cora usually makes the resolutions," he says with a teasing smile, "but I think mine is just to keep doing exactly what I'm doing."

"Oh, smooth," I tease, nudging him. "But that was your resolution last year."

He grins and pulls me closer, wrapping an arm around me. "Well, it worked out well last year."

"Hey!" calls Olive from across the room, interrupting us. "Who's up for a game of Wolf Valley trivia?"

At the mention of trivia, everyone cheers. Olive and Ryder always come up with the best questions, and it's become a yearly tradition, one that brings out everyone's competitive side. I can see Huxley rolling his eyes a little, but he's smiling too.

"Alright," I say, tugging Huxley toward the living room where the trivia is set up. "Think we're ready to win this year?"

"Only because I have you on my team," he replies, and I can't help but smile.

We settle in, Huxley leaning back against the couch

with me by his side, and Ginger sits beside me with Kip on her other side. Olive and Ryder are hosting, and they start the questions with a round of "Wolf Valley history."

"Alright, first question!" Ryder announces. "What year was the town's first general store built?"

Huxley raises an eyebrow at me, his mouth twitching into a grin. "This one's all you, trivia queen."

"1894," I answer confidently, and Ryder gives me a proud nod as he marks our team down for a point.

The trivia goes on, and even Huxley gets into it, throwing out a few answers and muttering jokes under his breath. It's one of those moments that feels timeless, like I could stay here forever, surrounded by people I love, the warmth of the fire crackling, the gentle hum of voices filling the air. When the trivia finally wraps up, Olive announces that our team has won, and Huxley leans over to kiss me on the cheek.

"Nice job, trivia queen," he says, his eyes shining with admiration.

Later, as the clock inches closer to midnight, Huxley and I slip away from the crowd for a few minutes. We find a quiet corner on the back porch, watching the snow fall outside. The night is quiet, with only the soft murmur of music and laughter from the party inside.

Huxley pulls me into his arms, his embrace warm against the chill of the night. "I can't believe it's already another year," he murmurs, his breath warm against my cheek. "Feels like yesterday we were just starting this whole adventure."

I smile up at him, feeling a familiar flutter of affection. "Time flies when you're having fun," I tease, and he laughs, his deep, rich chuckle filling the silence.

He looks down at me, his expression softening. "Cora," he says quietly, his eyes full of emotion, "I know I don't say it enough, but I love you. Every day, more than the day before. Even on the days when I don't say it, or when I'm too busy to show it, just know that I do."

Tears prick at my eyes, and I reach up to touch his cheek, my thumb brushing over the familiar lines that have deepened over the years. "I love you too, Huxley. Every single day."

He leans down, pressing a gentle kiss to my forehead, and I close my eyes, savoring the warmth of his touch. It's moments like this that make everything worthwhile—the quiet, tender moments when it's just us, wrapped in each other's arms, sharing a love that's only grown stronger over the years.

"Do you think they're going to come looking for us?" he asks, his voice soft with a hint of amusement.

I laugh, glancing over my shoulder at the party inside. "Probably. But let's stay out here a little longer."

He nods, pulling me closer, and we stand there together, watching the snowfall in the quiet of the night. The town of Wolf Valley stretches out before us, the lights twinkling in the distance, and I feel a sense of peace settle over me.

After a few more minutes, we hear the sounds of cheering from inside as the countdown to midnight begins, and Huxley and I smile at each other, caught up in the excitement of the moment. We slip back inside just as the countdown hits ten, joining our friends and family in the chorus of voices counting down the last seconds of the year.

"Three... two... one... Happy New Year!"

The room erupts in cheers, and I turn to Huxley, wrapping my arms around his neck as he pulls me in for a kiss. It's a kiss full of promises, of love, and of all the things we've shared and have yet to share. Around us, our friends and family cheer and laugh, the sound filling the room as we celebrate the start of a new year.

As we pull back, I catch Huxley's gaze, his eyes soft and full of love. "Happy New Year, Cora," he murmurs, his voice warm and filled with affection.

"Happy New Year, Huxley," I reply, feeling a swell of happiness.

We spend the rest of the night dancing, laughing, and celebrating with the people we love. And as the first light of dawn begins to peek over the horizon, Huxley and I find ourselves alone once more, standing on the porch as the party winds down inside.

"Another year," he murmurs, his arm around my shoulders as we watch the sunrise.

"Another year," I agree, leaning into him. "And I wouldn't want to spend it with anyone else."

He smiles down at me, his eyes shining with love. "Neither would I, Cora."

And as the sun rises over Wolf Valley, casting a warm, golden light over the town, I know that whatever the future holds, we'll face it together, just as we always have. Because with Huxley by my side, every year feels like the best year yet.

Want more of Cora and Huxley? Then be sure to check out this bonus scene set twenty-five years in the future!

Looking for Noelle and Ansel's story? Then check out Keeping Noelle today!

Love Wolf Valley? Check out the Wolf Valley: Grumps series!

WANT A FREE BOOK?

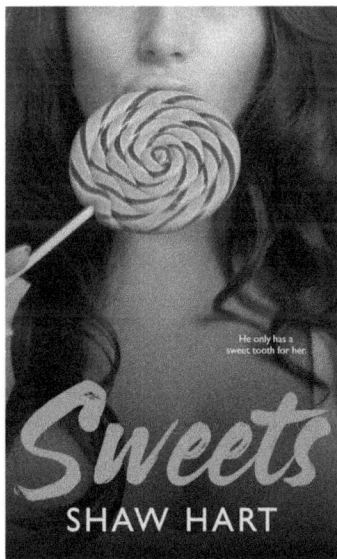

You can grab Sweets **Here.**
Check out my website, www.shawhart.com for
more free books!

ABOUT THE AUTHOR

CONNECT WITH ME!

If you enjoyed this story, please consider leaving a review on Amazon or any other reader site or blog that you like. Don't forget to recommend it to your other reader friends.

If you want to chat with me, please consider joining my VIP list or connecting with me on one of my Social Media platforms. I love talking with each of my readers. Links below!

<u>Website</u>
<u>Newsletter</u>

SERIES BY SHAW HART

Cherry Falls

803 Wishing Lane

1012 Curvy Way

Eye Candy Ink

Atlas

Mischa

Sam

Zeke

Nico

Eye Candy Ink: Second Generation

Ames

Harvey

Rooney

Gray

Ender

Banks

Fallen Peak

A Very Mountain Man Valentine's Day

A Very Mountain Man Halloween

A Very Mountain Man Thanksgiving

A Very Mountain Man Christmas

A Very Mountain Man New Year

Folklore

Kidnapping His Forever

Claiming His Forever

Finding His Forever

Rescuing His Forever

Chasing His Forever

Folklore: The Complete Series

Holiday Hearts

Be Mine

Falling in Love

Holly Jolly Holidays

Love Notes

Signing Off With Love

Care Package Love

Wrong Number, Right Love

Kings Gym

Fighting Fire With Fire

Fighting Tooth and Nail

Fighting Back From Hell

Mine To

Mine to Love

Mine to Protect

Mine to Cherish

ALSO BY SHAW HART

Still in the mood for Christmas books?

Stuffing Her Stocking, Mistletoe Kisses, Snowed in For Christmas, Coming Down Her Chimney

Love holiday books? Check out these!

For Better or Worse, Riding His Broomstick, Thankful for His FAKE Girlfriend, His New Year Resolution, Hop Stuff, Taming Her Beast, Hungry For Dash, His Firework

Looking for some OTT love stories?

Her Scottish Savior, Baby Mama, Tempted By My Roommate, Blame It On The Rum, Wild Ride, Always

Looking for a celebrity love story?

Bedroom Eyes, Seducing Archer, Finding Their Rhythm

In the mood for some young love books?

Study Dates, His Forever, My Girl

Some other books by Shaw:

The Billionaire's Bet, Her Guardian Angel, Falling Again, Stealing Her, Dreamboat, Making Her His, Trouble

9 798230 651581